Kiss the Bricks

Books by Tammy Kaehler

The Kate Reilly Mysteries
Dead Man's Switch
Braking Points
Avoidable Contact
Red Flags
Kiss the Bricks

Kiss the Bricks

A Kate Reilly Mystery

Tammy Kaehler

Poisoned Pen Press

First Edition 2017

10 9 8 7 6 5 4 3 2 1

Library of Congress Catalog Card Number: 2016955446

ISBN: 9781464207297   Hardcover
      9781464207310   Trade Paperback

Poisoned Pen Press
6962 E. First Ave., Ste. 103
Scottsdale, AZ 85251
www.poisonedpenpress.com
info@poisonedpenpress.com

Printed in the United States of America

To all the women who have been part of
(and who love) the Indy 500, especially the nine
women who have taken the green flag.

Most of all, to Pippa Mann
for her inspiration on and off the track.

Acknowledgments

At no time have I asked readers to suspend disbelief more than in this book where I ask you to believe an Indy 500 driver has time to solve a mystery in the month of May—trust me, they're too busy! That aside, the rest of the description of a driver's life during that time is as accurate as I can make it, thanks to a group of generous souls who I think of as "my Indy people" (whether or not you live there). Thank you to Meesh Beer, Tony DiZinno, Patti Edwards, Carolyn Meier, Jon Paulette, and Liz Wittich. Extra special thanks to Steve Wittich and Patsy White who got me better inside access and information than I ever dreamed of.

One woman stands alone in the "I couldn't have done it without you" category: Pippa Mann, five-time starter at the Indy 500, fierce competitor, crusader for breast cancer awareness, avid reader, and wonderful human being. She's my primary source for what it's like to be a participant in "The Greatest Spectacle in Racing," and, I'm honored to say, she's my friend. Thank you, Pippa, for your time and support. Any errors are mine!

Thank you to those who let me use your names, particularly those who made donations to worthy causes for the purpose: Beth Thomas (for "Lead-Foot" Lyla Thomas), John Dale (for Vallorie Westleton), Rick Hunt (for Maria Febbo), Rick Ollie (for himself), and Carolyn Meier (for Diane Wittmeier). Special thanks to Barb and Mary's real Uncle Stan for your stories and inspiration.

For helping me tune a rough-running manuscript, thank you to my beta readers Christine Harvey, Carolyn Meier, Rochelle Staab, and Bill Zahren. For unwavering support and early feedback, thank you to my agent, Lucienne Diver of the Knight Agency. For always pinpointing exactly what can be improved (and also telling me what works), thank you to my incredible, incomparable Poisoned Pen Press editors, Barbara Peters and Annette Rogers. Also at Poisoned Pen Press, thank you to Rob, Raj, Diane, Beth, and everyone else who takes such good care of me.

Finally, thank you to my family for understanding when I do and don't want to talk about it, for letting me go AWOL for a few months last year while panic-writing, and for never failing to cheer me on. I love you guys. And to Chet, thank you for our life. Here's to the fun that's ahead of us.

Indianapolis Motor Speedway

Indianapolis, Indiana

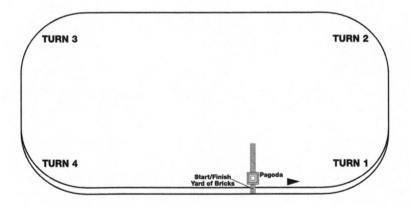

Chapter One

Present Day

Bald John looked giddy, which confused me as I pulled into the pits after our first practice for the Indy 500. He didn't speak, but helped me out of the car with a wide, goofy grin and unusually fumbling fingers.

Also confusing was my best friend, manager, and PR person, Holly Wilson, climbing over the low pit wall with a towel and a bottle of water—normally a crew member's job. I saw the stern look on her face and fear clenched my insides.

I shouted to be heard through my helmet. "What's wrong?"

She shook her head. "Everyone's fine. No one's hurt. I have good news and bad news. Bad news first."

Do we have to do this again? Now?

I yanked off my gloves, helmet, balaclava, and earplugs. I wiped my face with the cold, wet towel she'd brought and looked up and down the Indianapolis Motor Speedway's pit lane, seeing thirty-three other drivers talking with their engineers.

Why am I not doing the same?

I drank down half the water. As a babble of voices erupted from my Beermeier Racing team pit box, Holly glanced over her shoulder, worried.

My sense of unease increased. "Tell me."

"The bad news." She hesitated. "This is only the first practice. Where you are in the finishing order doesn't matter, because teams are playing with car setup. Position doesn't mean anything."

"I get it. I was last in this practice last year, but finished seventeenth in the race." I relived the overwhelmed feeling I'd had the year before, my first time driving at IMS and my first time attempting to qualify for one of the biggest races in the world. I'd nearly stopped breathing during the rookie test, when I proved I could handle speeds over 220 mph around the two-and-a-half-mile oval. The first full practice had been equally stunning, as I learned to deal with other cars on the massive track. In contrast, the practice a year later had felt good. I'd felt relatively comfortable with a car on the edge. I'd had fun.

"What's the problem?" I asked.

"Keep the bad news in mind."

I waved Holly on, bored of whatever this was. I wanted to talk to my engineer, though I saw he was busy with a small crowd of people—press?

Holly put a hand on my shoulder. "The good news." She broke into a smile. "Kate, you were the fastest in that session."

Her words didn't register. "What?"

She pointed at the scoring pylon, the tall, electronic tower that soared over the track displaying the running or finishing order. Sure enough, my number was at the top.

I blinked twice, but the digits didn't change. I sank down on the pit wall, unable to feel my legs. "Holy shit," I whispered.

"It's a damn good start." She laughed, then sobered. "But don't let it go to your head. Stay calm when you talk with the media."

I glanced at the group in the pits again and finally understood what was happening.

"You can be pleased," she went on, "but don't get cocky. The other teams—"

I grinned at her. "It doesn't mean anything for qualifying or the race. But it's sure as hell a better way to start than last place."

I turned back to the scoring pylon and the start/finish line of the legendary track. Position one: the number 82 car. Me.

Maybe this will be my year at the 500…

I had ten seconds to fantasize about drinking the traditional milk in the victory lane before my crew descended on me with back-slaps and hugs. After a few minutes of answering questions for the reporters going live on the PA or radio, I spent time talking with Nolan Oshiro, the genius engineer who made decisions about race strategy and technical details for me. But before we were done, a rep for the IndyCar Series, which I was driving in full-time that year, arrived to take me to the media center to talk with the press.

I hadn't ever been called to the ground-floor interview room of the media building—a shorter, longer structure next to the Speedway's famous pagoda tower—so I hadn't known the drill. As a result, the other top finishers had come and gone, and I faced a couple dozen journalists alone.

The bottle of cold water I clutched—my second—helped me rehydrate after losing about five pounds in sweat over the course of the practice session, but it didn't help me feel warm. Though I'd been overheated in the car, I already felt clammy from wearing a soaking-wet firesuit in the air-conditioned room. Plus I felt anxious, nervous.

The price of success.

At first, reporters asked the normal questions about how the car felt, if we had what it would take to win this year, and if I'd known I was that fast.

Then a voice spoke from my left. "I have two questions. What does this mean for you? And do you think it'll make more people take you seriously?"

"Is someone not taking me seriously? My name's on the car. What's not serious about that?"

The male reporter dug himself deeper. "There haven't been many women running the 500, and none of them have come close to winning."

"Third isn't close to winning?" I shot back.

Be nice, Kate. Educate, I reminded myself.

I tried again. "People take me seriously. Will this get me more exposure in the rest of the world? I hope so. I'd love to bring more attention to this great race, to the Beermeier Racing team, and to my sponsors, Frame Savings and Beauté."

"And to women drivers?" he persisted.

"Absolutely. Women can be fast and win anywhere men can."

A different man spoke. "Were you thinking about beating the other woman in the field today? And how's your relationship with Sofia Montalvo?"

Don't say she's a bitch. Don't say she's a bitch.

"Sofia and I are friendly, but I wasn't thinking of her or anyone else. I was trying to get the most out of the car."

The other female reporter wagged a finger in the air and winked. "You weren't out there focused on the statement you were making for women?"

I barely caught my snort of amusement. "I was thinking about hanging on, making adjustments with the anti-roll bars and weight jacker, and giving my team feedback to make the car better. That's all I *should* think about at more than two-twenty."

The questions returned to more standard lines—what did my speed today mean for the race and what would my team change on the car before the next session. Then someone suggested I was the first woman in the 106-year history of the Indy 500 to ever top the speed charts.

"Am I? Some of you know more race history than I do."

The reporters debated the question and the volume in the room escalated until one voice broke through.

"No, she wasn't," drawled a small, wiry man in his early fifties. He leaned against the doorframe, holding what looked like a change of clothes for me.

Everyone turned to him, and some reporters looked a question at me.

"Uncle—er, Stan Wright, from Beermeier Racing. Expert mechanic." I wasn't sure why he was there, but I'd found that Stan—who everyone on the team called "Uncle Stan," regardless of age or relation—always turned up exactly when he was most needed.

Uncle Stan smiled. "Just plain mechanic and sometime errand boy—checking up on you for Alexa." The last was directed at me, referencing Alexa Wittmeier, co-owner of Beermeier Racing, the team I drove for.

"You said Kate wasn't the first?" one of the youngest reporters asked.

Uncle Stan nodded. "Couple decades ago, PJ Rodriguez was the first."

Chapter Two

May 1987

The checkered flag flew to mark the end of the first practice for the 1987 Indianapolis 500, and the number 23 car's crew slapped each other's backs in disbelief. Noise from the small crowd on hand was drowned out by the roar of thirty-seven snarling V-6 and V-8 engines entering pit lane—but not before the crew heard boos mixed in with cheering.

At the front of the pit space, a crew member waved his arm up and down, and PJ pulled the car in. As she shut down the engine, the crew member approached, but PJ waved him off. He turned back to the pits, relief evident in the slump of his shoulders.

PJ unbuckled her belts and muscled herself out, perching on the rim of the cockpit, her feet on the seat. She pulled her helmet and balaclava off, shaking out thick, black hair, and wiped her forehead with a sleeve.

In contrast to other pit spaces, where crew members clustered around each car and driver, PJ sat alone. Her lips tightened briefly and she squared her shoulders before climbing the rest of the way out of the car, helmet in hand. Only then did she turn to look at the scoring pylon, frowning as she searched for her car number at the bottom of the list. Her first practice that year, only her second time attempting to make the race…she knew she'd be at the bottom of the speed chart. She looked again. Nothing.

Finally understanding, she looked higher on the pylon, her mouth dropping open as she followed the list of numbers all the way to the top.

Position 1: 23.

She froze, shocked. Certain there'd been some mistake. After a long minute, she turned her head and met the eyes of her race engineer, Jerry Watson. "Really? How?"

He shrugged and stepped closer to the pit wall, gesturing for a crew member to take PJ's helmet. "A fluke." He looked sternly at the joy spreading over PJ's face. "You did good—your fastest lap was 210.772 miles per hour. But don't get ahead of yourself. We've got three weeks of on-track sessions before the race itself. Anything can happen. Some of the favorites didn't even get out there today."

PJ waved an arm at the pylon, her enthusiasm undimmed. "But they cannot say I can't drive if I did this."

"They're gonna say whatever they want, kid. But you keep on believing." He glanced over his shoulder. "And brace yourself, because here comes the press."

Within seconds, PJ was surrounded. Men with notebooks in hand tumbled over the pit wall and swarmed the pit space, pressing in on her.

"PJ, did you know you were fastest while you were out there?"

"How did the car feel?"

"Did you really think a girl could go that fast?"

"Do you think you can do it again?"

She heard a guffaw, and a low voice. "Of course she can't. She'll probably collapse from the strain of this session."

"Do you think people will say you're too masculine if you go too fast?"

As the men invaded her personal space and their questions continued to rain down, PJ felt her breaths grow more shallow and panicky. She let the sound wash over her and focused on slow, smooth breathing. A moment later, she threw up her hands, bumping three notebooks out of the way.

"Enough," she shouted.

In the brief, shocked silence that followed, she spoke again. "One at a time. No, I did not know my speed while I was in the car. Still, I don't believe it. The car felt touchy and not so great in a couple of corners. Of course I thought I could go that fast. Being a girl—a woman—it has nothing to do with driving a racecar."

"Now you're getting all feminist on us—you one of those women's libbers, PJ?" one reporter asked.

"If you mean do I think women can do anything they want to do? Then yes. But that does not mean I don't appreciate men or want to—what is it? Burn my bra. Not that."

Another reporter eyed her chest. "I'll say. It looks plenty good where it is."

PJ crossed her arms and flicked a glance at the man's crotch before giving him a pitying look.

"Aren't you afraid of being seen as too manly?" That was from a different voice, on her other side.

She turned to face him. "You tell me, am I ever going to look like a man?"

He inspected her curves and grinned. "No, ma'am, but behavior ain't looks."

"I do not understand why, if I am a good, fast driver, anyone else is less of a man." She shrugged. "Maybe they need their manhood checked."

Some of the men muttered disapproving responses, but didn't say anything loud enough for her to hear.

A woman in the back spoke up for the first time. "Lyla Thomas for *Autoweek*. Can I get some background? Where you're from, racing history, that sort of thing?"

PJ was surprised at a woman being part of the macho press corps. "I am twenty-six, my father is Mexican and my mother is American. I was brought up in the United States, Colombia, and Mexico City. I started racing go-karts at the age of eight, and then I moved into sportscars, then to formula cars. This is my second year trying to qualify here at Indy, because I didn't pass the rookie test last year." She glanced at the scoring pylon. "But I am clearly capable this year, no?"

Some of the men laughed, grudgingly, she thought.

Lyla Thomas looked up from her notebook. "What does PJ stand for?"

PJ rolled her Rs. "Patricia Julieta Rosamaria Rivera Rodriguez."

The reporter quirked the side of her mouth up. "I see why you go by PJ."

PJ nodded at her as the questions started up again.

"Do you think the other drivers on track stayed out of your way?"

"Why would they do that?" PJ studied the man's feeble attempts at a comb-over.

"So you wouldn't get hurt," he replied. "Could that explain you being fastest?"

Another man slapped his notebook with the back of his free hand. "You're onto something. That's gotta be what it is." He turned to PJ. "What if they won't race you wheel-to-wheel?"

PJ couldn't help herself. "Then they are weak."

"You're talking about champions!" The men were indignant.

She shrugged. "If they are afraid to race me…"

A different reporter spoke up. "Kevin Hagan, Associated Press. What do you have to say to the fans who think you shouldn't be on the track? Who think you're taking a seat a man should have?"

"I say this is nineteen eighty-seven, and it is time for this conversation to be over. Women play sports. We race cars. Billie Jean King won the tennis match fourteen years ago, *por Dios*. If there's a man who's better than me, maybe he'd be standing here. Except that I was faster than your men today. Look at the list." She pointed to the pylon.

She heard a sharply indrawn breath and saw heads shake. Heard one man mutter, "Not going to get you more fans."

PJ met the eyes of anyone who'd look at her. "No one stayed out of my way today. I was faster. Maybe tomorrow I will not be—or maybe I will. But either way, I succeed because I work hard, not because someone gives me a gift."

She saw a young crew member signaling to her from the pit box. "You must now excuse me and move so they can take the car to the garage. Thank you for your time." She walked away, the young crew member scurrying after her.

The reporters shifted out of the way of the crew, except for Kevin Hagan, who lagged behind and sidled up to the mechanic climbing in the car for the tow to the garage. "How's she to work with?"

The crew member settled himself down in the seat. "You know."

"I don't know, that's why I'm asking. What's she like?"

The guy in the car glanced around and shook his head. "There's some as make it easy, and some that make you regret not knowing who the driver is before you sign a contract with a team. I'll let you guess."

"She don't make it easy?"

The crew member rolled his eyes. "Off the charts." He grabbed Hagan's arm. "And off the record."

The reporter nodded. "Anonymous source."

"Meet me in an hour behind the garage for a cigarette, and I'll tell you more."

"Done." Hagan smirked as the car was towed away.

Chapter Three

Present Day

As I changed into the dry clothes Uncle Stan brought me, my thoughts ping-ponged between my own achievement and that of PJ Rodriguez.

I still can't believe we were fastest today. That another woman was fastest decades ago—when there were hardly any women around. How much harder must it have been for her? And can I do it again?

"Good job today," Uncle Stan said, as I emerged from the bathroom, once again dry. "You figured the car out quick."

"I only hope we can do it again. You know what the secret sauce was?"

He chuckled. "Good driver's part of it. Other part's Indy magic. Sometimes it hits. But you can't ever count on it."

I didn't know what had gone so right with the car either. Our team, like all of them, had unloaded the car and taken a stab in the dark at setup. I knew the others would find speed in the coming days, and some of us would lose what we'd found—or at least not make the same gains. But I'd had this day.

Before Uncle Stan and I exited the building, another driver came through the doors. The Spanish-born Sofia Montalvo stopped, a patronizing look on her beautiful face. "I suppose I am to congratulate you?"

Sofia and I had first encountered each other two years prior, when I'd subbed for one of Beermeier Racing's drivers in the Indy Lights race at Long Beach. She'd been the only woman there at the time, and she hadn't welcomed me. In general, that was fine. I didn't expect to be friends or even friendly with every other driver I raced against. But few, male or female, greeted me with such disdain.

Women can tear each other down in ways men can't even approach.

Now we were both in the IndyCar Series, I often regretted we didn't have a mutually respectful and supportive relationship. But I couldn't do it alone, and I'd long since realized it wasn't worth the effort of swallowing her insults to make it happen.

"I never expect anything, Sofia. But I hope you ran well today."

"As if you care." She sniffed. "Enjoy this attention. It is the last you will receive. Your little team with its pitiful budget, and you, with your inexperience, soon will falter. And the cream will rise to the top of the milk, you see?"

"You think that'll be you?" I snapped.

"Perhaps. I have yet to peak, unlike you." She smiled and swept out of the room.

I made an aggravated noise. "I shouldn't let her get to me."

"But she works so hard at it," Uncle Stan commented.

I shook my head and pushed open the door to the plaza, where we discovered fifteen or twenty fans waiting. As I did every time I was nearby, I looked up at the iconic pagoda, a tiered steel-and-glass tower that soared over the start/finish line and symbolized the Indianapolis Motor Speedway. I worked my way through the crowd, answering questions, signing autographs, giving quotes, or receiving hugs. I was enjoying the interactions until one over-beered fan shouted from a few feet away.

"How much did you pay the other drivers to let you be fastest?"

A passing crew member from another team—which one, I couldn't see, due to the equipment slung over his back—nodded at the man who'd spoken. "Girls don't belong here. It's a sport for men, not for girls pretending to be men."

The rude fan toasted the crew member, sloshing beer out of his cup. "Exactly—I mean, are you a dyke or what? Because it's fishy that a chick who qualified thirtieth last year is suddenly fastest today. Like there was a conspiracy to get the princess and her team more attention."

"Am I a lesbian or a princess?" I murmured, signaling Uncle Stan to ignore the taunts.

The fans around me shouted at the blowhard to shut up and argued with him about my talent and speed.

"Do other drivers worry about racing you," he yelled at me, raising his head and voice to be heard, "because they don't want to wreck a girl?"

What century is this guy from?

I shook my head. "Drivers are worried about beating each other—male or female—not about wrecking each other. Plus, the idea of a conspiracy is absurd. No one's willing to sacrifice their team. We're all trying to do our best. Ask around, if you don't believe me."

Educate, even if it's a lost cause.

"And a word of advice. Respect will get you further than insults. We don't like being called 'chicks' or 'girls.'"

"Damn straight," said one of the women nearby, an angry look on her face.

"We know exactly what you think about us when you say that." A woman with spiky, hot pink hair turned to me. "Kate, don't waste your time with him."

The rude guy started to bluster about being persecuted for his opinions, and the men and women in the crowd shouted back. As the volume increased, I headed for the garage, encouraging others to follow me.

One of the IndyCar Series' defining characteristics was accessibility. Fans had many opportunities to get close to drivers, crews, and teams, from public autograph sessions to open paddocks. They couldn't walk into team garages, but they could stand at the door and watch the activity, take photos, and see drivers go about their business. They could approach us in the paddock. We liked being close to our fan base, but there were occasional downsides.

Uncle Stan shook his full head of white hair. "Some idiots never learn."

"You've seen plenty of them." I knew he'd been in racing for decades.

"Always been jackasses in the bunch, pardon my language. Plenty who refuse to change with the times. Fewer of them holding those wrongheaded opinions now."

I paused to scribble my name on a program a man offered up. "At least I have people willing to stick up for me."

The good-looking fan smiled at me as I finished writing and unleashed an Australian accent. "I'll stick up for you, protect you, whatever you need, Kate. Just let me know, day or night." He winked and handed me a card with his personal information.

Before I managed to respond, another man claimed my attention. "Kate, I want to thank you for bringing awareness to breast cancer. My wife's a survivor, and your efforts mean a lot to both of us."

I thanked both men and kept moving.

Uncle Stan spoke again as we passed the closed-up concession stands and entered Gasoline Alley, the name for IMS's garage area. "You have more support than PJ—she never had a strong fan base. It was a different time."

"When did she race?"

"In nineteen eighty-seven, she was fastest in the first practice for the Indy 500."

I stopped him with a hand on his arm. "Also the first practice? Thirty years ago?"

He nodded as we turned the corner to our row of garages. Before I could ask him more questions, we encountered a dozen people wearing Team Kate and Beermeier Racing shirts. They stood in front of our garage taking photos of my car.

"Congratulations, Kate!" It was almost a chorus as the fans spotted me.

After more photos and questions, I entered the garage where Alexa, my team owner, stood inside talking with a tall, well-built blond man in his mid-forties. As I got closer, I revised that estimate upward and wondered if his tight jaw owed more to a surgeon than to genetics.

Not nice.

He smiled, with lots of teeth. "Kate, Tom Barclay. Great job today."

I knew the name. Barclay owned the go-to firm of sports psychologists for racing drivers. "I worked with your group—Dr. Felicia Shields—years ago. But you and I never met in person."

His smile got bigger as he released my hand. "Glad we have now. Best of luck this year." He left the building with a wave.

The long Beermeier Racing garage occupied the space of seven separate openings: two for each car and one for the hospitality and office areas. There were no walls or dividers, except for partitions separating the office from hospitality and the rest. I entered the office area—a fifteen-foot-wide space containing folding tables and chairs, plus our driver lockers at one side—where my race engineer, Nolan, hunched over his computer, and I pulled up a chair to talk through the day's work.

Halfway through that conversation, Holly called me out to the front of the garage for an on-camera interview with a local TV station for the evening news. She managed to hold off the other media outlets looking for comment until after I'd finished debriefing with Nolan, but returning calls took another half an hour. Then I responded to congratulatory texts from my loved ones—my grandfather, father, and boyfriend.

Finally, when all questions and messages had been addressed—leaving social media aside for later—I sat still for a few minutes and watched the crew pull the engine cover off to check for oil leaks. I sipped water and admired the car. Low-slung, with swooping, aerodynamic lines, it had no bodywork around the wheels—hence an "open-wheel" racecar—and no roof over the cockpit. It was built for speed.

The bottom half was a medium green containing the Frame Savings and Loan name in large, white letters. The top half, including most of the nose, was white. Wide swaths of pink ran down both sides of the car, separating the white and green sections, coming together on the nose into a giant pink ribbon, the symbol of the fight against breast cancer. Logos for Beauté, my cosmetics company sponsor, and the Breast Cancer Research Foundation, Beauté's charitable partner, occupied the nose and rear wing, and there were a dozen other logos in various locations around the car, such as our equipment suppliers who gave us a break in pricing, and other companies or organizations that sponsored us at lesser amounts.

The green, white, and pink theme carried over into our team firesuits and the designs on our pit boxes and carts. Everything and everyone associated with my number 82 car looked alike, and more importantly, we all wore a pink ribbon for breast cancer integrated into our clothing. That sight always lifted my spirits.

I sat on one of the stools usually occupied by two old-timers who'd adopted our garage and focused on Uncle Stan. "You saw PJ race thirty years ago?"

"First team job was working on her car. 'Course, they didn't let me do much at the time." He grinned, showing the yellow teeth of a lifetime smoker.

"She was good? How'd she do in the race?"

"Never made it. Tried a couple of years. Got closest the year she was fastest, in eighty-seven. But she had talent."

"She'd have been only the second woman to try to make it into the Indy 500?" I asked. "I know Janet Guthrie was the first to race in the late seventies."

"There was Desiré Wilson in the early eighties—but she didn't manage to qualify. It was a rougher time then for women."

I studied him. "You felt sorry for PJ."

"Lot of pressure on her, and she didn't have male anatomy or lily white skin."

"Weren't there Hispanic or Latino men racing at the time?"

"A couple. Mostly white men from America, with a handful from Europe or South America. Not many different-looking people of any type. But she didn't care." He sprayed more cleaner. "You remind me of her."

"I'm not that unusual." I pointed to my black hair, pale skin, and blue eyes. "Basic white girl. Even being female isn't the same battle now." I reflected on the recent fan interaction. "Though it's not all easy."

He shook his head. "Not that. Your focus and determination. She wanted this, and she worked hard. Did whatever she could to make it happen. That's like you."

I was proud a crew member felt that way about me—and relieved he understood. Then I thought about the coincidence. "What happened to PJ? Could we get her here to talk about us both leading the first practice, thirty years apart?"

Uncle Stan sighed as he set down the cleaner and cloth. "PJ set the fastest time that practice. She was dead ten days later."

Chapter Four

May 1987

PJ knew the next days wouldn't be as great as the first one had been—couldn't be. But she didn't expect outright disaster.

Second practice: she crashed on her out lap, damaging the rear end of the car and finishing her day before it began.

Third practice: she brushed the wall coming out of Turn 4 three different times, and her team pulled her off the track thirty minutes before the end of the session. Last on the speed chart.

Fourth practice: she was five miles per hour slower than anyone else.

At the start and end of every day, PJ huddled with her engineer and team owner, discussing how to fix the car. As the days went on, the men appeared increasingly grim and PJ acted more and more worried.

"You made the same mistake three times in Turn 4, PJ. You look like a rookie," her engineer, Jerry, told her on the third day. "You're better than that. You need to get everyone out of your head."

PJ bit back a defensive comment. Then sighed. "*Madre de Dios.* I know. I don't know what happens to me. The car—"

"Some of it's the car, I'll give you that," Jerry returned.

Arvie, her team owner, put a hand on her arm. "Are you sleeping enough? Hydrating and eating well?"

PJ shrugged one shoulder, and the men exchanged concerned looks. They'd seen the crowd of people PJ fought through to reach the garages every day. They'd heard the questions. The insults.

Arvie spoke again. "The garage area's open to fans—I can't change that. But we'll protect you to and from the parking lot."

"There's no need. I can handle it." PJ gave him a weak smile. "A man could handle it. Besides, some fans have walked with me, defended me."

"I don't care," Arvie huffed. "I want you at the top of your game. Jerry, make it happen. Get one of the big guys—Jimmy or Donny."

"Not Jimmy." PJ's response was quick.

Jerry raised his eyebrows at her, but PJ shook her head.

"Donny, then," Jerry said. "He'll keep people away."

"Thank you. When they press in at me, I can't breathe." She wrapped her arms around herself.

"What else can we do?" Arvie asked.

PJ looked at the two men. "You are doing it now. Being patient with me. I'm sorry about the car, my driving."

"Are you sleeping?" Jerry repeated Arvie's question.

"Not well," she admitted. "When I go to the hotel or to a restaurant, there are people waiting. Reporters. Also regular men who make fun of me or tell me I'm worthless. Once in a while, there is a positive comment. But the bad words, the mean intentions, are always there."

Jerry and Arvie exchanged another glance. They'd seen the stories.

PJ sucked in a deep breath, then exhaled. Did that a second time and squared her shoulders. "No more complaining. I will be tougher than they are."

Arvie started to speak, "You don't have to—"

She shook her head. "They won't break me. Tomorrow, I'll be better, I swear it."

She was true to her word, picking up four miles per hour and staying out of the walls—even beating the speed of two other drivers that day. But she looked increasingly brittle. The team members who cared about her worried about the confident, aggressive girl they saw entering the garage and the nail-biting, distraught one they saw inside, out of the public eye.

No matter her performance—or lack of it—on track, the critical, jeering fans never let up. The stories in the media never stopped.

"Girl Driver Flames Out After First Day," and "PJ Proves Females Can't Drive Like Men," and "Can Girls Handle Indy Pressure?" ran the headlines in major publications.

The questions from the primarily male attendees at the track were usually cruder. Most asked if she'd faked her speed the first day or taunted her with her failures in the days since. Some got more personal.

One morning, PJ heard, "Why don't you get out of the way and let the real drivers have a chance?" and "Stay in the kitchen where you belong, sweetheart." But those were typical, and she didn't so much as break her stride.

Then one man shouted, "I don't even think you're a woman," which stirred up the group of eight or ten men around her—including Donny, who towered over her and kept a protective arm around her shoulders as they walked toward the garages.

"I wondered, too," called another male voice. "Show us your tits."

"Maybe she needs a doctor's note to prove she's a girl," said another.

"I've got a better idea—bend over and prove it to all of us," crowed yet another voice, a closer one.

PJ felt a hand grab her buttocks and another one fondle her right breast. That's when she stumbled, her face white and eyes glassy.

"Back off, assholes," Donny snarled as he shoved men away.

The men made kissing sounds and flopped their wrists at him. "Oooh, ladies, look, we've upset the mama's boy and his whore."

Donny and PJ shook off the crowd, arriving at the garage at a near-run. Once inside, he grabbed her shoulders with both hands. "Are you all right?"

PJ took deep breaths, which restored her color. "I am fine."

"I can't believe—I mean, I'm sorry for what they said."

She smiled at him and didn't mention the groping hands she could still feel. "Small minds won't break me or this team."

"We should tell someone from the track. They shouldn't be allowed to say that."

"It's all right, Donny. We leave it. We have better things to focus on today, like going faster." She gestured to the blue-and-green racecar next to them.

"I'm going to tell Arvie and Jerry."

She stepped back so his hands fell away from her shoulders. "Don't bother them. Focus on the car. It is all that matters." She moved closer to the car and stared into the cockpit. "The speed is all that matters. I can take anything if I can go fast."

PJ was last again in that day's session, slower than the next car by three miles per hour—a closer number than before, but not much good when the rest of the field improved their speeds every day and the number of days remaining before qualifying dwindled rapidly.

During the first two of four weekend days of qualifying, while half the field entered official times, PJ and the crew continued their work, making slow progress. The car improved. As Arvie remarked, "Given infinite time, we might have a top ten car. But we'll run out of days before the race to make that happen."

Jerry and Arvie stayed late many nights, going through every possible adjustment on the car and coming up with new approaches. One morning, the tenth day of practice, the Tuesday between qualifying weekends, they waited for PJ, eager to tell her about the problem they'd found and corrected. But PJ never arrived.

She wouldn't ever get the chance to try their fix. She'd never drive the Indy 500, never taste that kind of speed again. All of PJ's possibilities had ended earlier that morning when she fell from the roof of a fifteen-story hotel in downtown Indianapolis.

Chapter Five

Present Day

I still felt the gut punch of PJ's death the next day. I'd spent a restless night imagining the shock everyone in the paddock felt. Imagining the sight of her broken body on the ground outside the hotel. Waking up with a jolt from a nightmare of falling.

My eyes were gritty as I arrived at the track, and I carried my sorrow over PJ—maybe even carried PJ—with me, using it as motivation to buckle down and work hard. After the euphoria of our first practice, my crew and I expected the second practice day to be rough. We were right.

Tuesday's weather was overcast and cooler than Monday's hot, humid temperatures, and the adjustments we made to the car to compensate messed everything up. For a while, we trailed around at the back of the field, as I repeatedly took to the track and returned for more adjustments. No one was more frustrated than my engineer.

I caught sight of him during one stop and radioed to Alexa, the only one who spoke to me on the radio besides my spotter. "Nolan's got no more hair to lose."

She looked at him and smiled. True to form, Nolan's left hand clutched the fringe of short hair above his ear. Alexa pulled her aviator sunglasses off and rubbed the bridge of her nose. "Not the day to break the habit of a lifetime."

I watched Nolan's agitated movements and Alexa's calm, measured response and was grateful again for my team. Concerns, ideas, and pronouncements fizzed out of Nolan Oshiro like endless soda froth. Alexa Wittmeier, in contrast, moved in slow-motion, never getting wound up or overly excited—which made her ideal for talking to me on the radio as I circled the track at more than 220 mph. Alexa was a little more than a decade older than me, a successful veteran of IndyCar who'd driven for six years and then changed her focus to building her own team. She'd run it on her own for a handful of years before joining forces with Tim Beerman—a move that propelled the team from also-rans to serious competitors.

"We're trying to get you back up on speed. No one can work out how we lost it from yesterday." She slipped her glasses back on. "Changing tire pressure and taking more front wing out. Give us a sec. We'll send you back out to see how it works."

The answer, two laps later, was it didn't. But three more adjustments—plus more hair-tugging from Nolan—and we started to make progress. We ended the day in thirtieth place—a dramatic comedown from first the day before, but still not last of the thirty-four cars practicing. And we'd started heading in the right direction.

When I wasn't driving the car, my thoughts centered on PJ Rodriguez. Wondering what she was like and being sad for everything she missed out on. I'd searched for information online the night before, and I'd been transfixed by photos of her, partly because we were similar in appearance, with our short height and black hair—though she was curvier. But I was also caught by the look of determination in her eyes—a look I understood. I felt an instant connection to her that went beyond our shared accomplishment, straight to our experiences as women in a male-dominated world. With those photos, I felt I knew her.

Beyond images, my Internet search yielded basic information, but not much insight. However, some of our crew had been in the paddock at the time, on different teams, and they'd told me what they knew about PJ.

"I saw her in the garages and pits," said a fifty-something tire expert who went by Banjo and spoke in a slow Southern drawl. "She had the best and worst luck all at once."

Bald John—to differentiate him from the John who had hair—snapped his fingers. "I remember. If anyone was ever jinxed at the 500, it was her."

"You had more days of practice then, didn't you?" I asked.

Banjo nodded. "The whole month of May, not only the two weeks we have now. This PJ, who no one's ever heard of—Mexican, I think, and let me tell you, we didn't see many Hispanics or women in those days, so she stood out—she's fastest right out of the gate, first day. Shocked the stuffing out of everyone."

"Then nothing," Bald John said. "After that, she was barely competent on track. Dead-last, day after day."

"Then she was just dead." Banjo shook his head. "Killed herself. Couldn't handle the pressure."

"I don't understand how she stopped wanting it," I put in. "But it must have been tougher for her—Uncle Stan said she was only the third woman to try to make the race."

Bald John rubbed his polished head. "The stories around the paddock about her weren't great. Now I wonder if they were personal or simply the usual."

I sighed. "I know the usual."

The corners of Banjo's mouth pulled down. "They don't say nothing bad in our hearing, I promise you."

I smiled at him. "I appreciate that, but I know it happens. I'm a bitch because I'm focused and not afraid to be aggressive."

"PJ got labeled the B-word, too." Bald John shrugged. "Maybe she was."

"Or maybe she had to be to get what she wanted," I replied.

We definitely need a thick skin, I thought later, as I answered questions after practice for a small group of press. The regular IndyCar journalists covered the basics—how I felt about the car, what had changed from the day before, and where we'd go from here. Those questions were fine. As I'd heard one broadcast journalist put it, they allowed me to retain my dignity by asking for information without judgment.

The rest of the reporters weren't so considerate.

"Did the pressure of being fastest yesterday get to you and the team, Kate?"

"Can you actually find the speed to keep up with the rest of the cars who're picking up the pace?"

"Was yesterday a fluke?"

"Sofia Montalvo was faster than you today, so you've lost the title of fastest woman here. Any comment?"

"Are you aware you're polling behind Sofia for sexiest driver?"

I gritted my teeth and smiled.

Then I heard the last question. "Are you doing a PJ?"

I felt my smile fade. "What do you mean?"

A paunchy man with greasy, bowl-cut hair looked up from his notebook. "In eighty-seven, she was fastest in the first session and the next day, last. She crashed coming out of the pits that day, and you didn't, but still. She was last the next four or five days. I figure history's repeating itself."

I felt Holly bristle beside me, and I glanced at her.

Stay calm.

"What's your name?" I asked the journalist.

His Adam's apple bobbed. "Rick Ollie."

"Hi, Rick Ollie, I'm Kate Reilly. Which means I'm not 'doing a PJ,' I'm doing a Kate." I smiled, making it a joke, and saw answering grins from other journalists. "First of all, I qualified for and raced in one Indy 500 already. Second, track conditions changed, maybe we bumped something on the car, who knows? By the end of the session, we were making progress, so we'll be headed back up the order."

"Sure you will," I heard Rick mumble as I walked back into the garage.

Once safely away from press ears, I turned to Holly. "Who do these people write for? Is that how a journalist behaves?"

"Not that I don't agree with you, but he's not the only one asking the question." Holly glanced at her phone, and I knew what was coming.

"The Ringer has it?" Racing's Ringer was a blogger known for his anonymity, his inside scoops on the motorsports world, and his outrageous level of snark. The fact that I knew his real identity didn't stop him from making me a target, though he'd also defended me against attack at times. He wouldn't be able to resist this situation.

Holly nodded and turned her phone so I could see it.

I read the headline aloud. "'Time Travel or Supernatural Possession? Is Kate Channeling 1987's Doomed Girl Driver?'" I took a deep breath, smelling the mixture of hot rubber, race fuel, and solvent that permeated the garage. I exhaled and did it again. Didn't help.

Uncle Stan walked up and studied my face. "Didn't mean to depress you by comparing you to PJ. You're not her."

"Try telling that to bloggers and social media." Holly wiggled her phone in the air. "I'll post an upbeat message about today and see if we can head this off." She wandered away.

I turned to Uncle Stan, who looked confused. "The problem isn't you—though hearing what PJ did makes me sad. Makes me wonder if she thought she was jinxed."

"Plenty of her team thought so."

"How well did you know her, Uncle Stan?"

He rocked back on his heels. "Mechanic on her car, my first IndyCar job. Youngest guy on the pit crew. PJ and I were about the same age—maybe she was a couple years older. Both new. Won't claim we were friends, but we connected over being fish out of water in the garage."

"Who else was around then?"

"Some of our senior engineers." He scanned the room. "Banjo and Bald John, like they told you. Ron and Chuck."

"Are those our mascots? The two older guys usually sitting here?" I gestured to the two empty stools in a corner of the garage near my car. "What's their story?"

"Ron was involved as a kid for a lot of years, later owned teams—including PJ's. Then he got out for a while, and now he's back for the entertainment value, he says. Chuck started Gaffey Insurance years ago and recently turned it over to his son. He and Ron have been friends forever—still like being near the action." Uncle Stan nodded toward a woman straightening up the food table. "Ask Diane Wittmeier, she'll tell you stories."

"Alexa's mom?"

He nodded. "She worked for PJ's team doing hospitality."

Alexa called me over to confirm timing and other details for the next day, and after we were done, I went to Diane.

"Thanks for today's celebration cookies."

She beamed at me from behind her red-framed glasses. She had a sleek bob of ash blond hair that I envied because the ends curled under perfectly. Unlike mine, which went everywhere. "Sorry they didn't bring you more luck. But you'll find your speed again. I've seen it many times."

"Uncle Stan said you've worked in racing for a long time."

"My father was involved, so I don't remember life before the track. Grew up here and never left." She eyed me. "You're hearing the stories about PJ."

"You knew her?"

She sighed. "The poor kid."

Chapter Six

May 1987

The morning of the fifth day of practice, Donny returned to the garage alone. PJ's engineer, Jerry, saw him and frowned. "Where is she?"

"No idea. But her car's in the lot."

"Did you look around?"

"I came back here to tell you."

Jerry bit back an expletive. "You told me. Now go back and make sure you didn't miss her somewhere." He surveyed the garage as Donny left, then crossed to the food area where a slight woman in her early thirties rearranged snacks and utensils. "Diane, will you look for PJ?"

"Where do you think she's gone?"

"If I knew, I'd go there."

Diane raised an eyebrow at him and fluffed her blond, permed hair.

Jerry blew out a breath. "You can go places Donny and I can't. Girl places. Please, check the bathrooms or something. Anything."

Diane rolled her eyes. "Girl places? You can't do better than that?" She held up a hand and slipped on her Ray-Ban Wayfarers. "I'm going."

Fifteen minutes later, Diane sat down next to the lone figure in the grandstands, above pit lane near the pagoda. She pushed her sunglasses up to hold her hair against the light breeze. "You're tough to find."

PJ nodded, never taking her eyes from the empty track.

"You must have gotten here early today," Diane said, turning to look at the last vestige of the formerly all-brick track. The famous "yard of bricks" was a three-foot-wide strip—nine rows that crossed the track at the start/finish line, ran through pit lane, and continued through the pagoda plaza in the infield.

"It was simpler that way." PJ sighed. "They sent you to find me?"

"They're worried."

"That I am sorry for."

Diane shrugged absently as she tried to count individual bricks on the front straight. "What do you see when you sit here?"

PJ looked from right to left, up and down the long front straight, lined from end to end with grandstands. "I see history. Racing's history."

"Your own history."

PJ glanced at Diane with surprise. "I suppose this is true. My history also." She was quiet a moment. "If I half close my eyes, I can see those cars that came before me."

"So many dreams," Diane murmured.

"So many drivers—and now me." PJ faltered. "It used to give me hope."

"And now?"

"My whole career has been difficult, and I knew this would be harder." PJ shook her head. "I did not understand how much *more* this would be—but this place is so much more." She turned to Diane, gesturing wildly toward the track with one arm. "Of *course* this is more difficult, more pressure, everything, because the race itself is more everything. The Indy 500 is like a test. Only the strongest survive here."

"So it's been said."

"You do not agree?" PJ deflated again.

"You're right, I've seen it. This race is the most demanding test there is. But we keep coming back. Because every year, we get a glimpse of glory—of sport, achievement, success. Triumph."

PJ studied Diane, a trim female her own age. "You have been here many times?"

"All my life. My father raced here." Diane glanced at PJ. "He also died here, fourteen years ago."

PJ wrapped her arms around herself. "I am sorry. I should not ask."

"It was a long time ago."

They sat in silence, then PJ asked, "Is your father why you study the bricks?"

"He drove the 36." Diane smiled and pointed. "My mother and I wrote his name on the brick that's three rows in, six bricks down. I think of him every time I see it."

"Is it not difficult for you to be here?"

"It's hard. But it also honors him and what he loved. It's what I know—and in my blood. Isn't it the same for you?"

PJ sucked in a breath. "This is true. It is what I know. *All* I know."

"If you couldn't race, you don't know what you'd do?"

"If I do not race, I have nothing. I am nothing." She spoke the words as if they were a vow.

Diane opened her mouth, then closed it again.

"You think I am obsessed." PJ smiled. "Don't worry. I know what I'm doing, and I will succeed, eventually."

"We're all obsessed." Diane paused. "But I hope you have something else in your life—family, education, other interests. Because racing can be cruel."

"When the time comes to stop, I will be fine. But it is not yet time."

Diane glanced at her watch. "It *is* time to get to the garage."

PJ agreed and stood, looking more at peace than a few minutes before.

"Speaking of family," Diane said, "will yours be here for the race?"

"My family." PJ frowned as the breeze whipped her long, black hair. She pulled it into a ponytail and secured it with a band from her pocket. "My parents might be here for the race. I am not sure if I will allow them to come."

Diane tried to hide her surprise. "Are you more nervous with them here?"

"My father complicates things. He is powerful. Sometimes a bully."

Diane suddenly remembered a taunt she'd heard aimed at PJ. A bystander—racing fan, media, or crew member, she didn't know which—had shouted something about PJ's father and drugs. And tainted money. *Is he a Mexican drug lord?* she wondered.

PJ continued, "I love my father, but I do not agree with everything he does, and I do not wish him to tarnish what I do here. This is my world, not his."

"Family can be complicated, but they can also be a support."

PJ didn't respond, and Diane didn't press her.

As they walked past the first of three garage buildings, Diane nodded at friends and acquaintances from other teams. She was surprised to be met with looks that ranged from blank to hostile, instead of the friendly greetings she usually received. She glanced at PJ and saw her looking straight ahead, ignoring everyone and everything, including a catcall.

Diane turned to glare at the man responsible, a doughy white guy in a tee-shirt with the sleeves cut off to show prodigious underarm and back hair. Seeing her watching him, he licked his lips and rubbed his chest suggestively. She made a strangled sound and focused forward, as PJ did.

"It is better to not respond at all." PJ sounded almost amused.

"I knew you had to deal with rudeness, but I didn't expect it was so totally gross."

PJ giggled, a sound more fragile than joyous. "Most of it is totally gross. Gag me with a spoon, yes?"

"'Like, oh my God,'" Diane parroted.

This time, PJ's laughter rolled out, unrestrained. But even as she joined in, Diane knew she wasn't imagining its hysterical edge.

Chapter Seven

Present Day

I get her. I don't know what I'd do if I couldn't race either. Obviously, I wouldn't kill myself, I'd figure something out. Why didn't PJ?

I was still asking myself that question Wednesday morning, our third day of practice, when I discovered I had a serious identity problem. I'd gone to sleep as Kate Reilly and woken up as "The Next PJ."

My phone pinged nonstop with mentions on social media, linking to blog posts and articles. I was bombarded with additional requests for comment from new outlets picking up the story, as well as with texts from family and friends asking what was happening. Even my social-media-avoiding, FBI-agent boyfriend, Ryan Johnston, had gotten wind of it, texting me:

WTH is going on? You OK? Miss you.

As I clicked through the media mentions, my spirits sinking, I traced everything back to an article in a major, reputable motorsports publication. That article was fair, comparing me to PJ evenhandedly, and making clear our only similarities were our gender and posting the fastest time in the first practice session of our second attempt at the Indy 500. The reporter used the coincidence to draw attention to the relative lack of women in the Indy 500 in general—only eleven in the 200 years of racing—and included quotes from relevant parties, including the first, Janet Guthrie, and the eleventh, me.

I appreciated that write-up—felt flattered. But the social media trolls added two and two and came up with nineteen, seeing my slower practice the day before as proof I was PJ reincarnated or PJ Junior. That sparked a firestorm of tweets telling anyone at IMS to #CallKatePJ. Then someone suggested ways I was exactly like PJ, with the search term #KateorPJ, and hundreds jumped on that bandwagon. I had a lot of supporters, both male and female, ranging from articulate and normal to hysterical, belligerent, or outright sexual—if I counted people calling me "hot" or offering to have sex with me as support. But the positive voices were lost in a tsunami of comparisons to PJ.

I knew better than to let any yahoo with an opinion and a Twitter account bother me—I was used to shrugging off criticism of my driving, even when I got slammed for driving the same way as men who were praised. That was par for the course. But the comparison to PJ bothered me.

First, because she was the butt of the joke. Even the reputable media outlet's article described her as a no-hoper, there only because her father paid her way. And while that might be true, it was no more true for her than for five to ten male entrants *every year* in the Indy 500. But only PJ became the driver who didn't deserve to be there and couldn't make it. A couple trolls found insulting images of awkward, wimpy girls and posted them with the #KateorPJ tag. Someone posted a photo of a man doing a belly flop into a pool, referencing #KateorPJ, while others wondered if I'd jump if I didn't make the race. Reading that made me taste bile in the back of my throat.

For as much as I felt a connection to her, I still didn't understand what had gone on in PJ's head. What drove her to choose death over the racecar. I believed she'd had skill—certainly as much as hundreds of other Indy 500 entrants. And I hated that people made fun of her. It wasn't right if she wasn't here to defend herself.

I also felt unsettled by my identity being subsumed in PJ's. People were starting to expect me to perform poorly, because that's what she'd done. They felt vindicated by my slow showing the day before, because she'd done the same. Whether it was a joke or not, they wondered in posts if I'd even make it to the race, since she hadn't—ignoring that I'd finished seventeenth the year before.

In the space of thirty-six hours, the racing public no longer saw Kate Reilly, but an amalgam of Kate and a woman who'd killed herself thirty years ago. I was being judged on her record, not mine, and it made me angry.

Fortunately, I wasn't alone. PJ's family was also furious.

A call from IndyCar officials got Holly and me to the track earlier than planned that day to take part in a special news conference. We entered the media center's ground-floor room, where I'd met the press after the first day's practice, to find a dozen chairs arranged in a rough circle and three people who stood at our approach. The IndyCar marketing guy I recognized. The strangers were PJ's mother and brother.

Elena Rodriguez was small—shorter than me—with thick, snow-white hair and an erect bearing, though I noticed she leaned carefully on a polished, black walking stick. She must have been nearly eighty, thin and wiry, and still sharp.

She shook my hand with a firm grip. "It is a great pleasure to meet you, Miss Reilly."

"Kate. Please accept my condolences on the loss of your daughter."

"Thank you, and I am Elena." She turned to the man beside her. "My son, Antonio."

"Tony." In his late forties, he was tall, tan, and fit, ropey with muscle. Swap his dark hair—graying at the temples—for blond and he'd have been the picture of a California surfer.

The IndyCar representative encouraged us all to sit again, saying he'd give us a few minutes and then round up the media representatives for the press conference. Holly sat down with us, but almost immediately received a call she had to take and ducked out.

Elena spoke first. "Thank you for joining us. I know it's a busy week."

"I'm glad to. I'm sorry I didn't know about PJ sooner."

"Before you repeated her accomplishment," Tony said.

I nodded. "Hearing her story has affected me a lot."

"And you think you have heard her story?" Elena bit out.

I straightened, taken aback, as Tony put a hand on hers. "*Mamá*, please."

She softened. "My apologies. You are kind to care. But I'd like to know from whom you have heard PJ's story?"

"People who knew her or observed her that year, mostly team members." I paused. "I only know the basics of what happened. I've been trying to understand her thoughts or reasons, and so far, I can't."

"That makes a few of us," muttered Tony.

Elena elaborated. "Nothing explains my daughter killing herself. She had great faith in God, and as a Catholic, would never have considered suicide. But more, she was a positive person, optimistic, focused on racing."

"Too focused?" Tony asked in a way that made me think it was a discussion they'd had before.

Elena made an impatient gesture. "Kate knows a driver must be focused—even obsessive—to build a successful career. PJ knew what she wanted and went after it. As a woman you have to be even better, more focused, more funded to reach your goals, and thirty years ago in racing, this was especially true. To be only the second woman to make the Indy 500? Only ten years after women weren't allowed in the garages or pits?" She stopped, her burst of energy gone. "Even some in our family thought PJ obsessed."

Tony shrugged. "What did I know? I was a dumb teenager."

"From the stories I've heard," I began, "everything was falling apart. The car wasn't good, she'd crashed, and maybe she was losing confidence in it or herself. Plus people around her were hateful. She had little support."

Elena raised her chin. "She had weathered those storms before. Many times."

"She dealt with rude fans and awful crew every race weekend," Tony added.

"What if she got tired of fighting it?" I struggled to put the part I *did* understand into words. "I'm not everyone's favorite, either. I still get hassled about taking seats a man should have. But I can ignore it because the magic is still there when I get in the car. Because I'm good at what I do, and I can deliver for teams. But if that was gone? Or I thought I was losing it?" I could imagine that moment—imagine the terrifying chasm stretching out in front of me. I took a deep breath. "I'm not sure what I'd do."

"You would *not* do anything so foolish as kill yourself," Elena announced, her voice laced with scorn. "As PJ did not."

I was comforted, then confused. "Then how do you explain what she did?"

Tony sighed, crossing his arms over his chest and leaning back in his chair.

"Simple. She was murdered." Elena held my gaze for a beat. "You've caught killers before, so I want you to prove it."

I felt my jaw drop, and I wasn't sure how long I sat there, staring at her.

"She's serious," Tony added, forestalling my first question.

Elena leaned forward and took my hands. "Idiots in the public and some in the press are making a mockery of my daughter's memory and of you. They make a cartoon figure of PJ, ignoring her individuality and accomplishments. Then they replace your identity with this figure of fun. There is no more PJ. No more Kate Reilly."

"I'm not sure it's quite that bad," I mumbled, still processing the idea PJ might have been murdered. Might not have given up.

Tony raised an eyebrow. "Been on Twitter today?"

Holly let herself back in the room and immediately picked up on the tension. "What's going on?"

Tony pulled a chair closer for her. "My mother is trying to impress on Kate the severity of the hatchet job the media—professional and social—is doing on her character. Eliminating her identity and replacing it with a caricature of poor, suicidal PJ, who can no longer defend herself. Kate isn't sure it's that bad."

Holly grimaced. "It's probably worse."

I stared at her, my chest tight.

This can't be happening to me. My image destroyed by a woman who's been dead for thirty years?

"Every time I look, there's more and more talk," Holly said. "More stupid hashtags. More and more blog mentions."

I dropped my head into my hands.

"But that's what this meeting is about," Holly added, "combating the stories."

"I have another, better solution," Elena put in.

"I'd like to hear it, sugar." Holly sat forward.

"I want Kate to prove PJ was not a suicide, but a murder victim." Elena smiled. "Clear PJ's name, clear Kate's name. Everyone wins."

I straightened and saw the surprise on Holly's face mirroring mine—though hers was tinged with humor I didn't feel.

Elena sighed. "I ask much, Kate. But for thirty years, my daughter has been falsely accused. Maligned. Patronized and pitied as unable to handle the pressure. Now they make her—and you and perhaps all female racers—a joke. Please, will you help restore my daughter's dignity?"

Tears glimmered in her eyes, and I couldn't find it in myself to argue.

Chapter Eight

Present Day

Once ten hand-picked journalists joined us, the IndyCar Series rep started the discussion. "As you all know, in nineteen eighty-seven, PJ Rodriguez, a Mexican-American female driver for Arvin Racing was making an attempt at the Indy 500 when she charted the fastest time in the first day of practice. This year, Kate Reilly, American driver for Beermeier Racing, repeated that achievement. Incidentally, the speeds were 210.772 for PJ and 223.165 for Kate. As you all know, PJ committed suicide before she could qualify for the race."

Or did she? Do I believe Elena? Do I really think PJ was murdered? Doesn't that make more sense than PJ killing herself?

My insides churned as much as my thoughts did.

"We're here," the IndyCar rep continued, "so your outlets can get direct facts and information about the two drivers, as well as impressions and comments from PJ's family—Elena and Tony Rodriguez, PJ's mother and brother—and from Kate. We have not opened this up to a larger group as a courtesy to these three, though a transcript will be provided to the full media center. We trust you will treat them and events past and present with professionalism and respect."

An older reporter I'd seen around the paddock snorted. "Unlike some of our media brethren."

The others smiled, and I started to relax, helped by the fact that these journalists all sat back in their chairs, acting calm. They didn't press forward, asking accusatory questions, like the media had done as I left the pits that first day.

That's why they're the pros.

They started with questions about PJ: her upbringing, racing background, and family support for pursuing the Indy 500.

Elena handled most of the responses. "We were behind her completely. Miguel, her father, used his business contacts to secure the sponsorship she needed—in early years, he funded her racing, but as she got better, there was value for other companies." She smiled. "We didn't always attend the races, because PJ said we made her nervous."

"You were here that year," said Lyla Thomas, a woman in her sixties who'd introduced herself to us before we started talking. I'd heard of her before, a career journalist who'd also been a racer, earning a first-place trophy at Sebring, a fourth-place showing at Le Mans, and the nickname "Lead-Foot" Lyla.

"Miguel, Tony, and myself were here in eighty-seven," Elena confirmed.

"Where's your husband now?" Lyla asked.

Tony spoke for the first time. "He passed away fifteen years ago. A heart attack."

"Our condolences," she said, as the others murmured agreement.

"What did you think when you found out PJ had been fastest in the first practice session?" one of the other men asked. "And then that she was slowest the next few days, including crashing twice?"

Elena smiled. "To start, I remember we were excited for her. PJ was flying high, happy. 'I will show them, *Mamá*,' she told me. Then she was upset the next few days, as she could not figure out the car. 'It is a beast,' she said, 'but I will master it.' She couldn't understand why the car never improved, though she and her crew tried everything."

Another female reporter spoke up. "Kate, you've gone through some of the same ups and downs. What's your mental and emotional state been like?"

"A lot the same as Elena describes." I paused. "The first day was magical—shocking and thrilling. I was so glad to get that result and attention for Beermeier Racing, Frame Savings, and Beauté, who've been incredibly supportive of me. The days since have been frustrating. My team has been great, and they've been right there with me, working to make the car better. But we're all used to that. I don't expect to be at the top of the charts at Indy, so it was a bonus for everyone on the team."

The reporters smiled, and kept taking notes, some on paper notebooks, some in laptop computers.

"Kate, you said your team's behind you. Has your relationship with them always been good?" Lyla turned from me to Elena and Tony. "And can either of you comment on PJ's relationship with her team and if that might have helped or hurt her?"

Elena nodded at me to begin.

"The crew I'm working with has been great from day one. They're smart and dedicated. I know they've got my back, and they know I'm doing everything I can on track. I've been especially glad to be with them for the full IndyCar season this year—I think that's helped." I glanced at Elena and Tony. "I recognize how fortunate I am, because that may not have been the case for PJ."

Tony made a frustrated noise. "Let's take the gloves off. PJ's crew hated her." Elena protested, and Tony waved a hand. "Not every crew member. Some of them were supportive. But some of them hated her. In fact, I wouldn't be surprised if her ongoing car problems were the crew doing it on purpose."

I caught my breath, and most of the journalists looked surprised. Except Lyla and the older man.

Lyla furrowed her brow. "Wouldn't sabotage defeat the team's purpose?"

"So would murdering your driver, but that happened. I

wouldn't put anything past them." Tony sat back in his chair, arms crossed, a satisfied smile on his face.

A young reporter, whose tapping fingers had accompanied every word we'd said so far, stopped typing. "You think PJ was murdered?"

Elena sat up straight. "We do. We know she would never have killed herself."

"But the police closed the investigation as suicide. Thirty years ago," the kid said. "Did she leave a note?"

"No note," Tony replied.

"Who do you think killed her?" one of the men asked.

Elena looked from reporter to reporter. "Maybe you can figure that out."

"All we know is suicide would never have occurred to her." Tony leaned forward. "It went against her religion, and it wasn't her personality. We watched our great-grandmother die when we were young, and PJ told me she prayed that she'd go like her: peacefully, in her bed." He shook his head. "She wouldn't have given herself seconds of terror falling from a great height—she was afraid of heights."

"Are you sure her death was connected to racing?" Lyla paused, appearing to choose her words carefully. "A child is killed and one of her parents is a powerful businessman, as I believe your husband was, Elena? It's logical to ask if it's related to the parent—and I mean no offense."

Tony had flushed red as Lyla spoke, but Elena's hand on his kept him quiet. She nodded. "I would advise you not to believe all rumors you hear, but you are not far off base about my husband. Still, we are sure it was not any of his enemies."

Tony cut off the questions several journalists started to ask. "No one ever claimed responsibility. If a rival killed my sister for an advantage, it would have been taken—or if an enemy for revenge, he'd have openly reveled in my father's suffering. But there was no one. My father's business did not suffer, no one beat him in business for a decade, and no one crowed about revenge. It must be about PJ's role in the racing world."

The room was quiet for a couple beats, then the old guy turned to me, grinning. "It's been a couple years, Kate, but you used to have a reputation as a sleuth. You gonna figure out if someone did PJ in?"

I chuckled, though even to my ears it sounded forced. "I have enough to do getting ready for the biggest race of the year, don't you think?"

I wasn't sure anyone bought my act.

Chapter Nine

May 1987

"Arvie?" A crew member stuck his head around the divider and found the team owner. "Got people asking for PJ, but since she's not here, they asked for you."

Walking into the main garage area, Arvie spotted the visitors immediately and walked forward with an outstretched hand. "You must be PJ's family."

Her father, who Arvie only knew as a voice on the phone, turned away from his examination of a racecar and smiled. "*Sí, señor* Arvin. I am Miguel Rodriguez." They shook hands, and Miguel continued. "This is PJ's mother, Elena. Over there, already bothering your mechanics is my son, Antonio."

Arvie shook hands with the others, and glanced at the son, who stood close to one of the cars, but wasn't in the crew's way.

"*Oye*, Antonio," Miguel called.

The teenager trotted over, flipping a long sweep of dark hair out of his eyes. He grinned and pumped Arvie's hand. "Dude, this is totally awesome! Am I cool over there watching? And hey, call me Tony."

Arvie bit back a smile. "Just stay out of their way."

"Awesome." Tony went back to his observation post.

Miguel rolled his eyes. "My son thinks he lives in that *Valley Girl* movie."

"Your fault for sending him to school in California," Elena put in with a smile. She and her son had no accent at all, while Miguel's was strong but understandable.

Arvie studied them, seeing subtle-but-expensive watches, jewelry, and shoes. And a 5,000-dollar handbag on PJ's mother's arm. None of that surprised him. He'd already known there was money in PJ's family—because it took money to attract money. PJ wasn't paying her own way into the car, but she did have sponsorship from established, blue-chip companies in Mexico and Central and South America. He'd suspected family connections, and nothing he saw in the flesh changed his mind.

"PJ should be back soon—she's doing a photo op with a local youth group. But I'm glad to meet you all," Arvie said. "Have you been to the Speedway before?"

"Miguel was here last year," Elena said, "but only for one day in the stands, not in the garages. This year, I insisted, even though PJ won't like it."

Arvie raised his eyebrows. "How can she not want your support?"

"Too independent," Miguel grunted. He was a tall man, wearing jeans, a well-tailored navy blazer, and loafers with no socks.

Elena grimaced. "My daughter says we make her more nervous if we're here than if we're at home. But I can't miss her racing in the Indianapolis 500."

Arvie raised a cautionary hand. "It's not set in stone yet. We still have to qualify, and at least four cars won't make the field."

"About that." Miguel rubbed his hands together. "How do we guarantee it? More funds for better parts? Tell me, and we will make it happen. PJ must make the race."

Yessir, deep pockets, thought Arvie. "We have all the parts we need, and they're the best available. What we need is something money can't buy."

"Try me." Miguel raised an eyebrow.

His wife swatted his shoulder. "You can't solve everything for her."

"I can try."

Arvie smiled, liking them both. "What we need most is for the driver and team to have more time and experience together. They're starting to work together well—to bond. But sometimes it can be a slow process. It takes the time it takes."

Elena patted her husband's arm. "She wouldn't thank you for fixing it for her. She wants to do it herself. Win her own battles."

Tony had moved near enough to hear some of the conversation, and he laughed. "But *el jefe* must fix everything." He patted his father on the shoulder. "Let her succeed or fail on her own, Pops."

Arvie saw the look of frustration Miguel aimed at his son.

A classic overprotective father? Don't get involved. If curiosity doesn't kill the cat, it might take away its race funding.

PJ's father turned back to Arvie. "Is there nothing that can be done to help PJ? You said more time? I can pay overtime fees, no problem."

"That's covered, should it be necessary." Arvie shook his head. "I'm afraid it's up to PJ and the team now."

Miguel frowned. "I do not like to feel helpless."

"I understand." Arvie caught sight of PJ walking down the row of garages. "Here she is now."

Miguel and Elena stepped outside the garage in time to see two men get in PJ's way. When she stepped to the side, they blocked her. She stepped the other direction, and they blocked her again.

Elena put a hand on Miguel's arm. "Let her handle it," she said quietly.

Arvie wasn't sure that was a good idea, but he stayed put for the moment also.

PJ stood still, no expression on her face. Arvie and PJ's family couldn't hear what the men said, until one of them shouted, "We asked a question! If you're going to be a bitch about it, we'll treat you like one."

The other man mimed bending her over and pumped his hips back and forth.

Miguel moved before Elena could stop him. He reached the men in four long strides, spun the speaker around, and punched him in the jaw. The other man dropped his beer and started waving his arms and yelling. While PJ shouted at her father in Spanish and held onto his arm to keep him from doing more damage, a portly yellow-shirted security guard arrived at a fast waddle, blowing his whistle to break up the fight.

"Shit." Arvie stepped forward to talk to the yellow-shirt. "Get him into the garage," he instructed PJ and watched as she hustled Miguel out of sight.

"What the hell?" The man who'd been hit struggled up from the ground with help from his friend. "It's a free country. I can say what I want. That dude hit me!"

The yellow-shirt puffed up his chest. "That man can't leave," he said, ignoring the fact Miguel was already gone. "Security will need to talk to him. Get him back here!"

The team owner's job is never done.

Arvie held up his hands and spoke soothingly. "He's close by, and he'll be happy to talk with security. However, he is an angry father defending his daughter from rude, offensive remarks." He glared at the two clearly inebriated idiots. "From crude language no gentleman should use to a lady."

Arvie was right, that phrasing appealed to the sixty-something yellow-shirt, who turned a baleful eye on the two young offenders. "I see." He pursed his lips. "Maybe I'll call security to take you boys in."

The troublemakers were gone inside of twenty seconds. Arvie turned to the yellow-shirt with a smile. "Thanks, Earl."

"How much horseshit were you shoveling there, Arvie?"

"None at all, my friend. Sadly, none at all."

Arvie reentered the garage to find PJ standing with her brother near her car, talking to one of the new, young mechanics, Stan Wright. Her parents stood together by the office area, on the far side of the car. Miguel cast frustrated glances at his daughter.

Arvie went to his driver first. "You okay, kid?"

PJ lifted one shoulder in a shrug. "It's the same as yesterday or the day before."

"Are you dealing with it?"

"Dude," her brother said, "I'm telling you, she's *tough*."

As PJ smiled up at her brother, Arvie saw a lightness on her face that had been missing for weeks. "I think your family should stick around."

PJ closed up again. "No, I must do this myself."

"Your father…" Arvie began, but PJ overrode him.

"My father tries to control everything. It is not how I want to live my life." She glanced at her brother. "Tony understands."

Tony tore his gaze away from the engine in front of him. "I totally do, Sis. But you know the old man won't stay away. We're going up to Chicago for a couple days, but we'll be back next week."

PJ clenched her fists. "I must qualify on my own. It must happen because I am good enough, not because my father fixes it." She paused. "I know they will be here for the race. But qualifying is the battle I will fight. I will get there on my own."

Arvie nodded. "It's make or break for all of us to qualify this weekend or next. Do or die."

Chapter Ten

Present Day

My empathy for PJ grew with every story I heard about her. I knew what it was like to be leered at, groped, and propositioned. To be put down by teams, sponsors, and fans. PJ and I both had families that tried to define us—control us in different ways.

PJ struggled for her own identity with a controlling father, and I had to make my way in the absence of both father and mother. Yet I've still got it better than she did...

I was able to shut out the turmoil I felt about PJ when I got in the car, but regardless, our practice session on Wednesday was awful—and my actions only added fuel to the comparisons between me and PJ.

I was slowly getting more comfortable running in dirty air—disrupted airflow from other cars nearby—which was mostly what we'd do in race conditions. We worked on making the car faster, and I worked on how I could follow—if I could hang on through the turbulence with a little front wing underneath or outside the car next to me.

Primarily, dealing with dirty air meant figuring out how to combat push, or understeer, in racing language—the tendency of the car not to respond when you turned the wheel. Many drivers went low on the track, being as aggressive as possible, trying to work with the push and skate through a turn. Other drivers told

me if you tried that maneuver in past years and got loose—if
the back end lost grip, also known as oversteer—you could more
easily catch the car, by lifting off the throttle and chasing it up
the track. But with the new configuration of the chassis, not
to mention a full fuel load and tires that weren't totally up to
pressure, there wasn't much hope. Or so I learned the hard way.

Worse, I took someone else with me.

I went low in Turn 2, and the back end snapped. *Catch it,
catch it! Shit!*

The car careened up the track. *Catch it!*

I couldn't. Then I bumped someone else. *No, no. Shit!*

The back end of my car headed for the wall. Fighting, standing on the brake pedal even though I was sliding. Hoping to
grab traction. Turning the wheel. *Hands off the wheel!*

Crunch. *Back on the brakes.*

Rolling to a stop. Trying to find the breath I'd lost on impact.
Seeing the other car nosing into the inner wall down the track,
then driving away slowly.

Shit. Don't let them be wrecked, too.

My heart was in my throat as the safety crew helped me climb
out of the car at the exit of Turn 2. I'd screwed up. I owed my
team, the other driver, and the other driver's team big apologies.
It looked like only rear wing damage on my car, but I was terri-
fied I was wrong, that the damage would be more severe than I
thought. That I might have jeopardized our qualifying efforts.
Rationally, I knew we had another full day of practice before
the first day of qualifying. But at a minimum, this would be a
setback, and the other driver would be furious at me.

Back at the garage, I apologized to my guys and swore it
wouldn't happen again. They were surprisingly calm. As Banjo,
the tire guy, put it, "Hell of a lot better now than in the race
or even in qualifying." Thankfully, the other driver was also
understanding, once we'd gotten through the initial stiffness of
my approach and apology.

I stuck around in the garage that night until my crew kicked
me out, promising they wouldn't need an all-nighter to have

the car ready the next day. It took comfort food and a long, hot shower to start dealing with the guilt I felt.

By the next morning, Thursday, I'd pulled myself together. I was ready for a better day ahead. I had a momentary setback when I saw all my social media notifications and started reading posts—apparently the media trolls had picked up on PJ's family's murder accusation and were running with it. Reactions ranged from suggestions that I solve the mystery, to saying I already had, to wondering if I'd be the killer's next victim. I texted Holly, asking her to deal with it, and I turned off notifications.

Then I meditated for a few minutes and started the day over. Fortunately, my first stop involved cake.

My biggest sponsor, Frame Savings and Loan, a national bank, was dishing up anniversary cake as part of a celebration for their Indianapolis headquarters, and they'd started mid-morning to accommodate my practice schedule. There were more activities and speeches happening throughout the day for their celebration, but I'd only be there for an hour, long enough to say a few words about the race, thank them for their support, and pose for about a hundred photos.

Over the past two years of their sponsorship, I'd discovered a real affection for the people who worked for Frame Savings. The unwavering and enthusiastic support by its legions of employees was one of the most unexpected benefits of being Frame Savings' driver, and the Indianapolis celebration delivered more of the same. I continually marveled that such a solid, caring community had been created by a family I mostly hated—except for my father, his wife, and kids.

Fortunately, in the last two years, I hadn't had to interact with the Reillys I didn't like, not since a series of events had rocked the family and the bank's management structure. One of my cousins had been killed and an uncle was outed as leading a double life, as well as facilitating money-laundering and other shady activities. My father, James Hightower Reilly III, while slow to understand what was happening under his own nose, had figured it out and cleaned house—which meant I didn't have to dread sponsor appearances like this one.

Before I went inside, a savvy fan caught me. He was a small man with ears that stuck straight out from his head—a serious collector almost weighed down by the thick accordion file he held for me to sign on.

"Signature on two items." He wasn't asking.

On top was a flyer from the Frame Savings celebration happening that day. Underneath it was a photo of my car.

He gestured with his chin. "Date it three days ago, write 'Fastest'?"

"Did you take it that day?" I studied the photo. It was definitely this year's car, but I couldn't tell if it was from the first day of practice or not.

"Of course."

His abrupt tone amused me, and I wrote what he requested and moved on. No selfies with the driver for this guy. He was all business.

I entered through the staff door of the bank, a five-story, historic brick structure topped with classical moldings, and found my father waiting.

"Amelia and the kids send their love," he said, after I'd hugged him. "They'll be here for the race—and in a month, Lara will be here permanently. She's looking forward to spending time with you."

"She got the aerodynamics job?" I knew it had been my half sister's goal, after receiving a math degree with top honors, but I hadn't heard the final result.

My father nodded. "Now we'll have two children in one city—assuming you're staying in Indianapolis."

"For a while." Six months prior, when I'd been sure IndyCar would be my focus for the next couple years, I'd moved here to be closer to series and team activities.

"Good. As for this, you'll speak after me for about fifteen minutes, and then we'll have you cut the cake, take photos, and get out of here."

"Works for me."

"But first I have to introduce you to your biggest fan on our executive team—besides myself, of course." He waved over a fireplug of a woman in her fifties, who sported a sprayed-stiff helmet of poofy, blond hair and a ready, genuine smile. "Meet Charlene Menfis, one of our new regional VPs, and a rising star in the bank."

She pumped my hand. "So excited to meet you. I'm a huge fan of the Indy 500—I grew up in town and come every year with my family—and I'm all about the female drivers. Meeting you is the highlight of my weekend." She beamed at me like I was Santa Claus and she was three years old.

My father excused himself to check the stage, and I smiled at Charlene. "Thanks for the support. You've probably seen a lot of us over the years. How long have you been coming?"

"This will be my forty-third year here. I was eleven when my dad brought me for the first time as a birthday present—hell, that dates me! I had such a good time that first year, I begged him to buy us tickets for my birthday the next year, and the year after, and so on. It's my birthday tradition."

"You'll be in the Frame Savings suite?"

"Every chance I get." She gestured at her navy blue pantsuit. "Race weekend, I'll be head to toe pink or black and white checkers—most of it Kate Reilly gear."

"I appreciate it." Something clicked for me. "You would have been here the year PJ Rodriguez died."

She grimaced. "I'd been particularly excited about her, since she was close to my age and might have been only the second woman to run the race, if she'd qualified."

"What was the race like then? And what did people think of PJ?"

"It was grittier, more male. Less international. More open access, wilder, somehow." She thought back. "PJ wasn't mentioned much on race day—a minute of silence during the pre-race ceremonies—something along the line of 'a driver we lost this year.' But there was plenty of talk in the crowd about her."

That couldn't be good. "What did people say?"

"Some of it I'll never forget. The nice ones called her uppity, no-talent, and a token. The rude ones called her a whore, a slut who slept her way into a car, the C-word." She shook her head. "We've come a long way, baby, but as I'm sure you know, we haven't come as far as we need to."

"Sing it, Sister." I sighed.

Charlene smiled. "What shocked me wasn't hearing that from the public, but hearing it from the racing community. That year I had paddock access—they'd just built the new, concrete-block garages. I stuck my head into a lot of them, watching the crews work. Listening to people talk."

"You must have been pretty rare even as a fan in the paddock."

"There were women around, but not as many as these days. It was an education." She took a deep breath. "People from other teams said death was what she deserved, because even her physical assets couldn't make up for her lack of talent. That servicing men was all she was good for, and she never deserved to set foot in a car in the first place. That the only money she made people was by dying."

I felt pain in my chest. "That's awful. And cruel, to talk about money."

She nodded. "That's why I remembered it. My impression was lots of people had managed to profit from her death."

"Any idea who?"

"Not a chance." She laughed. "All I remember was her team owner and an insurance payout, because he was the most obvious person and that was the most surprising means. I'd never heard of insurance in racing before then, but people were impressed with how much money he'd gotten."

That's not much of a legacy for poor PJ.

A few minutes later, I stood with my father in the bank's soaring atrium, facing a couple hundred excited faces. He welcomed everyone and congratulated them on their milestone before introducing me. I talked about the car and the race, thanked them for their support, and explained our efforts to raise awareness and funds for breast cancer organizations. Hands waved, so I took questions, telling them what I thought our chances were—a top-fifteen finish would be a "win" for us—and what it's like to go wheel-to-wheel at more than 200 mph—exciting as all hell.

The third question, from a woman in the front row, threw me. "Everyone says you'll freak out like PJ Rodriguez. How will you make sure you make it to the race?"

I went blank for a moment, then cleared my throat. "No one should have any concerns about me making it to the race. I will be there."

"That's what she said," called a voice from the crowd.

What the hell?

Another voice agreed, "Are you sure you won't lose your nerve like her?"

"I'm not her. I'm me. I qualified for the race last year and finished seventeenth. I'm thrilled to be here again this year and happy with the car and team." I paused, feeling like I offered nothing better than "because I said so."

The audience stirred, and I could see concern on some of the faces close to me. Before my father could step closer and move us to the next activity, I spoke again.

"This is the chance I've always wanted. It's who I am and what I live for, and I can't thank you enough for helping me go after it. I guarantee you, I'll be in the race representing Frame Savings proudly—and I'll do everything I can to be in the hunt."

Chapter Eleven

Present Day

I thought about the exchange as I drove to the Speedway for practice.

How do you convince someone you won't lose your nerve? There's no argument against "But what if you get scared?" except time proving the questioner wrong.

I slammed the steering wheel with an open palm. "Besides," I shouted to my empty car, "it's sexist to ask me if I'll follow in her footsteps simply because we're both women. Are they asking men if they'll 'do a PJ?' Dammit, I hate that crap."

I breathed deeply, feeling marginally better and glad to have time alone in my car to vent all the things I'd never say in public. It infuriated me that people expected me to act a certain way because another woman had, but what made it worse was their underlying assumption—the proof PJ lost her nerve was that she killed herself.

But what if she didn't? What if the only thing people remembered about her was totally wrong? What if you went down in history as a coward, not a fighter?

I felt sick at the thought. I knew I wouldn't lose my nerve or stop wanting to push the limit in a racecar. Though I hadn't known PJ, from everything I'd learned about her, she couldn't have gone from total commitment to total defeat either.

You think she was murdered. Does that mean you're investigating?

I wasn't ready to admit it, and I spent the rest of the drive singing along with the radio to distract myself. As I parked, I saw a familiar figure locking his car door a few spaces away. I caught up to him before he'd gotten very far.

"Chuck?" I held out a hand. "I'm Kate. I'm not sure we've met yet.

"I don't think so." His green eyes twinkled at me as we shook hands. "I'm enjoying the hospitality of your garage."

"I'm glad. You've been in the racing business for a long time?"

"Decades, my dear. Gaffey Insurance, founded in 1979." His grin took ten years off his face. I pegged him as somewhere in his seventies, and still fit, for all his white hair and stiff walk. He winked at me. "You a customer?"

"I am, indeed."

I heard someone nearby call out, but I was lost in thought about what to ask Chuck about PJ. Then the guy called again. "Hey, PJ, don't wreck again today."

I heard male and female laughter and had to force myself not to react.

Chuck had no such hesitation. "Is that directed at you?"

I nodded, keeping my gaze straight ahead. "You've heard the talk?"

"Some. But I don't see why they would call you by her name, much less question your ability."

"It's become a thing to assume I'll imitate her in most respects." I flinched as I heard another man, closer in.

"It's PJ Junior, right? Can I get your signature?"

Though it went against every ingrained behavior, I ignored him and kept walking.

"Don't be rude!" The man jogged ahead of me, clutching his backpack to his chest. "I asked for your signature."

"No, you asked for someone else's. My name is Kate."

He smirked. "I think PJ Junior's fun."

"I don't." I stepped around him and continued walking.

"What a bitch," I heard behind me.

"Young man!" Chuck turned around before I could stop him. "There is no excuse for that kind of language or behavior. How would you like it if someone called you a rude and insulting name and then was angry you didn't approve?"

The man looked ashamed, but still defensive. "Can't she take a joke?"

"It isn't funny to make light of someone dying," Chuck replied. "Would you find it funny to be compared to someone who committed suicide?"

The man worried the hem of his vintage Indy 500 tee-shirt. "I guess not. Sorry."

I nodded and started to turn away.

"But can I have your signature? Kate?"

I kept the sigh internal and signed the photo he had of me in my car the previous year. Then a man walked up with his daughter, a twelve-year-old who'd been racing quarter midgets—small, purpose-built cars raced on oval tracks—for five years and already had a half-dozen wins to her name.

"I'm so glad you're out there," she told me, as I signed the back of her Team Kate shirt. "I'll be there one day, too."

I believed her.

Chuck had waited for me, and as we got moving again, I thanked him for the support.

"You handled even the rude fans with grace, Kate," he said as we walked. "I hope things don't become as intolerable for you as they did for poor PJ."

"You knew her?"

"I've always been close to Ron, and the community was smaller then—felt like it, anyway. I saw some of what she went through." He shook his head. "Actually, I almost got out after we lost her."

That surprised me. "She affected you that much? Did you work with her—did she have insurance?"

"No. Ron had coverage, of course, and I like to think it helped him after PJ…in the scramble with sponsorships and drivers."

He shrugged. "Insurance wouldn't have helped PJ. Seems like nothing could have. Such a senseless waste of human life."

"Her suicide made sense to you?"

He raised his eyebrows at me. "If you'd seen what she went through in the paddock—then to soar so high on the track, only to sink as low as can be?" He nodded. "It made terrible, awful sense. Don't you think?"

I played it safe. "How can I know? I have a hard time understanding how someone like me could choose that, when I never, ever could."

"You're a different person, my dear, thank goodness." He paused. "It was difficult to see the pain everyone went through. I found myself seriously considering if I wanted to remain involved in racing at all—knowing we could lose a team player without warning, on the track or off."

"Can't rule it out. We know it happens."

"I've come to understand it's the central heartbreak of racing."

"But you didn't get out," I said. "You stayed involved."

"I thought long and hard about a line of work where I could make a difference ahead of time, instead of picking up the pieces afterwards."

"Everyone needs support in those moments, as well."

"Hey, look, it's PJ!" another voice in the crowd called.

I grimaced. "Sure, we're different people."

"Trust me, you are," Chuck said, as he gestured for me to precede him into the garage. "Regardless of what small-minded people think, it's not all right to smear your name—and someone else's, too."

I appreciated his words, but people in the paddock didn't agree, because I heard a half-dozen references to PJ every time I stepped foot outside the garage. I was glad to get in the car for a reprieve.

We spent the hot, muggy practice session improving the car, millimeter by millimeter. We weren't anywhere near the top of the charts, but by the halfway point of the six-hour session, we'd jumped from thirtieth of thirty-four cars to twenty-first. That gave us a boost of confidence as we inched closer to qualifying weekend, everyone aware that with only thirty-three starting positions on offer, one team wouldn't make the show.

During one pit stop, Alexa radioed with a different message than usual. "Holly says to tell you your secret weapon is here."

I peered into the pit box—a tall, metal toolbox on wheels, with bench seating, desks for six people, and a canvas canopy. Sure enough, there was Gramps, fresh from being picked up at the airport by Holly. I waved and saw an answering grin on his face.

His smile was still there hours later after the practice session was over. I got out of the car and had a few minutes of conversation with Nolan and Alexa, who were as pleased as I was with the improvements we'd made. As we wound down, I thanked them for letting Gramps stay on the pit box in the shade.

"We're keeping him!" Nolan burst out. "The big gains we made happened after he got here." He turned and waved Gramps over. "He's our walking four-leaf clover."

I laughed, watching Gramps pick his way over hoses. With his short height, bowed legs, and merry expression, Gramps was the image of a leprechaun. But he was as Irish as strudel—of mostly German heritage, by way of New Mexico.

"Whatever works," I said to Nolan, then threw my arms around my grandfather.

"Ah, Katie, there you are," Gramps murmured, patting my back.

My throat got thick, and I didn't trust myself to speak. It was a rare race that Gramps attended these days—after taking me to every single one in my first decade and a half of racing—but he'd wanted to be with me for this go-round at Indy. I hadn't realized how much I'd missed him until I laid eyes on him. I squeezed him tight.

A few minutes later, we all went back to the garage, and Alexa and Nolan wrapped things up quickly for the night while I changed and grabbed my tote from my locker. I was digging through it for my keys when I discovered a folded piece of lined, yellow notepaper. I opened it and read the words.

"Son of a bitch," I muttered.

Holly poked her head around the lockers. "What is it now?"

I flapped the page at her. "Anonymous note. Threatening me. It says, 'Learn from PJ, or you'll be next.'"

"What the hell does that mean?"

"I have no idea. That I'll commit suicide? That I'll die?" I shook my head and crumpled the note, looking for the nearest trash can. "I can't take it seriously when it's a page ripped from a yellow pad. And I'm not dealing with crackpot racing fans today."

Holly took the paper. "Ignore it. Just like you need to ignore speculation that you might be investigating PJ's death."

Where did that come from?

It took me a minute. "The Ringer said something."

"Don't do anything about it, but in case someone brings it up…" She sighed. "He's reporting PJ's family's belief that she was killed and wondering if 'Sleuth Kate' is on the case."

I rolled my eyes. "He always did like his nicknames."

"Ignore it. Take Gramps to see his buddies. Talk later."

Focus on the good stuff, like Gramps being here.

I put my arm around his waist as we walked to my car. "Don't feel like you have to sit on our pit box all day, every day."

"I don't mess with superstition. I'll be there until my luck wears off." Gramps shook his head. "Tell me, how's Ryan these days?"

I smiled, thinking of Los Angeles-based FBI agent Ryan Johnston, the man I'd been seeing for a couple years. When I'd finally taken him to Albuquerque to visit my grandparents earlier in the spring, Ryan and Gramps had gotten on like a house on fire, in Gramps' words. I was surprised Gramps hadn't been in touch with Ryan himself.

"He's good. Busy with work. He's not sure he can get out for the race, but if so, it'll be last-minute next weekend."

"He'll miss a lot. Like Mug 'N' Bun!" Gramps took two skipping steps.

We were headed for the historic drive-in on West 10th that had been around for more than fifty years—plenty long, even if it was only half the time the Indy 500 had been running. A local institution, it offered everything from hot dogs, burgers, and grilled sandwiches to fried potatoes and breaded everything. But what kept people coming back was their homemade root beer. That and the history of the place.

I knew Gramps had been there many times in the past, during his long career as an electrical systems expert on a wide variety of racecars. Now retired, he still worked on a few special projects in the shop behind his home, and he hadn't been back to Indianapolis in decades.

"We're meeting some of your old friends?" I asked.

"A bunch of old farts like me. We used to get together regularly." He grinned. "I always liked it when we met here. I do love my root beer."

He was in his element an hour later, talking with his cronies, mug in hand—though I was surprised at the age range of the group sharing three picnic tables under the shade structure to one side of Mug 'N' Bun's main room. There were plenty of men in their sixties and seventies, like Gramps. But there were also men—and one woman—in their thirties and forties. Even a couple guys my age or younger who paid close attention, soaking up the wisdom on offer.

I settled at a table with my own root beer, burger, and fries, content to watch Gramps joking and laughing with his friends. It wasn't long before a good-looking man I guessed to be in his late fifties joined me with his own meal and introduced himself.

"Paul Lauth. My compliments on your better run today."

I nodded in lieu of shaking. "Thanks. You there with a team?"

"I'm working as a manager now, but I ran there a few times in the past."

"I'm sorry, I didn't realize."

He waved a hand holding a fry. "You can't know everyone who's entered the 500. But I wanted to tell you something— reassure you." He paused and ate the fry. "You're not PJ, so don't listen to all of that garbage."

I felt my eyes go wide. "I appreciate that. You knew her?"

"I was dating her."

Chapter Twelve

May 1987

PJ checked her watch. Paul was late, but she knew how unpredictable debriefing conversations could be after a practice session. Still, she was tired of waiting.

"You will be here for a few minutes?" she asked one of the mechanics.

He didn't take his attention from the engine in front of him. "We'll be here."

PJ flinched at his unfriendly tone and did her best to ignore the resentment on the face of another crew member. Defensiveness flared inside her.

Maybe I wouldn't do so poorly if you did your jobs better! Ay, pendejos, *did you never consider this is your fault as much as mine? How might this be different if anyone cared about me on this team?*

She swallowed those responses, thanked the mechanic, and exited the garage. She knew she was being unfair to her engineer, Jerry, and Donny, the crew member who escorted her to and from her car each day, as well as others on the team. But as hard as she'd tried, there were men on the crew who'd hated her from day one. She took a deep breath of air scented with hot metal and rubber.

I will let it blow over me like the wind.

She walked along the brand-new, concrete-block garage building that housed her team's cars and rounded the end, headed two buildings away to the garage structure closest to the track, where Paul's team had their spaces. She stiffened as she heard the first comments from passersby.

"It's that slow chick."

"That bitch, taking up a car one of her betters could use."

"Like who?"

PJ risked a glance toward the voices and saw a young woman—with long, feathered hair wearing running shorts and a tight tee-shirt—who hung on the arm of a shirtless, over-muscled man, looking adoringly at him. She repeated, in the same breathy tone. "Like who, baby?"

The man sneered under his thick, black mustache. "Any of them. Everyone knows girls can't drive as good as men can."

PJ snapped her eyes forward again, before the man saw her. Another male voice startled her, speaking right next to her ear.

"Don't listen to them." The tone was aggressive, but the words and face were kind. "You've got plenty of supporters, PJ. You get out there and show them the car doesn't care what you look like."

PJ suppressed her impulse to run and instead smiled at the man. "Thank you. That's nice of you to say."

He nodded and held out a program and pen. "Would you sign this for me?"

"With pleasure." She was relieved when he didn't try to detain her once she'd scrawled her name.

She kept moving, doing her best to tune out the chatter around her. She knew Jerry wouldn't be happy with her for walking through Gasoline Alley without Donny. But practice had been over for more than an hour, and the crowd had dwindled.

"Besides," she muttered to herself, "I'm tired of feeling I have no freedom."

She took another deep breath and straightened her shoulders. As she rounded the end of the garage, she saw Paul leaning against the wall in front of his team space. With a tall, willowy blonde plastered to him. Undulating, slithering against him.

PJ stopped abruptly, gaping, unsure whether to move forward and fight or turn around and give up. *No one could blame me for giving up.*

Before she could decide, Paul saw her. He pushed away from the other woman and jogged straight to PJ, who turned on her heel to leave before he reached her.

"PJ, God, that's not what it looked like. Wait." He sounded angry.

She kept walking, not trusting her tongue.

"Dammit, stop! Don't do this."

She whirled to him, only vaguely aware of curious onlookers. "Don't tell me what to do. Not when I see you with that woman. How many others are there every day?"

Paul grabbed her hands. "You know what it's like as a driver. There are always fans on you, wanting something, wanting you. It doesn't mean I want them, but I can't be rude. You understand that."

PJ made a sound that started as a laugh and ended on a sob, which shocked her. She straightened her spine. "No, I do not *know what it is like* to have fans wanting me. All people want me to do is go away. And from the people I trust—who I think I can trust—I cannot take betrayal."

"PJ, look at me." Paul spoke quietly. "Really look at me, and hear me."

She studied him, tall and handsome, with dark hair and cheekbones to die for.

He held her gaze steadily. "I'm not interested in the offers. I'm interested in you. I was coming to you when she stopped me, and I was trying to be polite."

PJ bristled and Paul stopped her. "I'll be rude next time, okay?"

"You do that, or you will be walking with a limp when I am through with you."

Paul grinned. "That's my girl." He laced his fingers through hers. "Let's get dinner and you can tell me about your car getting better."

Three garages away from PJ's team, they ran into a reporter for the broadcast network. The man greeted PJ and inquired after her day, then asked if he could speak with Paul for a moment. PJ went ahead to her team's office space, and Paul followed a few minutes later. As he approached PJ's garage, he heard a loud, frustrated voice.

"What if we weren't stuck with her?"

Paul froze outside the door as another man shushed the first. "Isn't she here?"

"She's off chasing after that driver. Or giving Arvie a ride in order to keep her ride." That was an older, more bitter voice.

The other man was clearly younger. More innocent. "You don't think—do you?"

"Why else is she here? It's not her driving skills."

"But, Jimmy," the younger man sputtered, "that first day she was so good."

"Probably whored out for the Timing and Scoring guys to put her up there."

Paul couldn't move. *PJ can't be in there listening to this, right? She must have stepped out.*

Jimmy went on. "I wish Arvie would get over it and replace her. With a real driver we might actually have a chance."

"You don't think she'll snap out of it one of these days?"

Jimmy scoffed. "We're lucky if we don't get bumped out of the field. Best case, we'll end up pretending we're happy going to the party for the last-row qualifiers. Unless Arvie gets smart and replaces her."

"Can he do that?"

"He can do whatever the hell he wants, if he stops being pussy-whipped." Paul heard the sound of tools clanking on the floor as the older mechanic kept ranting. "We keep doing this, undoing that, doing the other thing. Fixing shit that ain't broken, because the princess can't go fast. I'm damn sick of it. I'm done for today. She can figure it out."

"We can't—"

"Sure we can. Let's get the others together, then I'll buy you a beer."

Paul heard the men move down the long garage bay that housed Arvin Racing's three cars. He slipped into the garage and behind the dividers forming a makeshift office and changing area, hoping against hope the space was empty.

One engineer sat facing the wall, working with a calculator and a spreadsheet, bouncing away to whatever music played through his Walkman. As Paul moved farther back in the space, his heart sank. PJ was slumped in a chair, her eyes glassy with shock.

He crouched in front of her and held her cold hands, chafing them to generate some warmth. "They're ignorant fools. You know better. You know you've got talent, and you know Arvie believes in you."

PJ finally whispered, "My own team. I didn't think they hated me that much."

Paul hugged her. "Don't listen to them. Ignore them."

"But if I don't have my team behind me," PJ's voice cracked as she spoke, "what can I possibly do?"

Chapter Thirteen

Present Day

What would I do without a team behind me, believing in me? Anything? Could I even do as much as PJ had?

As I drove Gramps back to the apartment Holly and I shared in Carmel, a northern suburb of Indianapolis, I thought about Paul Lauth's story. About his response when I asked if PJ's suicide made sense.

He'd sighed. "Given the kind of harassment she experienced, the almost total lack of support? I've had to accept she couldn't see a way out."

"But it surprised you?"

"Shocked me and hurt." He'd paused. "I never thought she'd give up."

Gramps interrupted my thoughts. "That was Paul you were talking to, Katie?"

"You know much about him?"

"Always heard he was a nice kid—open, friendly. Maybe too good-hearted to make it big in this business."

"What does that say about me, Gramps?"

He cackled. "You're good-hearted. But you've also got motivation and the will to achieve—call it the killer instinct to go after what you want. Not everyone has that."

We both knew plenty of good drivers who drifted into coaching and other jobs after never managing to put together enough deals to be in a car. We also knew terrible drivers who had full-time, paid rides because of their skill closing deals.

I sighed. "It all comes back to business."

"Racing used to be pure sport. There were still areas where money ruled all decisions, but forty or fifty years ago, talented amateurs could get picked up for top rides. Plenty of automotive journalists raced, at least in sportscar racing."

"Journalists and even some electronics specialists?" I teased. I knew he'd raced in the 1960s with some success, but I'd never asked him why he stopped.

"It's not that I had teams throwing money at me to race. It was a sideline—a fun hobby that helped me get more work."

"Some hobby!" I glanced at him. "You nearly won the 12 Hours of Sebring."

His smile was wistful. "We were so close."

"Why didn't you keep racing?"

"Your mother was born, and Vivien put her foot down." He shook his head at my expression. "I know what you're going to say. Your grandmother can be strict."

"Hard-nosed, bullheaded," I contributed.

He chuckled. "She's got firm views on what's right and wrong. Appropriate. Plus she rarely changes her mind."

"And she won't let go of a grudge."

"Ah, Katie. I'm working on her."

"That aside, Grandmother made you stop racing when my mother was born?"

"I won't put it all on her. She brought it up, but I agreed. I wouldn't risk the possibility of not being there to see my child grow up."

We both fell silent. Gramps had watched his child grow up to have a child, and then he'd lost her when my mother died days after my birth.

"Or of seeing my grandchild grow up," he finally continued.

"I didn't mind stopping—after the first race or two. My heart wasn't in it the same way yours is."

"I'm not sure what I'd do if I couldn't race." I glanced over as I exited Interstate 465 onto Keystone Parkway and saw him shake his head.

"You're not that poor girl from thirty years ago."

"PJ Rodriguez. Of course I'm not," I replied.

"You've had more success than she did. And the world is different now."

"Did you know her, Gramps?"

"I don't remember seeing her, but I knew about her, especially after."

"Her family doesn't think she did it," I said.

"Kill herself or give up on racing?"

"For her, they were probably the same." I stopped at a light and turned to him. "The more I think about her, I don't believe it either. People said she was totally focused on racing. One hundred percent. More. And then she gave up?"

He nodded toward the green in front of us. "It was a tougher time. Maybe she didn't have the underlying grit after all."

I shook my head as I navigated into the apartment complex. "That's not what people have told me."

"Maybe she had other problems in her life. A history of depression. Katie, you can't know. And if not suicide, then what—murder? Is that easier to believe?"

"It might be." I let Gramps out of the car before pulling into my garage. But as I unlocked the door to our third-floor apartment, I thought about the connection I felt to PJ and thought anything was more believable than giving up.

Would I prove it? How?

I showed Gramps around his home for the next two weeks—our three-bedroom unit in a large, new complex. Holly and I each had bedrooms to either side of the central living room and entry space. The dining room, kitchen, and screened balcony were open to and accessed via one end of the living room, giving us a large, central common space. I carried his suitcase into our

third bedroom—a combination gym, office, and guest room—
and watched as he unpacked.

"I wish Grandmother had come with you."

He gave me a look.

I smiled. "I know. She's never come to a race before. But it
would be nice to see her. How is she?"

"She's fine. She misses you."

"At least we talk now." Which was more than we'd done for
a year after I cornered her for an explanation of what happened
between her and my father's family. After my mother died when
I was three days old, I was raised by her parents and had no
contact with my father or his family until I was twenty-four.
My father had one version of the story, and my grandmother,
I assumed, knew another. But she wouldn't talk to me about
it—all I knew from her was I should have nothing to do with
the vile Reilly family. Then she wouldn't talk to me again after
I accepted the sponsorship deal from Frame Savings, which
thoroughly entwined me with my father's family.

Two years later, she had unbent enough so we could hold
full conversations, if I didn't mention anything to do with my
sponsor. That kind of constraint didn't make for relaxing, comfortable visits home, and as a result, I'd made fewer and fewer
trips to New Mexico in the last couple of years.

I felt a wave of sadness at what I'd missed. "Gramps, what
are we going to do?"

"About Vivien?"

"Her reaction to me living my life. I miss you both."

"We miss you, too." He took my hand. "Whatever's going
on, you know she loves you."

"I love her, too. Both of you. But I can't blindly adhere to her
opinions, especially with no explanation. She shouldn't ask me to."

He sighed. "Go out to the living room. Let me get something
out of my bag."

A couple minutes later, he joined me on the couch, a large
manila envelope in his hand. "Vivien is slowly coming to
accept—not agree with, but accept—that refusing to explain

to you what happened back then only pushes you closer to that family." He grimaced. "I'm afraid she used unkind words about them. And your stubbornness."

"I wonder where I get it?"

He smothered a smile. "She finally agreed with me it's time you know what we shielded you from all these years." He shook his head. "She thinks you'll read this and be convinced to cut all ties with them, but I've tried to prepare her for that *not* happening."

"It would be tough now with all the contracts." I stared at the envelope, suddenly unsure I wanted to see what it contained. "Seriously, Gramps, why now? Why not two and a half years ago, before I got involved with Frame Savings at all?"

He was silent a long moment. "I wish I had an answer for you, Kate. But it wouldn't be the first time your grandmother thought she could change reality by refusing to acknowledge it."

"It's part of her charm?"

"And it's what gives you that killer instinct."

I had to acknowledge that truth, even if I didn't like it. Not for the first time, I wondered what my mother had been like, if she'd have bridged the chasm I often felt yawning between my grandmother's attitudes and mine.

Gramps looked down at his hands, worrying the already worn corners of the envelope. "You can't look at these now, though— not with the race and all of your obligations this month. You need to wait until you've got some time to deal with it." He blew out a breath. "Because the details are awful."

Chapter Fourteen

Present Day

I crossed my arms and tucked my hands into my armpits, study-ing the envelope Gramps held as if it were a snake. "I'm torn between wanting to rip it open this minute and wanting to light it on fire. I guess it's a case of 'be careful what you ask for.'"

"Katie, I wish I could spare you from this—we've tried to do that your whole life." The corners of Gramps' mouth pulled down. "But it's obvious that not knowing isn't the right answer either. You've got to lance the boil to start the healing."

I grimaced. "That sounds icky and painful."

"Just like this will be."

Do I really want to know? Of course I do. I can't live the rest of my life in the dark. Can I wait to open the envelope? Probably.

I nodded at Gramps, then reached for the envelope.

But he pulled it back, out of my grasp. "I know you, Katie. Patience isn't your strong suit, and I won't be responsible for messing up your Indy 500—or your season. I need your word you won't open this until you have a break in your racing sched-ule—and then you'll commit to reading it all."

Dammit, Gramps.

I frowned at him. "All right, I promise. But you've got to do something for me."

"Anything." He handed me the envelope.

"You may be sorry you said that. I need you to get along with my father." I saw the frustration and anger on his face. "You're going to run into him—at parties, in the garage, at the banquet, sometime. I need you both to be civil. To not cause any drama."

"Me? Drama?" Gramps tried to look innocent. "What about him? Can he manage it?"

"I'll have the same conversation with him when I see him, but I'm more concerned about it being hard on you." I reached out and took his hand. "I don't want to hurt you, and I hate to ask, but I need you to do it."

"For the good of your career, I know." He sighed. "I'll play nice—just don't ask me to be his new best friend."

Gramps was nearly put to the test when we arrived at the Speedway late the next morning. I was focused on the practice session ahead, on the changes we might make to deal with overcast skies and a cooler track. On hoping it didn't rain. Gramps was excited to spend the day in the garage and pits with the crew. Neither of us was prepared to see my father first thing.

We'd entered Gasoline Alley when I saw my father approaching. I turned to Gramps. "Go ahead to my garage—on the other side of that building. Let me talk with him alone."

"Gladly." Gramps scurried off, eyes on the ground.

My father watched Gramps curiously, then moved closer and kissed my cheek. "Is that your grandfather? I didn't know he would be here."

I nodded. "He's here through the race, staying with me."

"Is your grandmother with him?" His voice was carefully neutral.

"Grandmother never comes to races." My stomach churned as I imagined trying to handle my grandmother and my father in the same city.

"That's a bullet dodged," he muttered.

I winced. "I need to put you in a different line of fire. I'm hoping you and my grandfather can agree to be polite for the next couple weeks. I can't spend my time keeping you apart or worrying about shouting matches breaking out."

My father looked affronted, and I stopped him. "I'm exaggerating."

He nodded. "Did he agree?"

"He did."

"Then I can do no less." He pulled me in for a hug. "Don't worry about us. Focus on the race."

"Thank you." I pulled back. "There's one other thing."

He raised his eyebrows and smiled. "Something else you need? A loan? A kidney?"

I wished I could feel any levity about the situation at all.

"Gramps brought me a packet of information about my mother—the background on whatever happened all those years ago. But he made me promise not to open it yet, not while I'm focusing on a race." I hesitated. "He said it's going to hurt."

My father went blank and opened his mouth to speak twice before he got words out. "I hope you'll tell me if there's anything I can do to support you when you go through the information." He cleared his throat. "Also, I know I have no right to ask…"

When he didn't continue, I finished his thought. "If I can share it with you, I will. That's all I can promise without seeing what it is."

"Fair enough." He let out a long breath. "Having an explanation in your hands must be a shock."

I'd been trying not to dwell on the fact that the answers I'd sought for years were now tucked in a cubby on my desk at home. I'd had enough trouble going to sleep the night before with my imagination running on overdrive.

Did Grandmother and the Reillys fight over me? Was there more to the story of my mother's death? Who from my father's family was at the hospital? Who gave me away—and why?

My stomach gave another queasy roll. "It's unsettling. But I need to put it aside for now—this race is going to be stressful enough."

For a while, the car was my savior. I felt the familiar magic—when I got in and put my visor down, the rest of the world went away. I didn't think about family secrets or missing parents. I thought about air. Specifically, the airflow around my car and the dirty air caused by it flowing around other cars in close proximity to mine. Of course, at the Indianapolis Motor Speedway and at speeds topping 225 mph, "close proximity" could be five or six car lengths behind.

The practice session was good enough to restore my optimism. It was "Fast Friday," so named because all cars got an increase in horsepower and a single day to get used to it before a full weekend of qualification. Saturday runs would lock a car and driver into either the first through ninth positions or tenth through thirty-third positions, and Sunday runs would set our starting positions within those groups. Both were important days, but Saturday, "Bump Day," was do-or-die day, because anyone who didn't make one of the top thirty-three spots would be bumped from the field and wouldn't start the race.

Realistically, I had no shot at pole position or the top group. But I wanted to be solidly in the rest of the pack with a good enough speed that I wouldn't have to make multiple attempts or spend anxious minutes waiting to be bumped. The team had put my car back together so well from my accident I was relatively confident for qualifying—but anything could happen.

That day we dealt well with the extra boost, ending twenty-second on the speed chart, but fifteenth with the aerodynamic "tow" from another car. I'd managed to get behind other cars a number of times, working on my feel for handling in different airflows, and I'd picked up speed when I followed another car that was breaking the air for both of us. When I didn't have to create a tunnel through the air, I went faster.

That speed was encouraging overall, but it wouldn't help for qualifying, when each car took to the track alone for four timed laps. Still, we were in better shape than we might have been, given my mistake the day before.

I sat on the pit wall for a few minutes talking with Alexa and Nolan about how the car had felt over the full fuel runs (pretty good), where it had felt light in the rear (the middle of Turn 4), and where it had wanted to push or not turn (entering Turn 2). We talked about what speeds might be reached in group qualifying the next day (231 mph max) and what our target was (227) to be safe in the field of thirty-three. We also discussed strategy for making additional qualifying attempts if I didn't reach our target speed the first time, but I excused myself when Nolan and Alexa started to drill down on their spreadsheets, getting into excruciating detail of comparison speeds, track temperature, and time of day.

As I walked back to my garage, I ran into Alexa's mother, Diane, walking with a curvy woman sporting a series polo shirt and long, salt-and-pepper hair.

"We were coming to find you," Diane said. "Meet Vallorie Westleton, from IndyCar Timing and Scoring. This is our Kate, who did so well in first practice."

Vallorie and I shook hands as Diane continued, "Vallorie's been in racing as long as I have, even if she's a couple years younger. I know you're curious about PJ. Vallorie knew her well."

Chapter Fifteen

May 1987

Vallorie found PJ slouched against the wall inside her garage, arms wrapped around herself. "Have they gotten anywhere?"

PJ glanced at her friend. "They are not sure yet. Perhaps."

Vallorie nudged PJ over and leaned against the wall with her. She studied the mechanics working on the car. "The car shouldn't have changed so dramatically. It doesn't seem logical."

PJ raised her eyebrows. "What are you saying?"

"I'm not sure."

"Do you think someone has done this?"

"Deliberately?" Vallorie blew out a breath. "No."

"But you are not sure?"

"I don't think anyone's sabotaged your car deliberately. That would be *crazy*. But it's hard to understand how you could be the fastest and then the slowest."

"Conditions change. I crashed the car and the rear assembly was fixed. The other cars got faster. Perhaps I am losing my nerve." PJ said the last lightly, but Vallorie could hear the hurt in her tone.

A tall, lanky young man poked his head into the garage and jogged over to Vallorie, arriving as she told PJ, "That's bullshit. Utter bullshit, and I won't hear it."

PJ smiled, and directed Vallorie's attention to the newcomer.

Vallorie turned. "Tom, sorry. What's going on?" She saw him glance at PJ and introduced them. "Tom Barclay, an intern with my uncle's team this summer, and less of a pain in the butt than most."

He was older than a typical teenage intern, maybe mid-twenties, but PJ could see he was still wide-eyed at the glories of the racing world. She shook his hand. "Nice to meet you."

"Ditto." He turned to Vallorie. "Bill said to remind you to go to the bank and the cleaners tonight, 'or we're screwed.'" His face reddened. "That's a direct quote."

Vallorie chuckled. "Got it. Tell Uncle Bill it's covered. And thanks."

Tom left with a last glance at PJ and a wave for both women, and Vallorie wasted no time returning to the previous topic. "The idea you've lost your nerve is bullshit. You don't believe that."

PJ quirked her mouth in the faintest of smiles. "You are so positive."

"I know you. You wouldn't lose your nerve. The people saying so are fools." Vallorie grabbed her by both shoulders. "Tell me you don't think it."

PJ looked Vallorie in the eye for a long moment, then smiled. "Thank you, my friend, for your faith in me. I haven't lost my nerve or my desire to win. But I'm sad people think so."

Vallorie nodded as she released PJ. "If they wanted to talk about fear of spiders or roller coasters, I might believe them. But not speed or racecars. Not that you're suddenly afraid to race."

"They look for an explanation. The weak girl is an easy one."

Vallorie frowned. "I suppose so. I wonder…"

An amused male voice spoke from behind them. "What do you wonder?"

PJ and Vallorie turned to see PJ's team owner, Ronnie Arvin. Everyone called him Arvie.

"PJ," he said, then turned to Vallorie. "Val, I can't believe you left me this year."

"Arvie," Vallorie hugged him. "You know I couldn't turn down my uncle when he asked me to work for him."

"But you're with the old fogies. This is where the young, happening people are." Arvie snapped his fingers and pointed them at the two women.

"He's not that old," Vallorie protested.

Arvie laughed and flipped up the collar of his polo shirt. "But he's not pushing the envelope like we are. We've got the only girl driver. Young, talented crew members. Fresh ideas for sponsorship and marketing. If we can't win the race, we'll at least get lots of attention. Right, PJ?"

She nodded and started to speak, but Arvie kept going. "In fact, here are a couple of our new partners." He turned to welcome two men and a woman who stepped from the sun into the shade of the garage. "Gentlemen and lady, welcome!"

Vallorie started to move away. "I'll get out of your way."

"Please, stay," PJ whispered.

"Stick around, Val. You're as much a part of the family as anyone, even if you've deserted us." Arvie beamed at her. "Girls, meet Chuck Gaffey, Nathan Standish, and Libby Conroy. Everyone, this is my history-making driver, PJ, and a friend and former member of the team, Vallorie."

Everyone shook hands while Arvie kept talking. "My buddy Chuck has a small but growing company offering insurance for racing teams and drivers, with clever options for keeping us all in business. And Nathan and Libby represent a new chain of hotels and spas—they've come on board in a big way for PJ in this race."

"We appreciate your partnership." PJ shook everyone's hands.

"Have you been to one of our resorts?" Nathan asked.

"I have not, but I will look forward to experiencing it."

"Especially the spa—that's what all women want." Libby peered at PJ's face. "Getting so sweaty all the time in those helmets must be hell on your skin."

Does she mean my skin looks bad?

PJ eyed the tall redhead with the perfect wedge haircut. "The balaclava is the worst. But sweat," PJ shrugged, "it's a part of racing. I don't mind."

"Good for you, I'm sure." Libby's expression showed she thought the opposite.

Arvie jingled change in his pocket, the broad smile still affixed to his face. "See? The spa aspect of your resorts is a natural fit for female race attendees who'll be drawn to PJ's participation in the race—or it'll give the men good gift ideas. Don't you think, Vallorie?" He glanced at her, then returned to the sponsors again. "Val, here, may be young, but she's third-generation. Her uncle runs another team—that's who stole her from us this year. Her father raced, and her grandfather was a mechanic back when the mechanics rode in the car during the races."

"How interesting." Nathan sounded sincere. Libby looked bored.

"You bet," Arvie said. "Would have been more to insure then, eh, Chuck?"

"I'm sure my grandfather tried to make those deals." Chuck winked at Vallorie.

"You aren't new to the series, like us?" Nathan asked him.

Chuck shook his head. "My family's been in racing for years, but I didn't go the driver route. I've focused on filling a need I saw to provide care and security for participants and loved ones in case anything goes wrong."

"Insuring drivers, I never knew," Libby mused, though she appeared more interested in the neon yellow on her fingernails than the conversation.

"Drivers and crew against injury or loss of work—even teams against the loss of revenue. That's our new product."

Arvie clapped Chuck on the shoulder. "That's what finally got Gaffey Insurance on our cars. PJ, be sure to talk with Chuck about insurance, in case you don't have any—he'll get you a good deal."

"Yes, of course, I am interested." PJ nodded at Chuck.

When an official pulled Arvie aside for a question, Vallorie filled the silence. "Nathan and Libby, is this your first race? Have you been involved in racing before?"

While they chatted, Chuck moved to PJ and handed her a business card. "Don't feel I'm pressuring you. Arvie's like that with everyone."

PJ returned his smile. "Always enthusiastic."

Chuck laughed. "Exactly. No obligation. Let me know if you'd like information. Otherwise, I'll wish you luck and provide what support I can."

"That is very kind of you." PJ studied him, noting his friendly, open expression and piercing green eyes.

He shrugged. "I'm in Arvie's corner, and I like what you're trying to do. I hope you get back to where you were on the first day of practice."

"I wish the same."

Arvie returned from conferring with the crew member. "Chuck and Nathan, let me show you the car. PJ, show Libby around our hospitality area and the gift shop."

Vallorie saw the frustration on PJ's face and took pity on her. "Or maybe Libby'd like a tour of other garages? To meet other drivers? Mario Andretti's driving for Paul Newman's team next to mine. We can go see if they're there." She grinned at PJ. "Maybe we'll even run into PJ's boyfriend, who drives for my team."

Libby agreed with enthusiasm. Although PJ would have preferred to talk engines with the men, she knew her role in keeping sponsors happy, and she dutifully followed the two women out of the garage.

Chapter Sixteen

Present Day

She couldn't have killed herself. She wouldn't have.

Those words played on repeat in my head—interspersed with worry over qualifying the next day and anger over the documents Gramps had brought me—as I drove Gramps home that evening.

You'd better figure out what happened, before the social media trolls ruin your reputation with hers.

I realized Gramps' non-stop chatter had stopped. "Sorry, what did you say?"

"A whole lot, but you didn't hear it." He patted my shoulder. "What are you worrying about?"

"Qualifying. PJ and her family."

"You didn't tell me about meeting them."

"Only her mother and brother. Her father died some years ago."

He nodded. "I remember him. Big guy—height, bone, and brawn. But shrewd. They said he was a drug dealer."

"Really?"

"That was the scuttlebutt—where he came from, all the money. Lots of cocaine and marijuana going back and forth in those days. Literal tons of it. Some floating through the racing world."

"I'd heard rumors." I pulled into the apartment complex. "It always seemed far away."

I could see Gramps smile as he unfastened his belts. "Not far away. All over the paddock—even at the Indy 500."

I stopped him with a hand on his arm. "People in the paddock were using?"

"I'm reassured you're still such an idealist," he said, smiling. "I never saw too many. Mostly crew. But there were never busts for use in the paddock."

I finally responded as we sat at my dining table eating grilled chicken and steamed vegetables—plus pasta for Gramps, the one of us not in training and on a strict diet. "If people weren't using drugs much, how were they all over the paddock?"

"Some team owners smuggled drugs to fund their racing."

"That never works." I stared at him in shock.

Gramps laughed. "Hindsight is on your side. It worked for some of them for a lot of years. Probably worked for plenty we never found out about. But some went to jail. Like Arvie, PJ's team owner."

I inhaled sharply while trying to swallow and gasped for breath. Gramps whacked me on the back until I held up a hand to stop him. "Arvie? You mean Ron, the guy who's been around the team for the past couple weeks?"

Gramps nodded. "He's Alexa's father, and he got out of jail in the last year. Look him up on the Google." He scooped up another bite of noodles and saw my stunned expression. "How did you not know this stuff, Katie?"

"Because I didn't think to research drug-running in open-wheel racing. Why would I?" I shook my head. "My team owner Alexa's father? Smuggled drugs? Alexa has a different last name—so does her mother, Diane. Really, Ron? Why is it a secret?" I knew the answer to my question. "So there's no scandal around Alexa."

Gramps nodded. "She's worked hard to stay squeaky clean. People respect her."

"I can't believe the press hasn't jumped on this."

"There's plenty the media knows but doesn't report, for one reason or another—sometimes juicy stuff," Gramps said.

I tried to refocus. "Was there proof PJ's father was a drug dealer?"

"Only coincidence, like PJ being associated with Arvie, who was busted for transporting the junk a couple years later."

As I got ready for bed I realized Lyla Thomas had known the rumor about PJ's father—that's what she'd meant during the press conference when she called him a "powerful business-man." Lyla and I had spoken again that evening, before I left the track, and I thought back to that conversation, wondering what else I'd missed.

She'd shown up at my garage well after practice was over, and I'd answered her questions about how we'd do in the next day's qualifying run.

At the end, I turned the tables. "Tell me, Lead-Foot, how'd you get the name?"

She'd laughed, flipping her notebook closed and tucking away her pen. "The first time I ran at Sebring, forty years ago, some punk kid asked me how I did it and if I wasn't scared—mind you, I was basically a punk kid myself. I told him I'd slipped lead weight into my right shoe, to help keep it down on the throttle. The story stuck."

She surveyed the garage area, then turned back to me. "I was joking."

"Of course." I smiled, thinking of all the small things drivers and mechanics had done throughout the years to give them an advantage—real or perceived. I figured it might have been a joke or it might have been true. I'd never know.

But I'd bet she was a firecracker behind the wheel.

"I wanted to ask you more about PJ," I continued. "Were you surprised when she died? At how she died?"

"That they called it suicide?" I nodded, and she gave me a keen look. "Shocked. I don't ever expect a driver to take their own life, but especially not her. I'd have to agree with her par-ents that her death was murder, not suicide. What about you?"

I realized I was about to do what I'd warned Holly and

Gramps against—trust someone I didn't know. "Can I level with you, off the record?"

"Off the record now, first rights if there's a story someday?"

"Done." We shook, and I went on. "It starts with media turning me into PJ, because of the first test day coincidence."

She rolled her eyes. "The *real* media isn't doing a smear job on you."

"Which I appreciate. But some of your lesser relations are."

"I've seen the stories and social media hashtags. Uncreative idiots, parroting the obvious—repeating press releases or random opinions and not getting their butts out of the media center. You can't get the stories if you're not out here talking to people!" She stopped herself with a grimace. "Sorry. Soapbox. Back to you and PJ."

I smiled. "All the comparisons to PJ got me interested in her mental state. You know, I can relate to her in some ways—a woman here for the second year."

"Except you actually raced the first year. She didn't."

"But she had it rougher—people weren't as receptive to a woman then, right?"

"It wasn't so bad in sportscars. It was worse here, especially for an outsider."

"Because she wasn't white?"

"Being Hispanic or Latina, or whatever the right word is now, might have had something to do with it. But we had drivers from other countries—being a little bit ethnic and speaking Spanish wasn't the burden you might think." She paused. "She was an outsider because she was a woman, but also because she hadn't driven much in the U.S. The racing establishment here hadn't heard of her. She didn't know people."

I considered. "Did she have any support system? Any close friends?"

"Not that I saw. Her family. Her boyfriend, but he was busy with his team. Guys on the team who tried—Jerry, her crew chief, and Donny, the kid who became her unofficial bodyguard."

"Do you know where they are now?"

"Donny's working for our tire supplier, over in their Gasoline Alley shop. Jerry died a few years back."

I studied her, wondering if I could ask the big questions.

She caught the look. "You can trust me, Kate. I won't share your secrets—especially if I can scoop everyone else later."

Oddly enough, that reassured me. "Did you know anyone who really hated her?"

"Anyone who might have wanted her dead?"

"Or who benefitted from her death."

She tapped a finger against her cheek. "Plenty of people hated her, but for most of them, it wasn't personal, it was because she was a stranger and a woman. I'm not sure if they'd have gotten physical."

"Words are safer and easier."

"But sometimes more painful." She gave me another one of her penetrating looks. "As for who benefitted, I have to be honest and say almost all of us did."

"Us?"

"Everyone got publicity and recognition out of it. The team got more name-recognition, loads of sympathy, and better sponsors. Existing sponsors on the car got free airtime during the race. The race got more exposure. The TV network sold more ads. The racing insurance guy sold more policies. The memorabilia guys sold more photos, signatures, and model cars. The merchandise people sold more tee-shirts. Reporters wrote more articles. Hell, I won an award for an article I wrote. So did other journalists."

She spread her hands. "We all came out ahead."

Chapter Seventeen

May 1987

The crew got restless when PJ was half an hour late on Tuesday morning, the second week of practice. Arvie sent Donny back and forth to the driver parking lot and points in between. Diane Wittmeier searched women's bathrooms and other possible hiding places. They turned up nothing.

PJ's family arrived close to an hour after PJ was due, and they were immediately concerned. Her father relaxed when he heard PJ had been late on two other occasions, and he sent PJ's brother to look around. But PJ's mother knew something was wrong. She sat on a cooler in the corner of the hospitality area, gray-faced, wringing her hands.

The crew kept working on the car as teams around them towed their vehicles, tires, and other supplies out to pit lane. As the day's practice started, they heard the distant firing of engines, and they stood idle, smoking cigarettes and occasionally shooting dark looks at the car, Arvie, or PJ's father, Miguel.

Arvie and Miguel stood in the open garage door, talking in low voices. Everyone wore concerned expressions except for Miguel, who looked angry and defiant. The garage phone, in use all morning with calls back and forth to Series officials in the pagoda, rang again right after noon, and a crew member called Arvie over.

The three minutes he was gone changed him. With slow, unwilling steps, Arvie reached PJ's father, who stood, legs apart and arms crossed, braced for what the world would throw at him. Arvie rubbed a hand over his face. "I'm so sorry. PJ is dead." He paused. "They're saying she killed herself."

PJ's mother crumpled in on herself, and Miguel's body shook as if he'd received a blow. "No."

Arvie shook his head. "Downtown. Fell from the roof of a fifteen-story building. About an hour and a half ago."

Jerry, PJ's engineer, approached. "She jumped? Why? We were working things out. How could she do this?"

In a flash, Miguel reached out and grabbed the front of Jerry's shirt, and pulled him close. "You failed her," he growled.

The sound of Elena's sobs reached them, and Miguel released Jerry to go to her.

Arvie put a hand on Jerry's shoulder. "I'm sorry."

"Forget it. He's her father. I shouldn't have said…"

Arvie shook his head. "We're all going to bear the weight of this. Shit. What the hell do we do now?" He stared out at Gasoline Alley, and sighed. "Jerry, tell the boys? I'll try to figure out what we do next."

"Sure, but…" Jerry paused. "What do I tell them? Will we go on? Find someone else?" He grimaced. "I feel awful—disloyal—saying it."

"This is a business." Arvie straightened his shoulders and hitched up his belt. "We have to move on—tomorrow. Tell the boys to close up now. Today is for PJ."

PJ's brother, Tony, pounded into the garage, gasping. "*Papá?* They are saying PJ—I punched someone. Tell me it's not true!"

Arvie went to where the boy, looking younger than his sixteen years now, stood trembling in front of his parents, who were curled around each other. "Son, I'm sorry. We just got word. Your sister is gone."

Tony took gasping breaths and wiped tears away from red cheeks. "They're saying she killed herself. She wouldn't." He stared at sullen, downcast crew members. "She wouldn't!" he shouted.

"Kid, easy." Arvie put an arm around his shoulder and drew him close. Then he realized what the teen had said. "Where did you hear?"

"Near the pagoda. Yellow-shirts talking. Saying it was all over the media center."

Arvie swallowed a curse. "Mr. and Mrs. Rodriguez, Tony, I'm going to make sure you're taken care of. Let me make a call."

While Arvie handled the family, Jerry spoke quietly with the team, explaining what happened and reassuring them they'd still have a job the rest of the month. Crew members drew together in small groups to talk quietly and smoke more cigarettes. They cast furtive glances at PJ's grieving family.

It wasn't until Arvie took a golf cart and drove the family away—to a parking lot for their car and ultimately for the morgue in downtown Indianapolis—that the atmosphere changed. Jerry rolled down the doors on the two spaces housing PJ's car and crew, and the pall lifted. The first trickle of relief filtered through the garage.

An hour later, the first laugh rang out, and Jerry cracked down hard on the offender. "If you can't be respectful, get the fuck out of here," he snarled.

Jimmy pulled on his cigarette, the bead glowing red. "There's the problem. She pulled us apart. No way we'd be a team. I ain't saying I wanted her dead—God rest her soul—but I ain't gonna pretend I won't be happier with someone else, neither."

"You're a son of a bitch, Jimmy," Jerry responded. "And you've got a lot to learn. You might think that, but you never say it. You play the goddamn game and pretend when you don't feel it. Now get out of here. I don't want to look at you today."

Jerry scanned the garage. "If anyone else can't be civil about our driver—our late driver, who wanted nothing more than a chance with this track and team—then get out. Be here tomorrow, but get out of my sight now."

Responses ranged from sneers on the faces of men who left to nods of support and respect on others. Then Jerry saw someone who didn't belong, and he stormed across the garage to loom over a small woman in her thirties. "What the hell are you doing here?"

"My job, Jerry," Lyla Thomas said quietly. "I'm looking for basic facts. I don't want to credit the rumors swirling around out there."

"You can't print anything these jackasses are saying."

She could tell he was angry and panicked, and she shook her head. "Don't want to. I'm not about salacious response or gossip-mongering. I want the facts."

Jerry relaxed a little, his big shoulders slumping. "How'd you get in here, anyway?" Reporters had been knocking at the closed garage door incessantly, and they'd set up cordons at the other team doors to keep people out, as well as dividers to separate PJ's team space from the others.

"Sweet-talked my way past someone. Won't tell you who, doesn't matter. I won't screw you or PJ."

Jerry nodded. "All right." He fed her the basics of learning the news, Arvie taking the family downtown, and PJ's mental state the last few days. Lyla asked what would happen to the team, and he hesitated.

"I won't make you sound heartless."

He grimaced. "We'll go on. Got sponsors who've paid money to be in the race and a crew that needs to feed their families. But I have no idea who or when or how. Arvie will figure that out, starting tomorrow. As he said, today is for PJ."

"Fair enough. Use your name?"

"An official with the team."

"Copy that." She closed her notebook. "Off the record? The crew doesn't seem too broken up."

"Really off the record?" He sounded skeptical.

"I don't want to write about this. I want to know as someone who's been there, sort of. Though sportscars aren't as chauvinist as this joint, let me tell you." Color flamed on her ruddy cheeks as she faced him, annoyed now.

Jerry pulled up a chair and offered it to her, then sat down gratefully when she declined. He leaned forward, elbows to knees. "It wasn't easy. She wasn't easy—or maybe the crew wasn't. Maybe both. But she wasn't someone to bring us all together. Too brash, abrasive, arrogant for that."

Lyla's smile was sad. "Maybe she had to be to get this far."

"Thing is, I don't think she was that person underneath. I saw her hurt, scared, unsure sometimes, but only when she was alone—or thought she was. It's like she had to put on armor to deal with the rest of the world."

Lyla patted his shoulder. "Most of us do."

Chapter Eighteen

Present Day

I was a mess as we drove to the track for the first day of qualifying, eight days before the race—tired from another night of poor sleep and emotionally hungover from the dual whammy of PJ's death and the envelope from my grandfather. I'd spent another restless night eyeing the envelope on my desk and coming up with wild ideas about its contents—I wasn't really my father's daughter, I was adopted, I had somehow killed my mother, or someone else had killed her—before I'd taken the envelope and stashed it behind the canned goods in a kitchen cabinet.

You have to be on your game today, Kate! You can't let the drama affect you!

My breaths were shallow, and my heart rate was high. I swore at myself, then focused on slow, deep breathing. Focused on calm.

This is no worse than getting in a car jetlagged because you've flown halfway around the world to race. Suck it up. You're a professional, so focus. Nothing gets in the car with you.

Practice that Saturday started at eight, so Gramps and I arrived around sunrise, coffee in hand. We walked through Gasoline Alley together, and split up at my garage.

"I'll be there when you go out for your run. Do good, Katie." He kissed my forehead and walked off, whistling, to reconnect with old pals.

I entered my garage and was immediately swept into conversation with my engineer, Nolan. The hour after my arrival went by in a flash, and before I knew it, I was circling the track with the first practice group. We had a half-hour break, then we were back out with the whole field at nine. We worked on the car, trying to make it faster with every lap, until time was called at ten.

The car could be better, could be worse.

It certainly wouldn't be comfortable, trimmed as it was for maximum speed. Nerves danced the samba in my stomach.

I left the car to the crew and headed back to the garage for a dry set of clothes, food, and water. On my way back through Gasoline Alley, I ran into Sofia Montalvo, who looked down her nose at me. I ignored her and kept moving, which she didn't like.

"It is as I told you," she said loudly to the man with her. "Kate is so threatened by the success of other drivers, like me, she cannot even be civil."

I turned to her, plastering a surprised look on my face and not caring how fake it appeared. "Sofia, I didn't see you there. I was focused on important things."

The man with her smirked, and Sofia gave me a nasty, patronizing smile. "I will wish you luck today, as I'm certain you will need it." She tossed her head and moved off.

Whatever, you prima donna. We'll see what happens on the track.

Two steps later I felt eyes on me. I looked around and saw a crew member from R-9 Racing a few feet away, leaning against the side of a building and glaring at me. The crewmember who'd egged on the belligerent fan on the first day of practice. The one who said girls didn't belong at the Indy 500.

He had a scrunched up face out of proportion to the rest of his tall, wiry frame and leathery skin, courtesy of sixty years of too much sun exposure. He clutched his cigarette like it was life-giving, and he looked at me like I was the devil. I'd have walked past him without comment if he hadn't tried to spit on my shoes.

"Excuse me? Can I help you with something?" My tone was far from gracious.

His lip curled. "You got nothin' I want. But I got something you do." He reached down and jiggled his junk.

"No way in hell." I thought I might vomit.

"I think you do. Think you need a real man. 'Cause maybe if you got some righteous cock, you'd have all the thrill you'd need. You wouldn't make a fool of yourself in these cars." He leered, revealing crooked teeth, and looked me up and down, then rubbed himself again. "You're a hot little package, so I'd give you what you're asking for."

I felt violated, and I wanted to run away, as if I could physically distance myself from the idea that anyone, no matter what age, would think such things, let alone say them to my face. But I made myself stand still. I took a breath and stared him down.

"You're vile. And you're wrong."

As I walked away, I was immediately stopped by a fan for a signature. I felt the awful man's eyes on me, but I refused to turn around. I rounded the corner to the next garage—though it wasn't my row—and slumped against the wall.

How can he say those things out loud? How did no one hear that? How many people agree with him? How can I fight that attitude?

After a minute of feeling vulnerable and small, I pulled myself together, remembering the support of my team, family, and fans. Reminding myself the nasty crewmember was a single voice—an older generation. Not the future. Then I got angry.

It's qualifying day. I refuse to let one asshole ruin everything I've worked for. He doesn't get that kind of power over me.

Walking back to the Beermeier garage and receiving a text from my boyfriend wishing me luck finished soothing my rattled nerves, though tension among my crew had ratcheted up a couple notches. Some guys gobbled down sandwiches, while others obsessively patrolled the car, cloth in hand, polishing away grime. I spied Alexa's father, Ron, and Chuck sitting on stools next to the coffee machine eating ice cream bars, and I leaned against the wall next to them.

"What do you think of our chances today?"

Chuck shrugged and jerked a thumb toward Ron. "He's the expert."

Ron studied the car. "I think your chances are good. Car's solid, you're more comfortable in her, and the team's all pulling in the same direction."

"I hope so." Nerves skittered up my spine. "Were you as confident about PJ qualifying?"

"Never was." He hitched a foot up onto the stool's cross-bar. "The first year, she was so green, she couldn't pass the rookie test."

"That had to be awful."

"It happened." He shrugged, then glanced at Chuck. "It helped we had insurance to cover some of the costs—helped us both." Chuck nodded.

Ron went on. "The next year, we had higher hopes at first, but so many problems it'd have been a miracle if she made the field at all." He turned to me. "You've got more going for you."

"What made you hire PJ in the first place?"

He stared at the ceiling. "A lot of reasons. I met her father somewhere, heard about her, and was impressed. Thought she deserved a chance. I thought it was time to shake things up in the paddock." He turned to look at me again. "The environment has changed for the better now."

"Kate," Holly called from the office area, tapping her watch. My heart pounded.

Time to get ready for qualifying.

Chapter Nineteen

A short while later, I sat in the car, sweating. I was fourth in line to qualify, and my heart rate was in the stratosphere. I was focused on the six circuits ahead of me: an out lap, a warm-up lap, and four timed laps to determine if I raced the Indy 500 this year.

I should feel confident—I did. Somewhere under the nerves.

We adjusted and trimmed for speed—for yesterday's conditions. Will they hold up or will we miss on the setup? Will I be too slow or will I be hanging on for dear life?

Every member of my crew stood around me as we made our slow progression to the head of the line, rolling me forward as cars pulled out for their runs. Three ahead.

Dear God, don't let me make a mistake. Don't let me screw up the car. Don't let me screw up our chances to race. Stop it, Kate. You won't. You'll do what you need to do.

I moved my hand from the two anti-roll bar levers—one for the front and one for the rear of the car—to the weight jacker buttons on the steering wheel. These controlled minute adjustments in ride height, which affected weight distribution and stiffness from side to side.

But how has the wind changed, and what will that do to the car? Will I be able to go flat in the corners or have to lift? Will I be loose? Have push?

Racecars had two fundamental handling problems: understeer, when the front of the car wouldn't turn—it "pushed"—and kept wanting to go straight even with the wheel turned, and oversteer, when the front turned fine, but the back end was "loose" or wouldn't hold grip and would make the car spin out. Both the weight jacker and the anti-roll bars were used to fine-tune the car to find balance between both states—and drivers usually made small adjustments with both tools multiple times a lap. That was especially true at Indianapolis Motor Speedway, given the track's two-and-a-half-mile length, where wind direction could cause significant change in handling from one end to the other.

Two cars ahead. My heart rate increased, until all I could hear was the pounding in my ears. I closed my eyes and focused on my breathing.

In and out. Deep breaths. In and out.

I popped my eyes open, afraid I'd missed something important. Bald John shifted next to me and checked the position of the umbrella he held over me to block the sun. Still two cars ahead.

Keep breathing. You've done this before.

One car ahead. I focused on the nose of my car. Thought about the track. Worried more. The car ahead started and pulled out. First in line. I breathed as deeply as panic and tight belts allowed, ignoring the screaming voice inside me.

This is my only chance to make the race! Don't screw up!

The car on track started its final lap. My team started my engine. Waiting.

Breathe. It was time.

The race director, who'd stood in pit lane in front of me and every other car in line, stepped aside and waved me out.

Alexa spoke in my ear: "You've got this, Kate."

I couldn't breathe. I rolled onto the throttle and released the clutch, spinning the wheels, but keeping the car straight. My heart was still in my throat, but the blinding moment of panic passed, and I started to settle.

For efficiency's sake, my out lap happened while the previous driver took his single cool-down lap—that was the only time more than one car was on track during qualifying. The rest of the time, each driver had the track to him or herself.

You and the car. Feel it, figure out what you've got under you.

On my out lap, I put my foot flat on the floor and worked my way up to speed around the track. Down the front straight to start my warm-up lap, shift into fifth gear for my first time into Turn 1 at speed.

Time to see what I've got.

Turn 1 flat. Turn 2 flat, feeling a little slide, and bumping the rear anti-roll bar on the back straight. Building speed there, thinking about the coming lap.

Will I need sixth on the front straight? Will I be fast enough to carry sixth? Did we get the gearing right?

Through Turn 4, releasing my hands at the exit to get the best run down the straight to the line. Hoping for speed. Grabbing sixth gear. Crossing start/finish to begin my first timed lap.

"Green flag," Alexa radioed.

I reminded myself to breathe. Kept my foot as flat as possible on the throttle, feeling my way, ready to move my tools if necessary. I dipped low to the apex of Turn 1, shifting my hands left slightly. Unwound the same small amount, let the car drift out to the exterior wall of the track. Foot still on the floor, car under me. Stay at the wall. Now shift left to the apex of Turn 2, holding the car steady, feeling the hum of the engine through my butt and legs. Looking down the track, down the back straight.

Touch the apex of 2, unwind the wheel, drift to the outer wall, flying down the straight. Move away from the wall, center track. All alone out here, use the space. Take a breath. Drift out to the wall, then turn the wheel for 3. Feeling less resistance in the front, turning less than last time.

Weight jacker one click to the right in the short chute.

Out of 3 to the outside wall. Turning in for 4, more push from the front end. Nudge the front bar. Foot planted down the front straight, moving center track and then to the inside wall, flashing past the lineup in pit lane. Focused on Turn 1 again.

Alexa radioed as I passed her. "Three more."

The next two laps went by in a blur. Turn by turn the car got looser. In between screaming, *Too loose! Hang on!* at myself, I kept adjusting to compensate. First the jacker, then the roll bar, bit by bit, trying to keep the tires under me, holding onto the track, going as fast as I could. Not knowing my speed, only knowing the car felt slippery—hoping that meant quick. Hoping it was enough.

"One to go," Alexa called.

I held my breath, balanced the car on the knife-edge of speed and grip.

Leave it all on the track.

I couldn't keep my foot flat on the throttle anymore, not with tire wear. Not with it this loose. I downshifted to fifth and lifted subtly before Turn 1. Then gathered it up, taking Turn 2 flat, willing the tires to hold for two more turns. Move the tools, tiny lift before Turn 3. A tinier lift still before Turn 4. Throttle down—crossing the stripe.

"Checkered flag," Alexa called. "Average of 228.402. P12 right now, which means you're in the race."

Chapter Twenty

As I slowed on my cool-down lap, I pounded the wheel and shouted inside my helmet, releasing my tension. Celebrating, because that speed was a full mile-per-hour faster than we'd gone in practice. My heart still pounding, I drove down pit lane and stopped on the row of bricks for our official team photo—which happened quickly, while the next car took their laps.

The crew crowded around the car, Bald John helping me remove the wheel to get out and replace it when I was sitting on the edge of the cockpit, feet on the seat. I undid my helmet with shaking fingers and put on a baseball hat. The crew lined up behind me, the photographer snapped photos, and I did my best to smile, sure I appeared manic.

After that, I stepped out of the car and let the crew pull it back to our temporary pit space. I walked with them, thanking everyone for their efforts, then joined Alexa and Nolan in front of our timing and scoring screen.

"Do we need another run?" I asked. On this first qualifying day, teams could take as many runs as they wanted or had time for during the official session, but by lining up for a new run, the previous time was deleted—obviously a risk when you had a decent time recorded already.

Alexa shook her head. "You've got us in the field." She stepped out of the pit box to tell the team to take the car to technical inspection and then back to the garage.

"We're sure?" I looked to Nolan, feeling the first trickle of relief.

"You went out twenty-third." He checked the timing screen. "Two more in the books now, and you're still P12. Nine more to qualify. Even if they all get ahead of you, which they won't, you're still in the top 33."

"I say sixteenth—that's what I've got in the pool." Alexa grinned. "Get some rest tonight, and be ready to do it again tomorrow."

All over again tomorrow for position—but I've made it into the race! I felt exhausted and overjoyed all at once.

By the end of that day, the Indy 500's field of thirty-three was set. We didn't know what positions we'd start, but we knew who'd take the green. Unfortunately for one team, we also knew who wouldn't be racing. I couldn't imagine spending months to pull together sponsors, team, crew, and car only to miss the race itself. I felt for the people packing up at the end of that Saturday.

I'd ended up in fifteenth—winning Banjo the betting pool— though the only use for that result was to place me firmly in the group of cars vying for positions ten through thirty-three the next day. We weren't celebrating yet, because that wasn't the end of the job. Merely the first step.

I drove home alone, remembering what my run felt like in each corner of each lap.

The same again tomorrow would be perfect.

On Sunday, we'd only have one set of four timed laps to establish our final starting position. The pressure would be on.

As I entered our apartment, Gramps and Holly were serving up dinner. I tossed my keys and tote on a side table—but my aim was off, and the bag upended on the floor. I crouched down, swearing, then froze at the sight of an unexpected item— another folded piece of yellow notepaper bearing my name in block letters.

Not again.

"Hurry up, butterfingers," Gramps called.

I stood and turned, the folded paper in my hand.

Holly understood. "Shit. What's this one say?"

I read it aloud. "'PJ was murdered. Find out why or you'll be next.'"

"Is it signed?" Gramps frowned. "Do you recognize the writing?"

I handed it over. "Block capitals and no signature."

Gramps shook his head. "I don't like this."

"Me either. But they want me to figure out why PJ died." I took a deep breath and said it out loud. "And I have to do that anyway."

It took Gramps a minute. "Oh, no. No. It's not your fight."

"Except it is, Gramps. You haven't seen social media, but it's full of the idea that I'm the second coming of PJ."

He waved a hand. "A few idiots on their phones."

"It's more like hundreds of people having the conversation," Holly said, "thousands of people monitoring it, and hundreds of thousands of people seeing it."

"Plus dozens of blogs and articles and newsletters. You heard the people at the track calling me PJ—that comes from social media. The topic 'call Kate PJ' was trending this morning. I'm losing my identity!" My voice and level of hysteria rose.

"Katie," Gramps' voice was anguished.

I took Gramps' hand and moved us all to the table. "Eventually it'll be okay. But right now, everyone sees PJ. Everyone's waiting for me to self-destruct. Some are rubbing their hands together with glee waiting for that. Some are telling me I deserve it."

He paled and his jaw dropped. He turned to Holly, hoping she'd deny my words.

"True." She shook her head. "And unfortunately typical."

I made Gramps look at me again. "All those comments do is tell me I'm doing something right—but I'm sorry to worry you."

He gathered his wits. "I'd rather know what you're dealing with. My poor Katie."

"The problem isn't those comments," Holly put in, "it's that Kate is disappearing in the eyes of the racing world."

"We can't stand for that." Gramps thumped his fist on the table, rattling the serving spoons.

I smiled. "It's also about the lies. Everything people know about PJ is lies, and I've damn well had enough of lies tarnishing someone's name."

The others were silent, aware I was talking about my own history as well as PJ's. Holly, who'd been filled in about the family documents, glanced between me and Gramps. Gramps stared at his plate.

I blew out a breath. "Look, if PJ's memory were respected, no one would taunt me with her. Plus her mother asked me to clear PJ's name and restore her dignity. That's a tough request to ignore."

We turned our attention to our dinners—chicken parmesan for the others, plain grilled chicken for me. As Holly distributed the grilled vegetables, Gramps came to a decision.

"I'm going to help you." He nodded. "We'll clear PJ's name."

Holly grinned at him. "I'm in, too, sugar." She retrieved a pen and a pad of paper from her bag on the couch. "Let's bring the first meeting of Special Team Kate to order."

"That's got a nice ring to it." Gramps turned to me. "What do we do?"

Talk about the blind leading the blind. Am I really doing this? Are they helping me? I had *promised PJ's family to try. Try, Kate, that's all you have to do.*

I sat up straight. "What we need is information. To know more about who PJ was and what went on back then—especially in the ten days between first practice and when she died. And who benefitted from her death."

"When we find that person, we find who did it?" Gramps asked.

"We'll probably find multiple people who benefitted," I replied and watched him frown.

"Tell us who you've talked to already." Holly held her pen at the ready.

I walked them through what I'd learned about PJ, in the same order I'd learned it: starting with Uncle Stan, then talking with

Diane Wittmeier—Alexa's mom—and the woman from the Timing and Scoring group, Vallorie Westleton. I told them how Paul Lauth, her former boyfriend, had interpreted PJ's emotions and actions, and how the reporter, Lyla Thomas, described team reactions on the day PJ died. Plus what Ron had said about PJ.

"And Ron, who's been hanging out in the Beermeier garage, is really Arvie, PJ's former team owner, Alexa's father, and an ex-con," I added.

"What?" Holly's eyes got big, as Gramps filled her in on that part of the story.

Holly had written individual names on her notepad as I'd discussed each of them. She titled the list "Sources," then held it out so we could all study it. "Who else were you thinking of talking to, Kate?"

"I want to ask Ron more questions—I got started today, but ran out of time. He'd know how the team changed after PJ's death."

"To figure that out," Gramps put in, "we need to know who Arvie—Ron—replaced PJ with and how the new driver did in the race that year."

Holly chewed on the end of her pen. "Let's take tomorrow and talk to everyone we can. Gather basic information about who was there that year, who heard stories, and so forth—including who could be leaving you notes."

Gramps nodded. "Cast a wide net and see what we drag in—then we can plan who to talk to in more depth."

"We'll need to be careful." I told both of them. "We have no idea if PJ's killer is still around. Don't assume everyone's innocent."

"The racing paddock?" Gramps hooted. "There's hardly anyone innocent at all."

"We're talking about murder, Gramps," I said. "It's more extreme than cheating."

"Murder, drug smuggling, embezzlement, you name it." He shrugged. "In my experience, everyone's hiding something. And we never know how far someone will go to protect their secrets."

"We've got this," Holly assured me. "He's—sorry, Gramps— an old-timer, and they can get away with talking about anything to anyone."

"True statement." Gramps winked at Holly.

She went on. "You're naturally involved with PJ, so it's logical you'd be curious and asking about her."

"And you?" I asked.

"Me?" She tossed her hair over her shoulders. "I'm a gossip professional, sugar. This is in the bag."

I felt better. But only a little.

Chapter Twenty-one

Before Gramps took off the next morning at the track to find and question friends about the old days, he hugged me. "Don't worry about me. Focus on the car. I'll see you before you go out."

He was off with a jaunty wave, his bowed legs carrying him rapidly through the growing crowd. Watching him, I finally understood the concerns Gramps and others had in the past over my own sleuthing efforts. I shook my head and finished my journey to the garage, ignoring at least three people calling me PJ.

Once again, time accelerated as we got closer to when I'd run my laps. It was a phenomenon I experienced at every race: days started out measured and calm, moving at a normal pace. But as we progressed, everything sped up—time, activity, tension, and pulse rates. To be sure, my heart was beating at race pace by the time I rolled down pit lane.

My crew again fired the car when the driver before me started his last timed lap. I closed my eyes for a minute, feeling the rumble, taking in the sensation. Becoming part of the car. A few seconds later, I pulled away.

My out lap was smooth. The warm-up lap was almost a catastrophe.

Going into Turn 2 for the second time, I felt an unexpected gust of wind from the left, as the front end suddenly stopped turning. I turned the wheel more, only to have the front end feel like it was snapping over on itself. The car twitched violently,

back end coming around to the right. I worked my hands franti-
cally on the wheel, correcting, counter-correcting, and correcting
again to stay pointed down the track.

Not the wall. I will not get into the wall. Keep it straight!

I let the car travel up the track as much as it needed—as much
as I dared. I lifted, but as little as I dared, not wanting to ruin
my momentum as I headed to the green flag. I didn't breathe.

Somehow, I kept it straight. Stayed out of the wall, got my
speed back up. On the back straight, I took a breath and softened
the front anti-roll bar to help the car turn more from my inputs
and moved the weight jacker three clicks to the right to make
it turn less on its own. I held my breath again going through
Turn 3, but the adjustment had settled the car. Barely. I took a
breath on the short chute between 3 and 4. Held on in Turn 4.

Alexa called to me. "Good use of tools. Pull it together.
Green flag."

I pointed the car down the center of the track and swept
under the green. My timed laps had begun, and I had a fight
on my hands.

In the end, nothing bad happened during my four qualifying
laps, though I adjusted the roll bars and jacker a dozen times a
lap and made scores of tiny steering inputs. I gave it all I had
and did everything I knew how to do.

Alexa stayed quiet on the radio, except to say "Two more"
or "One more." As I took the checkered flag, she radioed again.
"Coming in this lap, Kate. Great effort with the car. Average of
227.832, for P5 now, with fourteen left to qualify."

I was disappointed, but reminded myself I'd have started
thirty-third if I'd gotten into the wall. Of the fourteen cars still
to post a time, the top nine—or Fast Nine, as IndyCar called
them—were guaranteed positions one through nine. The other
five could qualify ahead of me or behind me, though chances
were, they'd be ahead. The best I could start would be fourteenth,
the worst, nineteenth. *Still better than thirtieth last year. Row six
or seven is a hell of a lot better than row ten.*

I radioed back to Alexa as I rounded Turn 4 low on the track and lined myself up with pit lane. "Thanks to everyone for the effort. Sorry it wasn't a higher spot, but the track was tough today."

Alexa waited to respond until I pulled diagonally into our cramped, temporary pit space at the top of pit lane and got out of the car. "No apologies," she said. "You did everything you could—and the save you made on the warm-up lap was incredible."

"I wish I could have bettered yesterday." *Shake it off, Kate, and don't bring the team down.* I made myself smile. "But it's an improvement over last year, starting in the middle of the pack. I'm happy."

She patted my shoulder. "You've got good hands and instincts. This will be a solid race, I've got a feeling about it."

"I like the sound of that." I turned at the approach of journalists wanting my reaction to my qualifying effort.

When the press had gone, Holly and I gathered my gear and made tracks back to our garage. Halfway there, I saw PJ's former boyfriend walking toward us, and I sent Holly ahead with my gear.

"Hell of a save, Kate," Paul said, with a shake of his head.

"Thanks. Twitchy today." I shrugged. "I wanted to ask you something else. Was there anyone you remember who especially had it in for PJ?"

"That's a strange question. Why do you ask?"

I'd prepared for this. "I've gotten some weird communications—stranger than normal. These are threatening, and reference PJ also, like the sender will make sure I end up how PJ did. I wondered if it's someone who was around then. Someone who might have threatened PJ also and added to her stress."

"Helped drive her to suicide?" Paul asked.

Something like that. "Can you think of any messages that stood out?"

He sighed heavily. "She got death threats."

"I'd be surprised if she hadn't. I do." His eyes got big, and I smiled. "Some people still don't like women racing. But I also have loyal fans. I brush the bad stuff off."

"I wish PJ'd had more supportive fans. It makes a difference." He was silent, looking down Gasoline Alley. "There was one letter-writer who was creepy, and I told the cops about him. The rest were of the 'we hope you die' variety, but one guy said he would make it his personal crusade to ensure she couldn't damage the reputation of the race." He shook his head. "I've never understood that attitude."

"You and me both. Did PJ hear from that guy a lot?"

"Two letters. I've always thought he was partially responsible for PJ doing what she did. That, if he hadn't been so cruel, she might not have felt everyone was against her." He frowned. "She might not have abandoned everyone else in her life."

I saw how he'd been hurt by his belief that PJ had chosen to give up on him. Maybe finding her killer would help Paul, too. "Were there specific people in the paddock against her?"

"Some of the old-timers who're mostly gone now. Bill James, who ran JKT Racing, was awful. He constantly put her down."

I recognized the name. "I've heard he had it in for any female driver."

"His crew was just as bad—especially the head mechanic, Jimmy, who'd been on PJ's team. He and Bill both got quoted for the 'women can't handle it' opinion in a bunch of articles." He shook his head. "They've sure proven to be on the losing side of history."

Back in the garage, I sat down with Nolan, my engineer, for the same discussion we had after every on-track session—how did the car handle, what went well in qualifying, what went poorly, how could we do better, and how could we go faster. When I left him, he was staring at data on his laptop, one hand tugging at his hair.

I'd said my goodbyes to the crew when I spotted Ron digging in the cooler that contained the ice cream bars. I walked over as he sat on his stool and unwrapped a drumstick.

"After all the comparisons the press has been making," I began, "I'm curious about PJ."

He shook his head, his mouth full of sugar cone and vanilla ice cream. He swallowed, then spoke. "Still makes me sad—so many things I wish were different about those days. Things I wish I could change."

"Given the similarities, I wondered what it was like for her as a woman then." I paused and sent silent apologies to PJ and her family. "I identify with her, and I keep trying to imagine what could make her give up like that. Do you have any idea why she did?"

Ron ran a hand over his brush-cut white hair, and a frown further creased his lined face. "She didn't have—I think she didn't feel she had a choice. PJ had it rough. I thought I was supporting her, but I clearly didn't understand how bad it was."

He paused and looked intently at me. "This is a different time, but still, don't let anyone get you down. Live your own life—like PJ never got the chance to."

Chapter Twenty-two

Holly and Gramps had left the track together earlier Sunday afternoon, so they had dinner waiting when I arrived home. I celebrated qualifying for the race by adding a tiny scoop of mashed potatoes to my grilled salmon and steamed vegetables—ignoring the delicious mountain of starch on Gramps' plate—and afterwards, I filled them in on what Ron Arvin and Paul Lauth had told me.

Holly started a new list titled "Suspects" and wrote two names down. I agreed with Jimmy but protested Ron Arvin. I wasn't sure how to articulate why I didn't think he'd killed PJ.

The sorrow I'd seen on his face. The regret. But what would he look like if he had *killed her?*

Holly laughed. "Sugar, you're having the whole argument in your head."

"I don't want to believe it, but I agree it's possible." I sighed. "Ron did say he should have done more—though that could mean anything."

Holly turned to Gramps and raised her eyebrows.

"Like Kate, I'm not sure I believe it," he responded. "The Arvie I knew of was more gentle than that."

"He was still a drug dealer, right?" I asked.

Gramps shrugged. "It was the eighties. You had to be there. We knew drugs funded racing, but we didn't know specifics. We learned not to look closely."

How did my straight-laced, conservative grandfather ignore drug evidence?

He saw me and flushed. "It's not that I condoned it. I didn't think about it."

"Head in the sand," Holly put in. "Everyone in the paddock was the same. That's what I learned today." She described what the old-timer reporter she'd talked to had said, which was more about background and environment than about PJ in particular. Except it was essentially known that PJ's father had been Arvie's contact and supplier.

I processed it all. "But that's—I can't believe I'm saying 'only'—drug running. It's not killing someone you claim to like and jeopardizing your team."

Holly nodded. "But I heard the publicity generated by PJ's stunning practice run and her surprising death launched Arvin Racing into the big leagues of racing teams. Before that year, they'd run partial seasons and hadn't had a win. After PJ, they pulled in a recently retired, top-tier driver for that race and others."

Gramps chuckled. "Another guy who retires and immediately regrets it?"

"Exactly. For the next couple years—until Arvie was busted by the Feds—his team had big sponsor backing, ran two cars for full seasons, won lots of races, and was seen as one of the teams to beat." She frowned. "I like him, too. But he benefitted in a major way from PJ's death."

My boss and mentor's father, that's who I'm looking at for murder. Now I remember why investigating is painful.

Next, Holly and Gramps reported what they'd learned that day—which wasn't much. "No one liked her," Holly said. "But no one hated her. They didn't know her."

"It's hard to come up with a motive for her murder." I thought back over the killers I'd helped unmask. "In my limited experience, murder is the result of a strong emotion."

"Except for the proverb." When we stared at him, confused, Gramps elaborated. "'Revenge is a dish best served cold.' Sometimes things happen after hot blood cools."

"Did anyone want revenge on PJ for anything?" Holly asked.

"I suppose there could be cold-blooded reasons for killing." I heard what I'd said and grimaced. "Theoretically."

"We're back to who benefitted from her death," Holly concluded. "You said Lyla mentioned other people benefitting— merch and memorabilia guys, insurance guy, other reporters. One of my contacts, a long-time PR guy, also mentioned a sports psychologist who got real popular right after PJ's time."

"That would have to be Tom Barclay," Gramps put in. "He was the first and the best. Even Kate's worked with him."

"With the woman on his team years ago," I said. "I didn't realize he started back in PJ's time."

"I didn't either, but I looked him up online." Holly handed us a couple printouts. "He doesn't name her, but PJ is a pivotal part of his history. Her death was 'the spark that illuminated the path he would take in life,'" she quoted.

We read for a minute, then I set the pages down. "Without PJ's death, he might never have found his life's work—or if he had, he wouldn't have had such a great example of the value of working with a sports psychologist."

Gramps frowned. "I always thought the guy was slick."

"You never objected to me working with them."

"The woman you saw—Dr. Shields?—seemed fine." He shrugged. "No good reason to stop you, regardless. And it helped."

Holly made a note. "I'll figure out a way to ask him about his background."

Gramps piped up. "I'll look into the memorabilia guy. I don't know much about that stuff, but I'll find out."

I stood to clear our dishes. "I'll try to finish my conversation with Ron."

Gramps snapped his fingers, his eyes wide with excitement. "The Speedway historian. He'll know details. I'll find him tomorrow. Plus I'll find the evil Jimmy. Better me than either of you."

"I'll also ask around about whoever the insurance guy was," Holly said. "I wonder if it's Gaffey Insurance."

Gramps stood and stretched. "They're who you think of. But I don't know a lot about them."

"I've met Chuck—the owner and founder—before, but mostly I know his son, Josh," Holly said.

"I talked with Chuck. Nice guy." I explained how he'd almost gotten out of racing over the idea of losing team members. "Maybe he'll have other ideas about PJ."

Holly studied her lists. "Didn't Paul mention anonymous letters?"

"PJ had gotten some, and one stood out."

Holly picked up her phone. "What were the words he used?"

"Something about a personal crusade and damaging the race's reputation."

Holly scrolled. "'I'm making it my personal crusade to ensure you don't damage the reputation of the race.'"

"Sounds like it. Why?"

She glanced from me to Gramps. "Because I was reading from an e-mail you got. I keep them, in case of any problems."

"Smart." Gramps' forehead was crinkled with concern.

What the hell? "Is there a name or an address?"

"The only name is 'RaceFan4Life.'" She turned back to her phone. "But reading this, I'm not feeling him as a suspect. This is a good old boy who thinks women shouldn't be driving, and he's been spouting off about it for thirty or more years."

"I've met them before."

Holly and I called that category of comments the "send women back to the kitchen" group. They weren't my favorite, but they were easier to ignore than the "I want to have sex with you" category, which I'd started getting more of as I moved to IndyCar and became more known in the racing world.

"Speaking of spouting off, any reduction in the 'Kate is PJ' theme?" I'd left all social media responses up to Holly, so I wouldn't be distracted or distressed.

Holly shook her head, but didn't elaborate.

"Even though I qualified for the race—for the second year?"

"Negativity is more pervasive, you know that."

I did. I shook off my frustration and studied Holly's lists. "What are we doing? We should have a plan, but this feels random—considering anyone we can find who was around in eighty-seven, even if we don't think they could be the killer. Like Arvie. Even Uncle Stan."

"For that matter, sugar," Holly said with a wink, "Gramps."

Gramps was startled, then amused. "By all means, investigate my disreputable character."

Holly chuckled, then got serious again. "We're taking a second look. But you're right, we should talk to everyone we can find who was here then."

"It feels haphazard." I frowned. "How can we possibly figure out who killed PJ—if anyone did? And what if the killer's also dead by now? It's been thirty years."

Holly made a T with her hands. "Timeout. Do you think PJ committed suicide?"

I listened to my gut. "No."

She nodded. "If we believe that—which I do, too—then all we're doing is asking questions. Once we have information, we'll see where it points us."

"If it's to someone who isn't alive or here?" I asked.

"We'll cross that bridge when we come to it," Gramps replied. Then he took my shoulders and pushed me toward my bedroom. "Enough for tonight. *My* brain is overloaded with information, and I'm not the one who qualified for the biggest race of the year today. Time for some rest."

Tomorrow. It'll all be better tomorrow.

Chapter Twenty-three

Before heading to the track the next day, Monday, I had an early-morning activity arranged by my sponsor, Beauté. Along with one of the cosmetics company's executives, I visited a local cancer research facility to talk with scientists about their work, which was partially funded by grants from the Breast Cancer Research Foundation, Beauté's charitable partner. Then we went next door to the associated hospital to visit women—and a man this time, too—undergoing treatment for breast cancer. Visits like those made me proud to wear and carry pink on my livery, to honor everyone fighting their individual battles. I handed out dozens of pink checkered-flag plastic bracelets from Beauté and urged everyone to watch the race and cheer me on. I also took lots of photos and signed plenty of autographs.

Then I made a quick swing back to the apartment to pick up Gramps and head to the track.

As we got on the highway, he puffed up his chest. "I've got an appointment with the Speedway's historian this afternoon for information about how the team did after PJ. I also called a buddy and got the scoop on the memorabilia guy."

"You're sure it's the right one?"

"Definitely. They all have a specialty, and this guy, Dean Herrera, is known for signed goods, especially hard-to-find people from years ago."

"He's still selling? He'll be at the track's memorabilia show next weekend?"

"Better. He's based here—has a shop in Indy. I'll go talk with him tomorrow."

I frowned. "Holly and I'll be in Phoenix for Media Day. Make sure you check in with us before and after you go."

"Yes, dear." When I glared at him, he added, "It's a memorabilia store."

"And the guy could have killed someone."

He sighed. "Fair point. I'll text your sidekick. Why Phoenix?"

"It's close to home—closer to Albuquerque than other cities drivers are going to. And it's a good market for IndyCar, now we're back there with the spring race."

Every year, usually on the Tuesday after qualifying, Indy-Car sent the full field of thirty-three drivers to different prime markets around the country for a promotional tour. All of us making news that day meant an Indy 500 media blitz, and the days could be fun, if long. Holly had done extra work to fill my schedule, so she was going with me.

Gramps' phone chimed, and he swiveled his glasses to his forehead to peer at it. "Holly's texting." He paused as another chime sounded. "She got details on PJ's sponsors—boy, she's good at this!" I laughed as he kept reading. "PJ's personal sponsors were a Mexican trade conglomerate. The name doesn't matter because they lost money on the deal with PJ, went away, and never had anything to do with racing again."

"Sounds like a dead end."

"But the other sponsors on her car…that's interesting. I had no idea that's where they started." He went silent.

"Gramps."

"Sorry." He glanced at me, sheepish and a little cross-eyed without his glasses. "The sponsor on the car was the Standish-Conroy Group—that's the Standish Hotel chain and Conroy Spas and products. They started out back in PJ's day, and her car was the first they'd ever backed in racing."

"They've been a sponsor for ages, haven't they?" I tried to remember the little IndyCar history I knew. "We're visiting their resort in Phoenix tomorrow."

"PJ's car was the beginning. They stuck with Arvin Racing that year, and the marketing went so well for them, they stepped up to sponsoring the series—what became the Indy Racing League when the series split. Standish has been 'The Official Hotel of IndyCar' for decades, and they've made a point to open hotels near all the tracks IndyCar regularly goes to. They're an integral part of the series."

"Did PJ's death help them?" I slowed to show my credential to the security guard at the entrance to IMS.

"They got a huge boost in publicity, attention, and sympathy over her death," Gramps said. "Holly says they reference PJ's year when asked about the value of association with racing." He turned back to his phone. "They call it a 'phoenix rising from the ashes' situation, where tragedy turned into something positive."

"That seems harsh." I paused. "Nathan Standish and Libby Conroy?"

Gramps tapped at his phone as I pulled into a parking space. "They're still listed as running the companies."

"Someone mentioned them—sponsors who'd come on in a big way for PJ. And for themselves, clearly."

"You can't be mad at people for making lemonade out of lemons, Katie."

I turned off the car. "Only if they created the lemons in the first place."

Alexa had called a full team meeting for ten-thirty that morning, well before the scheduled twelve-thirty start time for practice. After Monday, we'd have no more on-track activity until Carb Day, Friday, when we'd get only an hour's practice to make final adjustments. After that, we wouldn't set tire to pavement again until Sunday's race.

Of course, no on-track activity didn't mean the team wouldn't be at the Speedway. I'd be in Phoenix on Tuesday and fulfilling sponsor obligations on Wednesday, but some of the team would be here. We'd reconvene Thursday to talk through plans and strategy—or meticulously work through the car doing final checks, depending on the team member's role.

After the meeting I had time before I needed to be suited up and ready for an interview with a local television show, so I headed for the tire shop, permanently located in Gasoline Alley along the main corridor leading to the track.

The single tire supplier for the whole series occupied four or five spaces of the low, squat garage building. I walked past the stacks of tires on display and approached a tall, heavily muscled man in his thirties wearing the tire company shirt and smoking a cigarette in an open garage doorway.

"Help you?" he asked, on an exhale. The nametag on his shirt said Bubba.

"I'm looking for Donny. Is he around?"

"Got a couple Dons." He took a drag. "Last name?"

"I'm not sure. A friend of mine said he'd be able to tell me about what Indy was like twenty or thirty years ago."

"*That* Don. Hang on." Bubba set his burning cigarette on the edge of a stack of tires and disappeared inside.

While I waited, a young man approached me, a big grin on his face. I saw the Budweiser baseball hat, work boots, and cigarettes in the pocket of his loosely buttoned plaid flannel shirt and braced myself for a PJ reference.

He stuck out a hand. "I think it's awesome you're out there slugging it out with the guys on the track. I just had a baby girl last month, and I want her to know no one can put limits on what she wants to do in life. Thanks for being that example."

As I reminded myself never to judge by appearances, Bubba the tire guy returned with a tall, rangy man, then scooped up his cigarette and wandered down Gasoline Alley.

Donny's slowly graying light brown hair was the only indication of his age. He had a baby face—open, innocent, and curiously unlined.

I introduced myself and told him I wanted to know about PJ.

He smiled. "I wondered if anyone would get around to me."

"Everyone keeps comparing us, so I'm curious about her. What she was really like. How she felt about things."

"Why she killed herself."

"It's the biggest question for me," I admitted. "Did you think she was the type?"

"Not at all." He shook his head. "It was so hard to believe—still is. You drivers are half crazy, you know."

I grinned. "Have to be."

"She was as focused and nuts about driving as anyone." He paused. "I've always wondered if she actually did it. The girl I knew—woman, sorry—wouldn't have given up. I mean, would you?"

I shook my head. "But we're different people."

"You've still had to deal with crap for being a woman in this world—men calling you names and saying filthy things about you, right? And *you* don't give up."

I studied him. "You liked her."

"I did." He stuck his hands in his pockets and met my eyes, smiling. "I had a crush on her. She had to deal with so much—threats, hateful talk, groping. I did everything I could to protect her—even from her own crew. Through it all, she kept her head up. Kept trying to drive that damn car. I knew it hurt her, but she kept going. She taught me something about courage."

It was the best epitaph I'd heard yet. "If she didn't kill herself, what happened? You must have thought about it over the years."

"I did. Never thought anyone would believe me, or I'd have said something."

"Her family agrees with you."

"Good to know. And you're investigating?"

Chapter Twenty-four

When I flinched, Donny the tire guy laughed.

"Let's say I'm asking questions for PJ's parents," I said. "Who do you think did it?"

"I've read a lot of true-crime over the years. Thought about PJ a lot." He shook his head, eyes on mine. "When it happened, I thought it was someone who hated her. A crime of passion. But now?"

A cold dish of revenge, Gramps said.

"Do you still think it was a heat-of-the-moment crime, or could it have been coldly planned for revenge or long-term advantage?"

"I've gotten older and learned more. Now I think it was about convenience and personal gain. It was easier or better to have someone else in her place. PJ gone meant something else improved for them."

I was impressed with his analysis. "Who?"

"If it was someone who hated her, I'd talk to a couple crew from Bill James' team that are still around. They were the worst then." He eyed me. "Still are."

"Let me guess. One of them is Jimmy?"

Donny's face hardened. "Asshole. I wouldn't put it past him to have screwed up the car."

"Someone else suggested sabotage." I wondered why I wasn't more shocked at the idea. "Would he have actually messed with the team's livelihood?"

"If he knew PJ wouldn't make it to the race anyway?" He shrugged. "I wasn't a mechanic. I don't know who did what. I'm throwing ideas around."

Something to ask Uncle Stan about. "What if the motive was personal gain?"

"Two people who made their names from PJ's death were Kevin Hagan and Dean Herrera."

"The reporter and the memorabilia guy?"

Donny nodded. "Hagan was a ghoul, creeping around here after PJ's death, asking questions. He got national exposure for the series of articles he wrote, but they were muckraking—digging up everything bad people said or thought about PJ and portraying her as a weak, cowardly female who couldn't handle the pressure."

"That's how suicide would seem to people. Not that I agree with him."

"It was awfully convenient for him to ride her death to big success."

"And Herrera?" I prompted.

"Also nothing I could prove. He was a young guy then, starting out in the business, hanging around the track a lot, buying goods and getting drivers to sign them. But he bought up as much PJ merchandise as he could the minute we got word of her death. Sold some immediately, then held onto the rest of it—hoarded it. When the talk started about her this year, because of you, he's the one with all the stock." He paused, frowned. "There's no way it could all be signed by her either."

"I heard he specializes in signed goods. Couldn't he have gotten her signature?"

"I was around PJ a lot. I never saw anyone approach her with the volume of stuff he's got for sale. Hell, the cumulative amount of tee-shirts and ticket stubs and programs she signed for everyone during those weeks wasn't near the amount of 'signed' goods he's got now."

"They're forgeries? What would be the point?"

"A few bucks on every item. Multiply that by dozens of items and hundreds of drivers and it could be a good business. I'm sure it all started with PJ."

I was still thinking about Donny's accusations an hour later as I strapped into the car. Then I hit myself on the helmet.

You're about to go more than 220 mph, idiot. Focus on the car.

The day's four-hour practice session was a chance for us to get used to a number of changes. For one, our cars were all returned to pre-qualifying horsepower levels, so we'd tune the exact setup we'd use for the next weekend's race. Specifically, we'd focus on "tow speeds," or how fast we could go in the aero draft of another car, since that's how most of our race-running would be done.

Another change was our final pit boxes. We'd started the previous week in temporary spaces by team, then for the qualifying weekend, we'd moved to abbreviated spaces that made room for qualifying activities near pit exit. Once we'd qualified, teams chose their pit spaces based on qualifying order, and we moved to them the next day. For all of us, a big part of practice today was about *finding* our new pit locations.

We'd also practice hot pit stops for the first time—doing them at speed during the practice session—and we'd all enter the pits directly out of Turn 4 to maximize time at speed on the track, instead of taking the warm-up lane from the back stretch, as we'd done the other days. I knew I had at least one instance of heavy tire lockup in my future, before I got the timing right.

When we started the practice session, the car felt marginal—twitchy and unstable. So we worked on it. And worked on it. Kept working, fuel load by fuel load. A couple hours in, I felt we were on the right path, though I wanted more time than I knew we'd have. I focused on getting more comfortable with turbulent air due to other cars around me and with managing the car throughout the fuel run—from different weight balance due to diminishing fuel, to changes in tire wear affecting handling. At least I was significantly improved from the year before.

That had been my first time at the Indy 500, and only my second race on a high-speed oval. From my other racing experience, I understood and could handle dirty air from a car in front of me—it was the air coming from the side that threw me. It took conscious effort to be aware of cars moving up to the right or left, to think through how my car might react to the change in airflow, and to be ready to react. I spent the entire race that year hyper-aware of my position and focused on airflow, unable to really relax into the feel of the car and move with it organically. I'd done fine in the race, especially for my first effort, finishing seventeenth mostly due to luck in avoiding trouble.

But since I'd run a couple more ovals that year and the full IndyCar season this year, I was finally thinking less and reacting instinctively more. I was still hyper-aware, but I felt more a part of the machine I sat in—not that I was always in tune with the car. But I was getting there—and the speed charts at the end of the day proved it. I'd managed eighteenth, my qualifying position, on the no-tow list, but I was up to eleventh on the tow list. That was enough to give my crew a boost as we headed into three days of no running, especially when it turned out I'd been the fastest of Beermeier's three cars. I heard my guys ribbing the other crews as I walked back to our driver area.

Mick Porier and Kenny O'Toole, the other two Beermeier Racing drivers, were already there, half stripped down. I nodded a greeting while keeping my eyes on my own locker. As I pulled open the door, I immediately spotted a familiar yellow, folded note. I unfolded it with shaking fingers.

"Avenge PJ, before it's too late," it read.

We were right. He wants me to find PJ's murderer, but he's not threatening me. Why won't he say this publicly?

"Excellent job today, Kate." Mick broke into my reverie.

"Thanks. You both, too." I tucked the note into my bag.

Kenny snorted. "It's bloody nice of the speed princess to notice the peons."

I smirked as I pulled off my racing shoes and socks. "I prefer speed queen."

"I'm abjectly sorry, your highness." Kenny spoiled his words by throwing a dirty sock at me.

They cleared out as I finished changing, and we all wished each other safe travels the next day. Mick was headed to Toronto and Kenny to Texas, and we agreed to text with the most ridiculous local scenery we could find. After a short chat with my race engineer on my way back through the office, I reentered the main area to find it mostly empty. I grabbed a bottle of orange juice from the cooler and crossed to Uncle Stan, who was cleaning a small metal part with a toothbrush at one of the benches.

"Where'd everyone go, Uncle Stan?"

"Plenty of time the next couple days to work on the car. Sent everyone off early today—probably the last day they'll get the time with family this week." He peered over his reading glasses at me. "How're you doing?"

"Car was okay, but I wish we had more time." I caught sight of Gramps down at the far end of the long garage, talking with another mechanic. "I've been talking to people about PJ, and I don't see how she could make the choice people say she made."

"Understandable." He set down the part and the brush and slipped his glasses into his shirt pocket.

"Her parents think she didn't do it." I studied his face. The years had etched lines into it, but his eyes still conveyed compassion and kindness. "And you're not surprised."

"Seen so much, hardly anything surprises me anymore."

"More than one person suggested someone deliberately made PJ's car run badly after that first practice session. Is that possible?"

Uncle Stan opened his mouth, then closed it, looking around the garage. I got the feeling he wasn't seeing the present so much as the past.

"I want to say no, because who'd do that? It goes against the whole purpose of a team." He scratched his head. "But if I think about the car's behavior, it's possible. The question is who was involved—how many and how far up the chain?"

"If the whole crew colluded, it'd be easy." My mouth went dry at the thought. "I wouldn't know any different if Alexa told me one thing and the crew did another."

"I can't believe Arvie would have gone along with it. He was upset those weeks as they fought with the car—and devastated by PJ's death."

"What if it was a single mechanic, or maybe two?"

He slowly nodded his head. "Could be done, depending on specific jobs. But to do that to your own team?"

"Who'd have been in a position to do it?"

"I'll find my old notes about who on the crew worked on which bits." He sighed.

"Sorry to bring it all up."

Uncle Stan managed a smile as he patted my shoulder. "Wasn't your doing, Kate. Wasn't PJ's either. But now I wonder if it was someone else's."

Chapter Twenty-five

During dinner that night, Holly, Gramps, and I compared notes again. Holly volunteered to research Kevin Hagan's journalism career, and Gramps zeroed in on Donny's accusation that Dean Herrera, the memorabilia guy, might be selling forged autographs.

"Be careful when you go to his shop tomorrow," Holly told him. "You don't know what you're walking into."

Gramps looked miffed. "You both act like I can't take care of myself, but I've been doing it for seventy-two years."

"Gramps." I put a hand on his. "We love you. Humor us and be careful."

The fight drained out of him. "The same to you two."

I cleared our empty dishes, waving Holly back to her seat when she would have helped. "What did you learn today, besides the sponsors on PJ's car?"

"I ran into Tom Barclay and introduced myself—I used you for that, Kate." I waved a hand, and she went on. "I told him you'd been thinking about working with someone again—I laid it on thick about stepping up to a bigger racing stage, more attention, and your interest in the similarities between you and PJ. I asked for his advice, and we set up appointment on Wednesday, when I'll pump him for how he ties into PJ."

I set out a bowl of grapes for dessert, ignoring the look of disappointment on Gramps' face.

"No ice cream?" His voice was plaintive.

"Help yourself. You know where it is." I rolled my eyes as he jumped up.

"I also learned there's been no one unusual in the team's office area or near your driver lockers," Holly continued. "Whoever left the notes for you is someone we know."

We digested that tidbit in silence, then Holly went on. "I saw Josh Gaffey, of Gaffey Insurance, and chatted with him."

I noted a gleam in her eye. "A good friend of yours?"

"We dated, years ago—when we were young and clueless." She smiled. "He's worked for his dad's company since before he went to college, and his dad retired a couple years ago. Josh runs things now."

"Did he give you insight on their business and PJ?" I asked as Gramps sat down with a heaping bowl of vanilla ice cream smothered in chocolate sauce.

"A bit. His dad started the company long before PJ—in the sixties. Josh did say the company took off in the late eighties, but he didn't know if there was a specific reason for that boom."

"Timing is interesting," Gramps said, around a mouthful of ice cream.

"I couldn't push for more without being too obvious. But I thought of a way to get more information on him and others." Holly paused. "I bet Racing's Ringer would help, with the promise of stories later."

I let my anger and annoyance play out before acknowledging it was a good idea. "He owes me."

Gramps was wide-eyed. "You know the Ringer?"

"I figured out who he was a couple years ago, and I haven't exposed him yet." I raised an eyebrow at Holly. "I'm still not sure why."

"Banking favors for times like this."

"I guess so." I turned back to Gramps. "Before Holly and I have to set our alarms to wake up stupid-early tomorrow, tell us about meeting with the Speedway historian."

"Before I get to that," he said. "I found Jimmy the crew member."

"Who's he working for?" Holly asked.

"R-9 Racing. They've only got one car, but it's a family-run team that's been around Indy forever. Usually turn in a respectable performance."

My stomach fell. "Is Jimmy tall, with a scrunched-up face and leathery skin?"

"I thought you didn't know him?"

"I don't. But he's made his opinions clear."

"I'm not sure I like the sound of that." Gramps frowned. "On the surface, he's a nice guy—salt of the earth, I'd have said, if I hadn't heard the stories. I told him I thought he worked on a car in the late eighties I'd done a wiring harness for. He hadn't—I knew that going in—but he knew someone who did, which led to a conversation about 'the good old days' over at least four cigarettes. The man smokes like a chimney."

Holly smiled. "I know you managed to bring up PJ."

"Piece of cake." Gramps winked at her. "I mentioned things being simpler back in that era—you could say what you meant and not worry about being politically correct." He sighed. "That seemed to be code for 'I'm a bigot,' because it opened the floodgates. He's no fan of female drivers or owners—doesn't mind if they're 'facilitating racing,' working hospitality or something."

"Holding umbrellas, no doubt." Holly said.

"He didn't say it directly, but he thinks the problem with racing today is women and foreigners taking over. It was hard to listen to."

I could imagine. "Did he talk about PJ specifically?"

"He praised her, if you can believe it, but only for realizing she couldn't cut it and 'doing the right thing' by killing herself." Gramps harumphed. "I needed a shower after the conversation."

"Any idea if he could have sabotaged the car? Or killed PJ?" Holly asked.

"He worked on suspension that year, and given who the lead mechanic was, it would have been tough for Jimmy to have messed anything up on his own. Maybe not impossible, but hard." Gramps shook his head. "Plus I didn't get that sense from him. He was sly enough when he talked about making PJ feel unwanted—he didn't keep his mouth shut to the media or the paddock. But he was righteous about her inability to manage the car. He even said she reaped what she sowed, like it was God's opinion she didn't belong in a racecar."

"If Uncle Stan confirms Jimmy's role, we can probably rule out sabotage," I said. "Not that it had much to do with murder anyway."

"And we know Jimmy was at the track when PJ was killed," Holly added.

I nodded. "But it was good to check. Thanks for doing it, Gramps."

"At least the Speedway historian was fun." Gramps perked up. "The stuff that guy knows! Everything about any car or team in the history of the 500. Amazing."

Holly hid a smile. "What about PJ's car and team? After she died?"

He cleared his throat. "Two days after PJ's death, the team announced they were hiring a former series champion who'd retired the year before: Sidney Wells. Sid's passed on now, but as the historian tells it, he was happy to come out of retirement for one last crack at the race he never managed to win in a long career."

"He didn't win it that year either, did he?" Holly asked.

"He came close. Ran third near the end before something on the car broke. Limped it home in twentieth." Gramps shook his head. "He did a couple more races with the team that year. No huge success, and after that, he stayed retired, so not a suspect."

"Probably not," I agreed. "Did the historian have any perspective on team and sponsor fortunes with PJ out of the picture?"

"He volunteered it without my having to ask, which surprised me—do sources often do that when you question them, Kate?"

Am I the expert? In this room, probably so.

"Sometimes. Usually it means they've had the same idea we're fishing for."

"He called the Standish-Conroy hotel chain a textbook case of how companies can benefit from motorsports sponsorship. From return on investment—that's the money, right?—to intangibles like public perception and brand sympathy." Gramps pronounced the unfamiliar marketing terms with care.

"Sounds like we need more information on Standish and Conroy," Holly said.

Gramps nodded. "The historian also said he'd never seen a team's fortunes on such a roller-coaster ride as Arvin Racing's that year. From the top in the first practice to the bottom in subsequent days, culminating in PJ 'opting out,' as he put it. Then back to the top with the publicity and the former champion's performance in the race. Arvin Racing was the toast of the celebration banquet and the darling of the press."

"The good news kept coming over the next couple years, didn't it?" Holly asked.

"They were one of the top teams until Arvie was busted," Gramps said.

I still found it hard to picture Arvie—or Ron—as a stone-cold killer, out for profit.

Then again, he ran drugs to pay for racing. You never know about people at all.

Chapter Twenty-six

Holly and I were up at what she called "dark-thirty" Tuesday morning, and we left our apartment to pitch-black skies. Even the birds weren't chirping yet.

We landed in Phoenix before seven local time, and within thirty minutes, I was in a makeup chair. By eight, I was on the set of a Phoenix station's morning show with two anchors and a sports reporter. By nine-thirty, we'd zipped over to one of Phoenix's top radio stations to record a quick interview and some promos. And by eleven, we were suited up at a local go-kart track with two sports reporters—a man and a woman—for the local affiliate of the network that would broadcast the Indy 500. We pre-taped a segment to air during the evening news, during which I'd be on set.

As Holly and I left the go-kart track and walked to our car, my stomach growled loudly.

Holly laughed. "We've got an hour, and I scoped out a local taco shack."

"I'll drive if you direct. Any word from Gramps?"

"He texted while we were in the karts to say he's off to the memorabilia shop, and yes, he'll be careful."

"I really hope he is." I tried to put the worry aside and focus on my own jobs for the day. The delicious tacos made it easier.

The Standish Hotel was our next stop after we ate. As we pulled into the resort's large, circular driveway in Paradise Valley, one of the ritziest towns in the greater Phoenix metropolis, we saw a slim woman in a navy power suit—an outfit that seemed unusual for the casual flavor of Phoenix in general—pacing in front of the entrance.

Holly popped out as soon as I stopped the car. "Shawna? Are we late?"

Our contact, Shawna Wilkes, glanced at her watch and started to nod before changing the motion to a shake of her head. "You're not. I'm anxious. Welcome."

As she ushered us into the hotel, waving at the valet to deal with our car, she explained her nerves. "The plan has changed for your visit, and we'll have quite a few more press here as a result."

Holly and I exchanged a glance. "If IndyCar is fine with the change, we're at your disposal," Holly said.

Shawna nodded vigorously. "IndyCar was great with it. In addition to our local executives, you'll meet with our founder, Nathan Standish, a long-time IndyCar partner."

Holly and I looked at each other again, our eyes going wide at the same time.

I found my voice first. "I'll be pleased to meet him and thank him myself for his consistent and generous support."

Plus ask a couple questions.

Holly spoke up. "I understand he had a business partner in the Standish-Conroy Group, is that right?"

Shawna bobbed her head. I wondered if it was a nervous tic. "Libby Conroy co-founded the organization with Mr. Standish. Her expertise was spa services, and that's why her name is on the day-spa portion of the business."

"Does she live here also?" I asked.

A head bob, curtailed. "She retired a few years before Mr. Standish and primarily lives in Hawaii near her children. She wasn't ever as involved in the day-to-day as Mr. Standish, but she provided some of the start-up capital at the beginning and the overall direction for the spas through the years. She's very clever about how to create a luxurious and pampering atmosphere for our guests." Shawna started nodding again.

A long walk through the resort ended in a corner room with two walls made entirely of glass, looking out over a lush golf course on the gentle upslope of what I learned was Mummy Mountain. We were so caught by the vision of the landscape that at first we didn't register the presence of a man standing at one end of the room.

"Here we are," Shawna chirped with nods. "Mr. Standish, this is Kate Reilly and her assistant, Holly Wilson."

He was tall, with uncompromising posture, a thinning head of white hair, and a face set in stern lines. He strode forward, extending a hand. "Kate, I'm pleased to meet you. And Holly," he added, turning to her. "Call me Nathan."

"I'll leave you all to it," Shawna said, bobbing her head as she left the room.

I turned to Nathan with a questioning look, which he answered. "I'll give you ladies a tour of the resort, then we'll join our local executives and press for a chat over dessert—created by our award-winning pastry chef. Then we'll talk with the journalists for a few minutes." He glanced at his watch. "I appreciate you've got a schedule to keep, and we'll maintain it, never fear. But I want you to understand the depth and breadth of what it means to be a Standish property." He turned humorless eyes to me. "It's important you fully understand as you go forward representing IndyCar and us as an integral partner."

"I'm delighted to learn more." I grimaced at Holly as Nathan moved to a door in one of the walls of windows.

Asking him questions wouldn't be as easy as I thought.

Fortunately, his austere expression softened as he drove a golf cart through the grounds of the resort and pointed out private villas set among a variety of trees and shrubs. When I admired some beautiful orange and purple flowers, he spoke at length about the different varieties of sage (the purple blooms) and bird of paradise plants (the orange) before he caught himself.

He smiled at me as I sat next to him in the front seat of the cart. "You've stumbled upon my retirement hobby, Kate."

Thank goodness, there's some personality.

"Was it an interest before you retired?"

"I had no time for anything quite so frivolous." He smiled again, staring straight ahead at the path. "'Frivolous' is how I'd have seen it then."

"How long have you been retired?" Holly asked, leaning forward from the backseat. "I imagine it must be a difficult transition."

He nodded. "Five years, and you're correct, but the daily grind of business had started to pale. The change of pace has been welcome." He wheeled the cart around a bend and off the path into a small clearing affording a view of the main building. He described the basic features of the resort: how many rooms and suites, how many meeting rooms for other functions, the spa facilities, the restaurants and bar spaces, and all other amenities on offer.

I was impressed. "When traveling for races, our teams operate with less of a budget. But I'll make sure to stay with you when I'm making my own choices."

"With your visit today, we're establishing you as a VIP member of the Standish family of properties, which will give you pricing discounts and benefits. You won't have any barriers to representing us with firsthand experience."

That kind of quid pro quo happened all the time, and I welcomed it. The hotel—or sports apparel company or nutritional supplement maker—gave me extreme discounts or freebies, and in return, I talked about them on social media, in interviews, or in person. I didn't mind, so long as the products were good enough that I'd endorse them anyway. The Standish resorts certainly qualified. "I'll be delighted to spread the word about the Standish brand."

He wagged a finger. "And the Conroy brand. We'll be sending you home with certificates for spa services, so you can experience those and speak knowledgeably about them, as well." He glanced back at Holly. "Enough for the two of you, since we want your PR person on board, as well."

"Why, thank you for the thought, sugar," Holly flashed a blinding grin that Nathan couldn't see. "I've drooled over the Conroy Spa in Indianapolis for some time now, but never made it in."

"You're welcome. For our part, we're glad to have another female driver in the series—we expect you'll be more willing to talk about our spa services than most of the men." He waved a hand. "Plenty of wives have been involved, but they don't have the reach or clout of a driver."

"There have been women in IndyCar for a long time. They weren't interested?" I asked.

"Some were, and we had good relationships with them. But for a lot of years, the women have been mostly foreign-born and haven't had much following here in the United States, where we have our properties." Nathan pulled to a stop next to the golf course, between the green of one hole and the tee of another. He shifted in his seat to face me. "You're the all-American female driver, Kate. As such, we want you positively disposed to our brand. I don't say 'representing,' as we're not offering a true sponsorship opportunity. I'm sure you understand."

"I'm happy to work with Standish-Conroy in that framework." I paused, my mind busy. "In fact, I commend you for being open to the idea of working with female drivers. You've done that since the beginning of your association with IndyCar, going back thirty years now, correct?"

"Starting with the unfortunate PJ Rodriguez. I wondered how long it would take for you to ask about her."

Chapter Twenty-seven

I must have shown the surprise I felt, because Nathan Standish responded. "It's logical you'd be interested in her, given your similarities—though you've found more success. And I presume you won't come to such a precipitous end."

"Guaranteed," I replied. "Can you tell me anything about her?"

He paused and stared out across the golf course. "She was reserved. Many called her aloof or accused her of thinking she was too good for everyone else. But I always saw her as shy and insecure. Unsure how to reach out." He turned to me. "She didn't have your charisma or your ability to engage people."

I appreciated the compliment. "Surely it was more difficult for her then?"

He let out a long, slow breath. "It was such an interesting time, full of contradictions. On one hand you had the old views about women and racing only changing at a snail's pace. On the other, it was a great era for racing in the United States and for many of us who chose to partner with it."

"Was eighty-seven the first year you were involved?"

"And nearly the last," he said.

That surprised me. "Why?"

He pursed his lips. "It was the idea that all our efforts rested on a single person—our fortunes would rise and fall with that person, subject to the whims of fate that day."

"Or the whims of that individual," Holly noted.

"I wasn't a fan of the uncertainty—not for the brand we were trying to build, at least." He grinned, looking boyish. "I enjoy gambling as much as anyone—love a trip to the horse races. But I wasn't ready to go into a weekend not knowing if my fledgling company would come out a winner, a mid-pack journeyman, an also-ran—or worse, an instigator of trouble."

I pondered what he'd said. "By sponsoring the whole series you back everyone and you always back the winner."

"It wasn't my first thought," Nathan replied. "I was ready to get out after PJ's death and all the chaos that resulted from it."

"Isn't all publicity good publicity?" Holly asked.

"It can be said," he admitted. "But I want to get ahead through hard work and honest support, not notoriety."

"I can't blame you," I said. "You stuck with racing by sponsoring the Series."

"We've been happy with it as one of our main marketing efforts, along with tennis and golf. It's been an unusual approach, but it's worked for us."

If his story was true, Nathan didn't seem like a candidate for PJ's murder. I glanced at Holly, who shrugged, which meant she thought the same. "I'm still curious what the paddock and the racing world were like in PJ's day—I keep searching for more information—more context that might help me understand her."

Nathan checked the time. "I'd be happy to share my recollections, but we're in danger of running over your tight schedule today."

Dammit. "Will you be in Indianapolis for the race?"

"I will be—I never miss it, frankly—though the IndyCar series filled my schedule." He paused, studying my face, and I felt he was seeing through my cover story to the real reason I was asking questions about PJ.

"I'd be delighted to buy you coffee or a cocktail whenever we both—all," he said, including Holly, "have free time. But I can also dig up the case study I wrote that year, which might give you some of the insight you're looking for."

"Case study?" I asked.

He shrugged, the first break in the ramrod-straight posture I'd seen. "I call it that. I was documenting our different marketing efforts, but I also fancied myself a bit of an amateur historian." He made a self-deprecating face. "It's also a survey of other business interests, investment, and expansion in the context of the Indy 500 in the late 1980s. As well as any successes and failures. Would that be of interest to you?"

"It would, thank you," I managed.

Are you kidding me?!

I thought more about Nathan as Holly drove us from the resort to our next stop. "I wouldn't count him—or his partner, Libby, for that matter—as a suspect for killing PJ. Not if he almost got out of racing."

"I wish we could have asked outright who benefitted."

"I thought about it, but I couldn't come up with a good reason for the question. Maybe his notes will be useful." I looked out the window at roadside cactus. "Did you hear from Gramps?"

She nodded. "He's home from the memorabilia shop where he had a long conversation with Dean Herrera. Plus Gramps bought two signed items of PJ's and says we might try to get more and compare signatures. Something about research saying if signatures are identical, they're likely to be fake."

I smiled. "Leave it to Gramps."

"Did you think about talking with Scott about helping us?"

Scott Brooklyn was a sports reporter by day and the anonymous, rumormongering racing blogger Racing's Ringer by night. Much as he annoyed me, I knew, at heart, he wasn't totally evil. "It's a good idea. Since he lives in Indianapolis, let's make him buy something PJ may or may not have signed from Herrera's store."

"Should we also ask him for background on Gaffey Insurance?"

"And the reporter and the sports psychologist. If I'm calling in a favor, let's cover all the bases. I'll e-mail when we get to the airport tonight."

We made it to Phoenix International Raceway right on time for our next appointment and had fun "racing" golf carts around the track with PIR's president and some of their senior staff. We hammered it up for the cameras that followed us—and preceded us and rolled along side-by-side, reporters hanging out of track vans and trucks to get their shots. After that stop, we went back toward downtown to the local television station for a more interesting interview than normal, due to our pre-taped segments from the go-kart track.

Finally, Holly and I returned to the airport in time to grab a sandwich and hop a seven o'clock flight home. Thanks to onboard WiFi, I spent the three-plus hours of flight time catching up on details for the next two days of activity, responding to media outlets who'd requested comments or quotes, and e-mailing Scott Brooklyn. With the time change, we landed after one in the morning, exhausted.

My "day off" the next day, Wednesday, was theoretical. I wasn't going to the track, but I had a full slate of errands, chores, and visits to the local community lined up for the afternoon. It was also the last day to get a workout in before the race, so despite a lack of sleep, I got myself up early enough to hit the gym. When I returned to the apartment, I found Holly and Gramps at the dining table examining old marketing materials with a magnifying glass.

I poured a cup of coffee and sat down next to a signed ticket stub, milk bottle, and pair of gloves—then realized the latter were familiar.

"Gramps, you bought my signed gloves?" I didn't understand why he'd pay money for something I'd give him any time he wanted. I sipped my coffee, hoping the caffeine would bring more clarity.

"They weren't expensive, and I don't have anything from your Star Mazda days. Plus it helped my cover."

I picked up the milk bottle, which was signed by AJ Foyt, one of only three four-time winners of the Indy 500. The ticket was for 1967 and signed by Dan Gurney.

"You went all out. What do you have from PJ?"

"A ticket from eighty-six and a program from eighty-seven." He swiveled them around on the table to show me.

Holly's phone rang, and she went into the living room to take the call.

I raised an eyebrow at Gramps. "Where'd you get the lens, Sherlock?"

He laughed and held the magnifying glass up to his eye, making it look enormous. "Office store. I've been doing online research—amazing what you can find these days—so I thought I'd try my hand at detecting."

I got up to refill my coffee. "Did you come up with anything?"

"I think both of PJ's items are forged—poorly, if I can catch them." He leaned over the ticket with the magnifying glass. "You can see pencil lines underneath the ink, one of the main methods forgers use. They trace it in pencil, then go over it with ink."

"Do we need other people to buy more PJ signatures to compare?"

"It's probably a good idea."

"Then the question is, if Herrera's a minor crook, does that also mean he's a murderer? Did you get more information from him?"

"All I managed to ask was how long he'd been in business— thirty-two years at that location. There wasn't a good opening to ask him more."

"We'll see if we can figure it out another way."

My phone buzzed in my hand and distracted me from Gramps' study of signatures. Lyla Thomas had e-mailed me a scan of an old article.

"Thought you might be interested in this," she wrote. "It was an interview I did with PJ in May of '87 that isn't online. It may give you a different perspective on her."

I opened the attachment to find a photo I hadn't seen before. PJ stood on her racecar—one from a lower-level open-wheel series—in victory lane, her arms in the air, fists pumping, and face suffused with triumph. I was transfixed by the vision of her in her element, decidedly *not* looking weak and pathetic.

Lyla's interview with PJ was brief, one of the typical "Getting to Know Driver X" variety, though Lyla had infused it with more style and less "what's it like being a woman." She covered basics like PJ's racing background, but she also dug deeper.

> *Lyla Thomas: Do you have any pre-race rituals? Any superstitions?*
>
> *PJ Rodriguez: I take a moment just before I put my helmet on to look down the track and breathe it in. I also pull out my St. Christopher medal—that's the patron saint of travelers, athletes, and drivers—and kiss it for luck.*
>
> *LT: What does it mean to you to be here at the Indy 500?*
>
> *PJ: Everything. It's been my dream since I strapped into a go-kart. I used to watch men compete and read about the history of the race. I didn't care women hadn't been here until eight years ago—I wanted to be part of it. Now I am.*
>
> *LT: Why do you race?*
>
> *PJ: I have to. It's where I feel the most like myself. Where I feel in control. Where I feel free. It's not only about the winning—though I like that very much! But there's something magical that happens when I'm on the track and in tune with my car. I'm alive out there.*

I knew how PJ felt. I studied her photo again and again experienced the joy of her moment. I knew that feeling. I'd *felt* it.

That's how she should be remembered. That's why we're trying to find out what happened to her.

Chapter Twenty-eight

When he responded to my e-mail, Racing's Ringer, aka Scott Brooklyn, suggested we meet for coffee that morning. Holly spent the hour before we left scowling at the mirror in our foyer.

"I'm working on my badass expressions," she told me, and I hid my grin.

As I drove us to the coffee shop, we prepared our talking points and requests as if readying for war, which wasn't far off the truth, given prior interactions. Scott was a smart guy and a talented writer—and even more skilled at digging up facts and rumors in the racing world, in part because he promised sources anonymity. I couldn't let anything drop that I wasn't ready to talk about.

"Will you keep it from him that you're looking into PJ's death?" Holly asked, as we got out of the car.

"No chance. But I want his guarantee he won't post anything until we're ready."

"I've got your back." She nodded toward the door, where Scott stood waiting. "Game faces on."

In recent years, Scott Brooklyn had stopped chasing full-time funding and full-season seats in racecars—choosing instead to compete once or twice a year in the longer endurance races like the 24 Hours of Daytona or Le Mans. As he'd given up his driving dreams, his broadcasting career had picked up, and he now worked the pits for major networks at IndyCar races and the occasional NASCAR race. For a guy in his mid- to late-thirties, that was a good career trajectory. Of course, what the official biographers didn't report—or know—was his sideline as the hottest racing blogger of the past decade. I had to give him grudging credit for remaining anonymous, even if I didn't always approve of what he posted.

I studied him as we approached and decided he was more settled and comfortable with himself than in years past. He'd always been handsome, with a killer smile and a way of looking at you with total absorption that drew you in. He had the beginnings of laugh lines and gray hair mingling with dark blond at his temples, which actually improved his looks. Compared to when I'd first met him, three and a half years ago—after a mutual friend was hauled away for killing two people—he looked great.

"Ladies." He took our hands and pulled each of us close for a kiss on the cheek. "It's good to see you both."

Really? "Good to see you, too."

Scott laughed and held the door open. "I promise not to bite, Kate. Unless you want me to."

Flirting? I snapped my head around to Scott, and he winked at me.

"Sugar," Holly drawled, "you can't blame us for being gun-shy."

"I bear you no ill will today." He sobered. "Never have done, honestly."

I remembered, vividly, the attacks on me and my abilities his site had gleefully posted all those years ago. "Even at the beginning?"

He shrugged. "It was never personal. It was what was being said. I lose credibility if I don't report what people are saying."

"Convenient," Holly muttered and walked to the end of the line to order drinks.

Once we'd picked up our caffeine of choice—lattes for me and Scott and a mocha for Holly—we found a table and sat down.

Scott raised his cardboard cup. "A toast? I pledge I mean you no harm and I'll support you as far as I am able to, given the constraints of my site."

I put my hand on my cup, but didn't pick it up yet. "Your blog won't attack me?"

"I can't promise that—I'm being honest," he added, as he saw my expression. "It wouldn't look right if I praised you and never covered anything negative. But if you stay out of trouble—or murder cases—the negative stuff won't come up. Kudos for keeping your nose clean the last couple years, by the way." He glanced from me to Holly. "Do we have an agreement? A truce? Friends?"

"I can do a truce. Maybe even friends." I tried the idea on for size and my gut didn't argue. "But I have my own conditions."

"Let's hear them." He gave up waiting for a toast and drank some of his coffee.

"Promise me you won't publish anything we tell you without asking us first. That's the big one."

He put a hand to his heart. "You pain me."

"Suck it up," Holly advised him. "Friends don't rat out friends."

"True." Scott grinned. "But can I ask if I can publish? Convince you to let me?"

"You can try."

I wish you luck with that.

He nodded. "Fair enough. Is that it?"

"Sometimes I'm going to want background information or your insight." I chose my words carefully, but he was no dummy.

He raised an eyebrow. "What kind of information does Sleuth Kate need this time? I knew you couldn't have hung up your deerstalker."

I gritted my teeth. "Do we have a deal? Or will I throw this in your face?"

"What's in it for me?"

"I don't expose the biggest secret in racing and tell everyone who you are."

He laughed and picked up his cup. "You make a compelling argument. A toast to our truce. And friendship."

We bumped cardboard—Holly and I more warily than him—and drank.

Holly narrowed her eyes at him. "You've mellowed, Mr. Brooklyn."

He nodded. "I stopped worrying people would uncover my secret—and got comfortable with the idea you wouldn't expose me. I started to enjoy it more. Plus I'm happy in general."

"I'm glad for you." I even meant it.

"Thanks." His eyes were warm as they met mine. "I'm glad to see your career doing so well. Great first practice session this year—woke everyone right up."

"Have you gotten your pit lane assignments yet?" Holly asked. The three pit reporters would split coverage of cars on pit lane, each responsible for a mostly contiguous group of five to twelve pit spaces, depending on the amount of work required to cover the likely stories coming out of the teams.

He nodded. "I'll be covering your pits, Kate, so I expect you to put on a show and give me a story I can get on the air with."

"I'll do my best."

He leaned forward and lowered his tone. "Now we're friends, and I'm operating under the seal of the confessional, what do you want to know?" I hesitated, and he added, "You asked for help in your message. I assume you're investigating PJ's untimely death thirty years ago and you want background from me. How'm I doing so far?"

Holly sighed. "On the money."

I glanced around and saw the people nearest to us working on computers with earbuds in their ears. No one paying attention. I tried one last time to find duplicity in Scott's face. None. I forced myself to relax. To trust.

"Basic information. What do you know about the reporter, Kevin Hagan?"

He raised his eyebrows and leaned back in his seat. "Hmmm, Hagan."

"Don't read anything into this." I got tense. Defensive.

"No interpretation until you say so," Scott reminded me, covering my free hand with his. "Trust. Friends, remember?"

"Sorry." I sipped my latte.

"Trust and secrecy is a two-way street." Scott pointed his empty cup at each of us. "You won't disclose me as your source, right?"

"Cross our hearts." Holly scribbled in her notepad.

Scott nodded. "Kevin Hagan. Celebrated as one of motorsports great journalists, but those in the trenches with him think he's a hack. A blowhard."

"Not that good?" Holly asked.

"Others are better. But he's got the aura, the buzz, and the awards from decades ago. And he never lets anyone forget it." He thought for a moment and answered the questions we hadn't gotten to. "Was he around then? Absolutely. Did he profit from PJ's death? Totally. Could he have killed her for his own benefit?"

"Well?" I prompted, after he'd been quiet for thirty seconds.

"If he could have predicted her death would help his career, I wouldn't put it past him. But was it a sure outcome? I'd say it's hard to tell. Who else?"

"Chuck Gaffey, Gaffey Insurance," I said.

"He founded his company before PJ's era and, after some shaky early years, kept the business steadily booming throughout his career. Retired and turned the reins over to his son, Josh, five-plus years ago. Hard to say if he benefitted from PJ's death or not. I'd have to look to see when his business expanded."

I stared at him. "How do you know this? You weren't around the paddock then."

"Actually, I was. Dad was a lead mechanic and I was starting out in karting, so I tagged along whenever possible. I was there that year, a precocious eight-year-old kid. I even met PJ. " He stared across the room, serious for once. "She was sweet to me."

"I didn't realize," I said.

"That's why I'm glad to help you. With lips zipped." He nodded. "I'll look up Hagan and Gaffey in my files at home."

"You've got files?"

He laughed. "You wouldn't believe the data I've got compiled."

"Well, shit, sugar," Holly slapped her hand on the table. "Sounds like you got some sharin' to do."

Chapter Twenty-nine

After leaving the Ringer and dropping Holly at her car, I swung into action, making three phone calls for interviews, stopping at the local Beauté headquarters, and meeting two other Indy 500 drivers for a couple local appearances. I wrapped up the afternoon with a visit to a local television station that sponsored and broadcast the 500 Festival Parade. Held the day before the race every year, the event had the normal complement of bands and floats, but it also offered something other city parades didn't—the full field of Indy 500 drivers.

I was at the station to promote the race and parade, as well as to reveal live, on air, the names of three heroines in the cancer fight who'd receive a VIP experience at the Indy 500—plus one winner who got the bonus of riding in the Festival Parade with me.

As balloons and confetti dropped in the studio, and the anchors wished me well in the race, butterflies started up in my stomach. *Two days to last practice, three to the parade, and four until the Indianapolis 500!*

I had one remaining event for the day, a team party held at the Beermeier Racing shop in the town of Speedway, near the track. While I drove myself, Holly, and Gramps there, we caught each other up on the day's activities and investigations.

"Racing's Ringer has archives of information on people in the racing world?" Gramps asked. "Isn't that creepy?"

From the passenger seat, Holly swiveled around to look at

him. "The Ringer reports news, of a sort. I guess he has to be prepared for anything."

"He's going to share information?" Gramps sounded skeptical.

"That's what he said," I put in. "Now we're all *friends*."

"You trust him?" Gramps' voice went up an octave.

"So far." I frowned and met Holly's eyes. "I'm still not convinced."

"Your gut trusts him, but your head gets in the way." She turned back to Gramps. "He's going to send us background info on the people we asked about—he didn't say he had something on everyone. But he figured he could dig up something useful."

"Tell Gramps what he said about the people today," I told her.

Holly dug for her notebook. She filled him in on Hagan and Gaffey, then flipped the page. "The Ringer says Dean Herrera, the memorabilia guy—who I also met today—besides sporting the most prominent ears in racing, is a complete douchecanoe."

We heard sputtering from the backseat, and I glanced in the mirror to see Gramps trying to repeat the word.

I laughed. "Translation—he's a slimy jerk."

Holly kept reading. "No one in the industry likes Herrera, but he's been around so long and he's gotten to be so good at marketing—he jumped on social media way before everyone else—that he's not going away. He's known to be underhanded in deals, pushy when it comes to other vendors and even athletes."

"Did the Ringer say anything about forgery?" Gramps asked.

"He didn't bring it up," I replied, "but we asked. He recalled rumors now and again. Nothing ever proven."

"What do you do if you prove it?" Gramps asked. "Take it to the cops?"

I thought about it. "If he's selling fraudulent goods online, that makes it FBI."

"Sounds like you should call Ryan," Holly told me.

"I'll add it to my list. Tell Gramps what the Ringer said about Tom Barclay."

"Another charmer." Holly's tone was heavily sarcastic.

I was confused. "I don't remember the Ringer saying that."

"He didn't. That's my assessment after meeting with him."
She flipped another page in her notebook. "What the Ringer
said was this: Good guy. Been the go-to sports psychologist for
racing drivers for at least twenty-five years. Covers all sports,
but specializes in racing. He was degreed and about to start his
general consulting practice when PJ—apparently—killed herself.
That event gave him the idea for starting his business. He's been
the pioneer in destigmatizing the idea of 'getting help.'"

"The Ringer likes him," I added.

"Why don't you, Holly?" Gramps asked.

She hesitated. "He's full of himself. Knows all the answers
and can do no wrong. Everything stems from him—no one is
as smart as he is."

I thought back to meeting him. "You could tell so quickly?"

"When we spoke today, everything was about what he'd done,
with not a word about his staff. His walls were covered with
photos of him with clients—all men. He called everyone who
worked for him 'kids'—worse, all females were 'girls' or 'gals.'"

"I hate 'girls,' but I hate 'gals' more. Mind you," I caught
Gramps' eye in the mirror, "if you're over seventy years old, you
get a pass. But there's no excuse for anyone younger to think it's
okay."

"Noted," Gramps said, his eyebrows halfway up his forehead.

Holly twisted around to pat Gramps' knee. "You always get
a pass, sugar." She almost toppled over as I exited the freeway,
and she faced front again. "My impression is Barclay's outwardly
charming and smooth, delighted to be the big man in his business, and happy to have new clients. My gut feeling is narcissist."

She studied her notebook again. "That's all the Ringer had to
say, except the obvious—the big beneficiaries of PJ's death were
Ron Arvin, plus the replacement driver and Standish-Conroy,
the sponsors on the car."

"Maybe we can talk to Ron tonight," Gramps suggested.

Holly nodded. "I'll tackle any of our other sources or suspects
who're there."

I stopped at a light on Crawfordsville Road. "Except tonight's about having fun and celebrating. Let's not make it all investigation all night, deal?"

"Deal," they both echoed.

We entered the Beermeier Racing building through the lobby where a woman I didn't recognize checked names against a list. She marked off Gramps and Holly's names and waved us through, wishing me luck this weekend.

"I guess my fame precedes me," I commented as we stepped into the race shop. It was a large, open, warehouse-like space, two stories tall, the floor usually packed wall-to-wall with racecars and tools. Tonight it was full of temporary tables laden with food and beverages, as well as hundreds of team members, sponsors, and guests.

"If it's not fame, it could be the ginormous poster." Holly pointed to a more-than-life-size image of me standing next to my car that hung high on one wall. Two others, for Mick and Kenny's cars, adorned other walls.

"Festive."

Gramps clapped his hands together. "I'm getting a beer. Ladies?"

Holly spoke for both of us. "The man's a genius. Lead the way."

After we each got our hands on a beer—the one I was allowing myself that week—I left them to their own devices while I fulfilled my obligation as a Beermeier Racing driver. I worked my way through the room, chatting with sponsor after sponsor, partner after partner. As I spoke with representatives of one of the team's major backers, the biggest furniture company in the Midwest, the official photographer caught up with me and asked if I'd pose with the group. Then she wanted me posed with the people next to us, which turned out to be the team from Frame Savings—also known as my father and his family. After the flashes temporarily blinded us and the photographer moved on, we were able to chat.

As he usually did, my half brother, Eddie, overwhelmed me with a bear hug. "Huge congratulations on qualifying, Kate."

"A great job." My half sister, Lara, moved in for a quick squeeze.

"My turn." My father's wife, Amelia, pretended to push her daughter out of the way and hugged me also. Then she looked me square in the eye and nodded toward my father.

"He's worried for you," she said. I knew she was talking about the information from my grandmother, not the race.

My father stepped forward for his own hug and as I moved back, I felt a tap on my shoulder. I turned.

Here it is.

"Gramps." Though I'd prepared for the moment, tension still coiled in my gut.

Gramps stood very still, his eyes darting between my face and my father behind me. He swallowed. "Sorry to interrupt. You've got a special guest who's just arrived."

I nodded, not really hearing his words. Thinking more about needing to make introductions.

Then my guest, who had his back to me as he talked with another partygoer—neither of whom I'd seen behind Gramps, given my focus on family drama—turned around and smiled. A familiar, comforting smile. One I'd missed more than I realized.

"What are you doing here?" I didn't think about anyone else. I went straight into my boyfriend's open arms.

Ryan Johnston had been an FBI agent for eight years and my boyfriend for two. It hadn't been easy arranging times and places to be together in those years, given he was based in Los Angeles and I was in Indianapolis, when I wasn't traveling around the U.S. for races and sponsor obligations. But we'd grown slowly closer, as friends and lovers. I rested my head on his chest, inhaled his familiar scent—a mix of woodsy citrus and Ryan—and let the relief of his calm, intelligent presence wash over me. The feel of the muscles in his chest and arms as they tightened around me triggered a visceral response.

How long since we've seen each other? Too long.

Then I remembered the group standing behind me. I straightened and met Ryan's eyes. "Ready for this?"

"Always." He smiled and took my hand.

I turned around and towed him two steps forward, to the people who hadn't spoken, but who at least hadn't run in opposite directions. "James and Amelia, you've met Ryan, but Eddie and Lara, you haven't. Ryan Johnston. My half-siblings."

Ryan stepped forward to shake hands with all of them, while I turned to Gramps and put an arm around his shoulders. I took a deep breath.

"Gramps, this is James Reilly, his wife Amelia, and their kids, Eddie and Lara." Gramps was stiff, but I plowed ahead. "My grandfather, Horace."

Chapter Thirty

Everyone froze for a single second. My father retreated behind the blank, aloof façade I thought of as his "banker face." He and my grandfather both had to be thinking about the past, and I wondered what images flashed through their minds.

Before either man spoke, Amelia stepped forward, her face radiating warmth as she took both of Gramps' hands in hers. "I am so glad to meet the infamous Gramps. Kate speaks so lovingly of you, and she has so many stories of her wonderful childhood with you and your wife." She bit her lip, then plunged ahead. "I hope I'm not being presumptuous telling you what a beautiful woman you've raised. Thank you for that."

I felt Gramps relax and knew he'd been moved by her words. He nodded and thanked her with a gruff voice.

Eddie and Lara stepped forward together, both with friendly, uncomplicated smiles on their faces. Eddie winked at me before he spoke. "We're so glad to meet the most important man in Kate's life." He glanced at Ryan. "Sorry, bro."

"True statement," Ryan replied.

My father still hadn't moved. He finally nodded once, a curt, shallow movement. "Horace."

Gramps echoed the movement and expressionless tone. "James." Then Gramps turned to me, took my arm off his shoulder, and kissed my cheek. "It's okay, Katie."

Then he turned around, took a step forward, and offered my

father his hand. Neither man spoke, but they did shake, and I felt some of the tension leave the group.

Gramps stepped back and nodded generally at the group. He turned to me, and I could see distress brewing under his veneer of calm.

"I'm sorry—" I started.

"*You* have never done anything wrong, Katie. And maybe, just maybe, he didn't either." He glanced around, taking in the Reilly family, who were now chatting with Ryan. "I knew this would happen this weekend—even before you asked—and now it has. We'll all deal with it later. For now, I'm getting another beer."

I nodded, hating his pain, but not sure what to say to make it better.

He chucked me under the chin and managed a real smile. "I'll be fine. You keep enjoying the party. Make sure you've talked with all of your sponsors and team, and catch up with Ryan. I love you."

"I love you, too, Gramps." I let him go, staring after him.

"He'll be okay." Ryan moved to my side. "He's as tough as his granddaughter."

I leaned against him for a moment.

What I wouldn't give for just a couple minutes with Ryan, someone who I don't need to impress, placate, or worry about....

I turned to my family. "If you'll excuse us, I'm going to give Ryan a tour of the shop."

Eddie waved his hand. "We'll be here."

I dragged Ryan through the crowd to the rooms at the back of the building—a couple offices and storage rooms. All locked, and worse, the hallway was full of people waiting in line for the one-room bathroom—including Holly, who squealed and dragged Ryan close for a hug before letting us continue. Exasperated, I headed for the rear of the shop, for the human-sized door next to the full-height rollup through which racecars and equipment were loaded in and out. The people door was propped open by a sandbag, and I worried we'd find a crowd of people outside in the wide alley between the two Beermeier buildings.

A quick glance showed no one—at least that was the impression I got between stepping foot in the loading zone and when I was pinned against the block wall of the building and kissed senseless.

After a minute—two? five?—Ryan let us both up for air, cupping my face in his hands and leaning his forehead on mine. "I missed you."

I smiled. "I thought you weren't going to make it this weekend. What happened?"

He pulled back enough to give me a saucy look. "You bought that story? I wouldn't miss this for the world."

I opened my mouth to reply, but before I could, we heard a sob. We broke apart and saw two huddled figures at the end of the building, against the wall. We ran toward them, Ryan's hand moving to the gun at his waist.

The sobbing figure was Alexa Wittmeier, my boss, on her knees next to the still figure of her father, slumped on his side on the ground. Even in the poor exterior lighting, I could tell Ron Arvin's face and head were bloody. That his head rested in a pool of blood. That Alexa's hands were covered with it.

"Alexa." I sank to my knees next to her—though I had the presence of mind to stay well away from the blood. "What happened? Did you call an ambulance?"

Alexa shook her head, trying to draw enough breath to speak. Ryan circled around Ron and pressed two fingers to his neck, then shook his head.

He's dead?

I felt blank. Couldn't find other words to think or say. I put my arms around Alexa and pulled her close, as Ryan called in the cavalry. When he was done, he leaned close to my ear.

"You haven't touched anything, right?" he murmured.

"No. What can I do?"

He put a hand on my shoulder and squeezed. "Stay with her. We need someone to keep people from coming out here. I can do it for now, but I'll need to talk to the authorities when they arrive."

"Text Holly. Have her meet you at the back door. She'll do it."

I rocked back off my knees and into a seated position, pulling Alexa with me. She stared at her bloody hands, then slumped against me, still weeping.

Ryan frowned. "I was thinking of someone more like a big, burly security guard."

"She might be only five feet tall, but no one's going to mess with her. Get her out here, Ryan. She'll do what you need." I heard the exasperation in my voice, and I grabbed his hand to stop him from moving. "I'm sorry. I'm…"

He kissed the top of my head. "I know."

Alexa got quiet and pulled away from me. "I'm sorry to fall apart on you."

Lacking tissue or handkerchief, I used the cuff of my long-sleeved shirt to wipe the tears from her cheeks. "It's the only reasonable response. I'm so sorry."

She stared at her hands. "I need to wash."

I thought about evidence. "Let's wait for the police. They'll be here soon."

She shrugged and wiped her nose on her sleeve, like a kid.

"Did you see anything, Alexa?" I asked.

"I came looking for him, because someone said he'd gone out this way, and I found him like this." She started to cry again, big silent tears that slid down her face. "I didn't see anyone or anything. Only him."

I reached out and held her again, as she kept talking. "He was still alive when I got here. I leaned over him, and he saw me. Knew me." She hiccupped a breath. "He said my name and he said 'sorry.' Then he was gone." She looked blindly at her father's body. "I held his hand. It was all I could do." She crumpled as we heard the first sirens.

Fifteen minutes later, Alexa and I remained in the same position, but everything around us had changed. Holly watched the door to the shop, a fierce expression on her face. Gramps stood next to her, arms crossed, his face grim. The police had strung yellow crime scene tape to block access to the loading zone and alley. And Ryan stood talking with the guys in charge, a few steps away from us and Ron Arvin's body.

Alexa had mostly calmed again, helped by the packet of tissues Holly brought over. As we watched an ambulance pull up to the mouth of the alley, lights flashing but minus a siren, Alexa stirred. "I need to stand up."

I helped her, keeping an arm around her waist until I knew she was steady.

"Let's move over there," I suggested, pointing to the wall of the building opposite the shop—inside the taped-off area, but well away from the official activity and the body.

She looked down at her father. "It's hard," she mumbled, and I saw tears streaming again. "If I don't stand up, if I don't step away…it didn't really happen, right? I can stay in that moment and not deal with everything that comes after."

I didn't say anything, but leaned into her for comfort.

She took a shuddering breath, still looking at the crumpled, bloody figure on the ground. "I know he messed up. I know he did awful things—and paid for them—we all paid for them. But he'd learned, and he regretted everything." She turned to me, eyes beseeching. "Underneath it all, Kate, under the opportunism and the momentary greed, he was a good man. He was my daddy." Her voice broke on the last word.

My own eyes filled with tears at the devastation on her face. "I'm so sorry. At least you had him in your life." I pulled her in for a hug, realizing what I'd said.

At least she did have her father in her life. More than I'd had.

I shook my head. Not the time for my own family drama.

"Come on." I urged her away from the body.

I stayed with her until Ryan approached with a tall, slim man with gray hair and a young face. Lieutenant Noble focused on Alexa, and Ryan led me away.

"You all right?" he asked.

I nodded, looking over at Ron's body. I'd been so focused on helping Alexa cope, that I hadn't dealt with the fact of someone

I knew bloody and dead in front of me. Three feet away from me. I shuddered. "That poor man."

Ryan put his arms around me and rested his chin on the top of my head. "Did Alexa see anything? Anyone?"

"No," I said into his chest. "And she didn't do it."

"I don't think she did. I saw her inside a couple minutes before we got out here. I told the officers she wasn't gone long enough."

"She got to him right before he died. He said her name and apologized to her."

"For what?"

"She didn't know or didn't say. Maybe for what he'd done in life." I pulled away, maintaining my grip on Ryan but able to see his face. "He spent time in jail for running drugs. He used to own a team, and that's how he funded it. He was even PJ's team owner—I told you about PJ."

"I know."

When Ryan didn't ask any questions, I studied his face as he watched the activity around the body. I pulled a hand free and punched him in the shoulder. "You knew all of that. You ran him. Why would you run Ron?" I thought a moment. "You ran Alexa?"

He grimaced and focused on me again. "Call it an occupational hazard and a protective streak. I wanted to know you'd be safe. Sue me."

"Why didn't you tell me?"

"*That* would have been abusing my position and privileges." He held up a hand before I could object. "But if you'd been in any danger or you'd said anything was hinky, I'd have shared the information."

I sighed. "It's a great welcome for you, isn't it?" I felt sick with grief for Ron and Alexa and awful that Ryan had shown up only to deal with something like work. I also felt the first trickle of panic that this whole situation could jeopardize me, the team, my car for the race on Sunday.

How selfish is that?

"Forget me." Ryan put his hands on my shoulders and made me meet his eyes. His warm, lovely, and too perceptive brown eyes. "What the hell's going on here?"

Chapter Thirty-one

I blew out a breath. "The usual is what's going on."

"Racing, with a little murder on the side?" Ryan frowned at the cops and crime scene people. "Are you a magnet?"

"I don't ask for it."

"I know, it finds you."

"When can we leave? I'll explain everything back at the apartment." I caught sight of Gramps and Holly at the back door of the shop. "We'll all explain."

Ryan checked in with the police and a couple minutes later we each spoke with a different officer about what we'd seen before and after entering the alley. A few minutes after that, we were free to go. We couldn't enter the shop building, as the police were clearing it of people, so we headed for the line of caution tape that held a small crowd at bay. I ignored the camera flashes and the handful of voices calling my name and zeroed in instead on Diane Wittmeier, huddled against the building at the edge of the crowd.

"Kate," Diane called, as I approached. "Is my girl all right?" She was jittery, bordering on frantic.

I ran the last couple steps and hugged her. "She's okay. Talking with the cops."

I'd thought plenty about what Alexa was going through, losing her father, but I hadn't considered Diane losing her ex-husband. I squeezed her hands. "I'm sorry."

She blinked back tears. "Thanks. I wish…a lot of things. Right now, I'd like to be with Alexa. Do you know when she'll be done?"

I turned to Ryan and explained who Diane was, and he made arrangements with an officer to take her to Alexa.

"Now, let's get out of here," Ryan murmured, his hand on my back guiding me through the crowd.

Holly rode back to our apartment with Ryan in his rental car, and Gramps and I sped off in mine. We were quiet for the first ten full minutes.

Gramps finally let out an explosive sigh. "Hell of a thing. Did you see him?"

I clenched the steering wheel. "I did. Ryan and I both found Alexa next to him." I saw the tableau again—the slumped, bloody father, the kneeling, grieving daughter. It would take a lot to wipe the scene from my mind.

"I'm sorry, Katie."

I reached over and found his hand. "Me, too."

"Crazy time for Ryan to show up—right as there's a murder? I guess you'll have to tell him about our investigation?"

"Seems that way."

Gramps nodded, staring at the highway ahead of us. "Maybe he'll help."

I'd settle for him not being mad.

While Ryan stowed his bags in my room, Holly pulled out her notepad and possibly-forged PJ autographs, and Gramps set up spoons, bowls, and ice cream. I leaned against the half wall between the living and dining rooms and drank two large glasses of water. Ryan exited the bedroom rubbing his eyes, and for the first time I noticed the fatigue in his expression.

"Want some ice cream, my boy?" Gramps asked. He dug into the carton, the tip of his tongue between his teeth.

Ryan grinned. "A small bowl." He crossed to the counter and doctored his scoops of vanilla with a quick squirt of chocolate sauce.

I filled my glass again and sat down at the table with him. As Holly and Gramps joined us, Ryan waved his spoon.

"What's going on? How were you investigating this death before it happened?"

I froze as his words hit me. I'd been so caught up in the horror of Ron Arvin's death, I hadn't considered the impact.

"Why's that question a shock?" Ryan asked.

I shook my head slowly. "We weren't investigating his death."

"No one else died around here, or I'd have heard about it." Ryan surveyed the people in the room and the supplies on the table. "And this has all the signs of an investigation. You're only missing the secret decoder rings."

Holly sighed, elaborately. "Only because you won't tell me where you got yours."

Ryan plunked his spoon down in his empty bowl, and I jumped in before he could speak. "Let me start by saying I didn't go looking for this. I was asked—pressured. I don't know where I'll get with it, but I said I'd try. And these two wanted to help. We're being careful."

"What's the crime?" Ryan's tone was mild.

"Oh, it's murder," Gramps put in.

Everyone opened their mouths to speak, and I topped them all. "Thirty years ago."

I saw Ryan get it. Saw his mind work. His brows drew together. "Who asked?"

"Her family." I explained everything that had happened from the first practice to the erasure of my identity for PJ's in the media to the meeting and press conference with PJ's mother and brother. "It's not that I think I—we—*can* figure out who killed her. Or maybe we'll end up with a good idea but no proof." I struggled for words.

"There's more behind it than thinking we'll catch a killer," Holly put in.

"I need to understand PJ." I pushed back from the table and paced the kitchen. "When I first heard about her—which wasn't until after the first practice—I felt a bond. We'd both done this lucky, flukey, amazing thing, thirty years apart. I admired her for doing it that long ago, with the extra battles she fought. And then when I heard she'd committed suicide…I couldn't make sense of it. It didn't fit."

"Why not?" Ryan asked. "Not all individuals are built the same way."

"Because I understand who she was and who she had to be to get to that point—this point, the same point I'm at. And I simply can't understand how she could change so fundamentally that she would take her own life."

Ryan nodded. "Because you couldn't."

"Yes, but it's not me projecting on her." I saw his expression. "It's not. I got curious about PJ, so I started asking people about her—to understand, to know more about her. And every story I heard convinced me it wasn't in her nature to give up." I stopped moving. "She wouldn't have given up. Someone made that choice for her."

"I'm not criticizing or even disagreeing," Ryan said, "but do you have evidence to back that up?"

I shook my head. "Only opinion, unless Ron Arvin's death is an indication."

Ryan picked up Holly's notes. "You'd worked on who benefitted from PJ's death, and Arvin did?"

"As well as others, to different degrees," Holly said.

Ryan yawned, then apologized. "I've been up for twenty-two hours. I'm taking you seriously, but can we sleep on it?" He glanced around. "We could all use some rest."

"I've got a call at ten and I have to be at the track by twelve-thirty." I considered. "Breakfast and discussion at nine?"

Holly nodded. "Special Team Kate out for the night." She disappeared into her bedroom, and with a wave, Gramps headed for his own.

Ryan took my hand. "Special Team Kate?"

"Decoder rings on order. Thanks for not yelling."

He sighed as I shut the bedroom door. "I don't like it. But I understand."

"Does that mean you'll help?"

He dropped down on the bed, flat on his back, groaned as he covered his eyes with his hand. "I'm going to regret this, but yes."

I pressed myself along the length of his body. "I'll make it worth your while."

His lips curved as he ran his hands down my body. "How?"

"We'll get you a ring, too."

Chapter Thirty-two

Gramps, Holly, and I lingered over the egg casserole Holly had made for breakfast. Ryan ended a call as he reentered the room. "The initial impression was Arvin's death was a mugging gone bad—watch and money missing." He scrutinized each of us in turn. "And none of you will repeat this."

"Aye, aye, Captain." Gramps stood to collect empty plates.

"Except we don't think that's true," I replied, frowning. "Why pick him? Why pick that location? It's not where muggings happen."

"Opportunity?" Ryan offered.

"That won't wash," Holly said. "I saw plenty of people in and out of that back door earlier in the evening for a smoke. All wore more jewelry and expensive shoes than Ron. He was targeted—and not for theft."

I nodded. "The only thing that makes sense is he knew something about PJ's death—involved or not—and someone went after him for it." I raised my eyebrows at Ryan. "Don't you think?"

He leaned back in his chair and smiled. "I'm playing devil's advocate. Making you test your theories."

His implicit approval was nice, but I still felt at sea. "So what's next?"

"We've been focusing on who had motive to kill PJ." Holly spoke slowly. "Do we assume the same person killed Ron?"

"Doesn't it have to be?" I asked the group, but mostly Ryan, who shrugged.

Gramps sat back down in a chair after cleaning the counters. "I can ask around to see if Ron was into anything bad or if he was keeping clean."

Ryan and I leaned forward at the same time, but I beat him to the punch. "Gramps, Ron was killed. Don't show up the next day asking why someone did it."

I glanced at Ryan, who nodded, but didn't speak.

"Do I look like a complete buffoon? On second thought, don't answer that," Gramps said. "Ron had become a team mascot, sitting on his stool in the corner of the garage. Some guys even had him touch parts before they bolted them down—you know how superstitious racing folks are."

Holly and I nodded. Superstition was rampant in the garages, though I didn't particularly subscribe myself.

Gramps went on. "I'm suggesting I take over Ron's stool. I'll make it a tribute to him, and get the guys talking about him, to help the sadness of losing him. I should be able to worm around to who showed up to talk to Ron and what they talked about. Won't that be safe enough, nervous Nellies?"

Ryan nodded. "Don't get complacent. Remember a killer could be anyone, big or small, young or old, male or female. The second you feel uncomfortable—get out of there. Don't second-guess yourself—go to the bathroom or take a call. Go somewhere and contact me. Keep your cell phone on you at all times."

As the conversation continued, I excused myself for a thirty-minute call with an Albuquerque radio station. When I returned, I found everyone poring over the different memorabilia items purchased from the sketchy dealer, Dean Herrera.

I got myself more coffee. "Ryan, did you ever work on a forgery case?"

"I worked on a couple that got turned over to the forgery investigators." He pulled one of the ticket stubs closer and examined it with the magnifying glass. "There might be something here."

Gramps went pink, and I grinned. "Not to burst your bubble, Gramps, but isn't this small potatoes? Would the FBI care?"

Ryan turned to me, bemused. "We *care* about them all, Kate."

"Sorry."

He laughed. "He's selling online, which makes it Internet fraud."

"Forgery doesn't have a damn thing to do with murder, though." Gramps stood up and stretched his back.

Ryan sat back in his chair. "I've come across it as a basis for murder before—to protect the business. But given you said Herrera bought PJ's goods after she died, I'm not sure it makes sense."

The others kept talking, but I was distracted by an e-mail that arrived. "The Ringer sent details." I pulled the information up on my laptop and set it in front of the others.

Ryan read the first name from the e-mail. "Kevin Hagan, reporter."

"The Ringer doesn't have much more on him than he told us," Holly mused.

"Except for occasional allegations throughout his career of skirting too close to the line of stealing a story or becoming it," I added.

Gramps cocked his head. "What does that mean, 'becoming the story'?"

"Journalists are supposed to be objective," Holly explained. "To report the facts. But if they're personally involved, they skew the story—or worse, they manufacture the story—and can't present an unbiased perspective. It's editorial, not reporting, yet he's praised as the last, great motorsports beat reporter."

"Was he there last night?" Ryan asked.

"I don't think I'd recognize him," I replied.

Holly nodded. "I think he was, but I can also ask the team who was checked off the guest list."

"That'd be useful to know in general," Ryan said.

"Handled." Holly pointed to the next name. "Chuck Gaffey, Gaffey Insurance."

I scanned the same details on my phone as I paced nearby. "The same as the Ringer told us in person, a rocky start the first few years, including a rumor of mishandled funds, but well established and considered the pioneer and gold-standard by the nineties. One new product introduced the year before PJ. Business interruption insurance for racing?"

"I'd heard of it, but didn't realize it'd been around for so long." Holly tapped her cheek. "That must have been the payout to Arvin Racing we've heard about. But it benefitted Ron, not the insurance company…"

She kept talking, but I didn't hear her. I couldn't hear anything over the roar of blood in my ears. I stood, frozen, until Holly took my phone and read the next e-mail I'd received from the Ringer. I hoped the message would be different the second time. It wasn't.

"'Kate, in the spirit of friendship,'" Holly read, "'I'm coming to you first before posting this anonymous tip I received. A credible source tells me you're desperately seeking the help of professional counselors before the race this weekend, because the stress of the spotlight is making you crack up and causing those around you to fear for your mental state. Since I didn't see anything shaky about your psyche when we met yesterday, I thought it only fair to ask for comment. Any rebuttal?'"

I clenched my fists. "That son of a bitch Tom Barclay."

"Wow," Holly said. "Just wow. What the hell?"

Ryan frowned. "Who's Tom Barclay and how do you know he's the source?"

I waved a hand at Holly to explain, stormed to the couch, and kicked it.

"Not with your throttle foot," Gramps yelled.

Holly sounded bitter. "Tom Barclay is on our list. He's a sports psychologist who claims PJ's death as the start of his career—he says it was the inspiration, the spark for his career. I met with him yesterday to get background on his services. My excuse was Kate might be interested in working with his team again—she worked with them years ago, so we didn't think it'd be a big deal."

"Not your fault, Holly. We trusted his professional ethics," I bit out.

I don't need this added stress three days before the race.
I took a deep breath.
Then don't allow it to stress you out.
After another minute of focused breathing, I calmed down.
"First, let me reply to the Ringer." I paused. "How about this? Tell him I'm laughing off the suggestion. I was happy to work with a trusted sports psychologist a decade ago, but I've been fortunate throughout my career to have a strong support system that helps me stay strong enough mentally and physically to meet the challenges of the racing world. As big as the Indy 500 is, and while I'm more excited for it than other races on the schedule this year, when the helmet goes on, it's any other day at the racetrack. But I appreciate everyone's concern and support. See you on Sunday."

Holly typed as I spoke. "Perfect."

"Still gonna punch that guy if I meet him alone somewhere." Gramps stomped over to refill his coffee.

With the Tom Barclay drama handled—for now—we turned back to the Ringer's information.

"Dean Herrera. Cheating memorabilia guy." I read aloud from the e-mail. "The truth is no one in the paddock likes Herrera. He's highly intelligent—which he makes sure everyone knows—with horribly awkward social skills he revels in. Thirty years on, he's become slyer and smugger, say those who've known him the whole time."

"He seems like a creep," Holly said. "But if he did kill PJ to improve his business, you'd think he'd have planned it better— bought all her merchandise and had her sign it before he killed her."

"What do you think of him?" I asked Holly and Gramps.

"He was smug—patronizing the old guy." Gramps looked annoyed. "He thought he was pulling something over on someone too far gone to notice."

Holly nodded. "But he's only about my size, physically, so I don't see him overpowering PJ or Ron."

Gramps shook his head. "With ears that stuck out like a cartoon."

"I met that guy. He had me sign a photo supposedly from the first practice this year." I wondered how many forged Kate Reilly signatures it might spawn.

"Ears aside, size doesn't matter if you have a weapon," Ryan said.

Holly shrugged. "It's an awkward fit for me, him as the killer."

"Fair enough." Ryan scrolled down to the last name on the page. "Who's Nathan Standish?"

"I didn't ask the Ringer about Nathan." I shook my head. "We already knew his business boomed after PJ's death. But it wasn't him. He was too sad about PJ dying, said he almost got out of racing after her death."

"But he didn't," Ryan noted.

"What are you getting at?" Holly asked.

"To be careful trusting what suspects say, especially about themselves." He paused. "Always question what anyone says. It's easy for Standish to say he was so sorry for PJ's death he almost quit, but it might be a convenient interpretation of past events. Or what he's convinced himself to believe. Or his cover story all along."

We all fell silent, considering his words. I thought through the conversation with Nathan, probing my memory for inconsistencies or different interpretations.

"I still don't think Standish is the guy." I glanced at Holly. "He seemed genuinely sorry for her death."

Ryan nodded. "He could be lying. You've met killers before who seemed normal."

"Why are you doing this?" I demanded.

"Not to stress you out." He frowned. "To push you to think more analytically. To think about more angles. It's not that I think Standish is guilty, and I believe you believe he isn't. But I want you to know why you think so."

Holly helped me out. "It was the break in his voice when he said he wanted recognition for hard work, not notoriety. His eyes were shiny with moisture. He wanted to do the right thing and succeed accordingly, not take shortcuts."

At that, Ryan conceded the point. I stayed grumpy with him for pushing us—though I knew he only did it to help—until I got to the track.

Racecars make it all better, even if they're not running.

Chapter Thirty-three

The action that day, the Thursday before the race, was all about drivers, sponsors, and media. And brewing thunderstorms.

The weather was always a question in Indianapolis, and unlike other kinds of tracks, no one raced in the rain on ovals—even grooved rain tires wouldn't give us the grip we needed. In past years, rain had put off qualifying sessions and shortened, post-poned, and even split the race itself across two days. Delays were tough on everyone—especially the fans who often had time off work and travel plans set in stone. We all did anti-rain dances throughout the month of May.

Please don't rain on Sunday. Please don't rain on Sunday.

Gramps, Holly, and I headed for the garage, as usual—Ryan had remained at the apartment to work—and I approached the Beermeier setup warily, after the trauma of the night before. I wasn't sure if I'd see Alexa there, and half-wondered if I'd see anyone there, but the team was business as usual, if more sub-dued. Alexa sat at her computer in the office area, her back to the room, and I paused next to her.

"How are you? Anything I can do?"

She turned, her eyes red-rimmed and puffy. "You did plenty last night, and I didn't thank you for it. I'll be all right." She poked the man next to her. "Let's talk about the car. Nolan?"

I pulled up a chair, and the three of us spent the next hour going over details—schedules, settings, and strategies. After that, I headed for the plaza below the pagoda for an hour of media availability and an hour spent signing official race merchandise—official programs, mini-helmets, and more. My hand hurt before I was halfway done. Two more hours of interviews and team duties, and I was finally dodging the raindrops with Gramps and Holly, headed back to my car.

"Did you learn anything in the garage today?" I asked Gramps.

He buckled his seatbelt. "They all liked Ron and liked having him there to question about car stuff—or sometimes opinions on strategy or history. They like Chuck, too, but he's good more for stories of people in racing, not so much the engine or mechanical knowledge. Ron was there every day, and Chuck most days, and Ron also got a steady stream of visitors—of the older generation. People he'd have known when he was running a team, is my guess."

I glanced at him. "Did they know any names?"

"That was tough, because there were so many. The best they could do was say 'everyone.' It sounds like most other team owners stopped by, plenty of other engineers, some drivers—Paul Lauth, PJ's old boyfriend was one. And loads of other people. Some reporters, but Ron wouldn't talk about his time in prison. He was done with it."

"Any idea if Hagan was around?" Holly asked.

"I didn't know how to ask. Maybe tomorrow." Gramps glanced at me. "That Tom Barclay was around a couple times, though, and the crew knew who he was."

"Asshole," I muttered.

Gramps grinned and laced his fingers over his small belly. "Indeed. I couldn't find out about Dean Herrera either, but I'll try tomorrow. For now, I've been accepted as the gossipy old-man replacement."

"Aww, sugar," Holly said, "you're number one in my book."

Back at our apartment, I got on the phone with a local radio station for an on-air interview. By the time I made it out to the kitchen to set the table, Gramps had already told the others what he'd learned from sitting on Ron Arvin's stool that day. Ryan stepped in before I could, warning him to be careful. He also talked Gramps through useful questions to keep the conversation moving in the direction he wanted—focused on Ron and who he interacted with—without appearing to be questioning them.

"You can ask Uncle Stan what he's seen, Gramps," I said. "He won't wonder why you're asking."

"Does he know you think PJ was murdered?" Ryan asked.

"Not explicitly. But I wouldn't be surprised if he's figured it out. He's a smart guy, and he's seen a lot. He was the first to tell me about PJ."

Ryan's attention sharpened. "He was there at the time?"

"A junior member of her crew," Holly responded.

"You don't have him on your list as a suspect?" Ryan focused on me.

I couldn't entertain the idea for even a moment. "Uncle Stan's no killer."

"How often have you said that before?" Ryan asked. "Did you consider him?"

Holly and I exchanged glances, then looked at Gramps, who shrugged. "I don't see it either," Gramps said.

I turned to Ryan. "We didn't talk about him as a possible suspect, no. But he didn't do it—either killing. I'd stake my life on it."

"You may have done so." He sighed. "I'm only worried about who you've let into the secret of your investigation. The more people who know, the more potential danger to you of the wrong person finding out. Plus you want to be one hundred and ten percent sure that whoever you let in isn't a suspect."

Holly nodded. "I'll add another 'no' vote for Uncle Stan. He was there, but he didn't gain anything from her death, and he was pretty cut up about it."

"Honestly, I think he had a crush on her, like the other guy, Donny," I said. "And Uncle Stan…I've seen him catch spiders and take them outside instead of killing them. He rescues beagles, and he's the one person who's always got a kind word about everyone—even the assholes. He's not that guy."

Ryan raised both hands. "Point taken. Hopefully you see mine also."

"Don't ignore what's in front of our faces because it's familiar," I said.

Holly made a sound. "I forgot. I have the item that the Ringer picked up at Herrera's memorabilia shop. But I haven't compared it to the others yet."

We were all quiet for a minute, eating the steak and vegetables—plus garlic bread for the others—Ryan had prepared.

I thought about the blank road ahead of us. "What next? We've found people who got something out of PJ's death… so what? We can't ask them what they were doing on a specific date thirty years ago."

"Why not?" Holly asked. "It's not every day you hear a driver in paddock is dead, let alone a woman who's killed herself. People might remember where they were or what else was happening when they heard."

Ryan nodded. "It's worth a try."

"That means we need to know exactly when PJ died." Holly told me.

"I'll contact her brother."

Gramps put down his fork. "We've decided Ron's death is connected, right?"

I glanced at Ryan, who kept his expression blank. *Your show*, his look seemed to say. I turned back to Gramps. "Probably. Why?"

"People might not remember thirty years ago, but they'll remember two nights ago." He pushed back his plate. "We need to know that, too."

"Easy now." Ryan's face was no longer neutral, but serious and worried.

"Is he wrong?" I asked.

He sighed. "I get twitchy when you're excited about hunting for the perpetrator of a deadly assault in the last couple days."

I raised an eyebrow. "Murder is murder, isn't it? Thirty years ago or today?"

Ryan muttered what sounded like "Smart ass" under his breath. "It's all violent crime. But one is more recent and vivid."

His words brought back the image of Ron Arvin's battered head and the sound of Alexa's weeping. "True."

Ryan rubbed his eyes. "I had a vision of you three running around with magnifying glasses and notebooks asking everyone where they were at 7:38 Wednesday night, the moment Ron was killed."

I frowned at him. "That's not giving us any credit."

"You're right, and I'm sorry for that. But you all have to admit, you have more enthusiasm than training."

"Can't argue." Gramps chuckled as he got up to clear his and Holly's plates.

"But what you don't understand," Holly said, "is we have *sources.*"

"Sources, like you wouldn't believe." I grinned. "Holly can tell you anything about anyone in the paddock almost as soon as it happens."

Holly smirked. "I've already got a list of confirmed party attendees from the team PR person. Plus, I was able to pin down when most of our people of interest left—or last verified sightings. We can compare those with our own observations, double-check with one or two other trusted people, then cross-check with what we find out about their whereabouts thirty years ago. Maybe that'll give us something without having to deploy the magnifying glasses."

Ryan laughed. "Holly, if you ever want a career at the FBI, say the word."

Chapter Thirty-four

Holly handed me the list of party attendees. "Tell us everyone who was also around thirty years ago."

"I didn't see half these people last night." I ran my finger down the list. "In alpha order, Ron Arvin, Tom Barclay, Scott Brooklyn—I didn't see Scott, did anyone else? Also Chuck Gaffey and his son, Josh—does Josh count as having been around back then? Kevin Hagan, Paul Lauth, and Don Strange—he's from the tire company, so that must be the Donny I talked with. And Lyla Thomas, Vallorie Westleton, and Diane Wittmeier."

"Don't forget Gramps," Holly said, winking at him and writing down the names.

I thought for a moment. "This list doesn't include the team, who were also all at the party. I know Uncle Stan, Bald John, and Banjo were there in PJ's day."

"Kate and Gramps, do you remember seeing Barclay or Hagan at the party?" Holly asked.

"I know Barclay, but not Hagan." I turned to Gramps. "Do you know what either one looks like?"

He shook his head, and Holly made a disgusted sound. "If we could organize, we might be dangerous. Let me find photos."

She pulled out her phone while the rest of us finished clearing the table. I was wiping it down when Holly showed us a photo. "Kevin Hagan, reporter extraordinaire."

"*That* guy," I said. He was coarse-featured, with a thick jaw, prominent chin, and a heavy brow that made him look like he was constantly scowling. "He acts like he looks, asking questions as if he knows the answers and getting angry about boilerplate responses."

I turned to Ryan. "In drivers' defense, there are only so many different responses to 'How's the car feeling and what do you think of your chances in the race?'"

"The team said they saw him leave with the main group of attendees after the police arrived," Holly reported. "Did either of you see him?"

Gramps nodded. "Early in the evening, at the buffet. He liked the meatballs."

Ryan took the phone from her and studied Hagan's face. "At the end of the night, at the tape line. Watching the police activity."

Holly nodded. "Pretty good for someone you don't know at all."

"The jawline and attitude are hard to miss," Ryan said.

"Hagan was there and could have done it. And he was around thirty years ago and he benefitted from PJ's death." Holly put a double star next to Hagan's name. After a moment, she put a line through Ron Arvin's name at the top of the list.

"Go to the previous photo," Holly directed Ryan. "Recognize him? That's Tom Barclay."

"He's familiar." Ryan frowned. "The all-American boy going to seed."

"Nothing a little Botox won't cure, sugar," Holly said.

Gramps studied the photo. "He left the party as Ryan was arriving. You must have passed him in the parking lot."

"That means he left before Ron was killed?" I asked, hearing disappointment in my voice.

Is Barclay the killer? I already think he's sleazy, why not a murderer?

"If you didn't see him get in his car and drive away," Ryan said, "we don't know he left. He could have walked around the building to meet Arvin."

Holly added Tom Barclay's name to the list with another double star, explaining to Ryan, "We know he was working for another team in PJ's day, and he got the idea for his life's work—and obviously successful business—from PJ's death."

"Would he have had the forethought to kill her to generate the idea?" Ryan asked.

I frowned. "Probably not. Still, scumbag spreading rumors about me to drum up business for himself? He stays on the list."

"Fair enough." Ryan grinned.

I checked the list. "I don't see Dean Herrera's name."

"Go back one more photo," Holly said. "That's Herrera. Anyone see him?"

"Was he there?" I asked, as we all studied the photo on Holly's phone.

"He was." Holly looked smug. "He tried to breeze into the party, but they wouldn't let him in without an invitation. He gave them attitude, said people from one of the team's major sponsors were waiting for him inside, and the team—fortunately Banjo was there with Cindy—would be in trouble if they didn't let him in. He tried to walk through the door, but Banjo stopped him."

"Banjo's protective," I explained to the others. "And big."

"Did Herrera leave then?" Ryan asked.

Holly shook her head. "He left the lobby, but stood in that small, front lot, by the walkway. One of Beermeier's retired drivers came along and Herrera got him to sign a photo. That's when Banjo escorted him off the property. They say he got into a white van parked across the street and stayed there for some time. They weren't sure when he left."

Ryan glanced at the photo again. "Does the shop have security video that might show the street?"

"There's an idea." Holly raised her eyebrows. "I'll have to ask."

I gestured to names from the party list. "What about the other people?"

She picked up the paper. "Ron Arvin, not relevant. Barclay, we talked about. Scott Brooklyn?"

I shook my head. "Not a suspect."

"That's the media guy?" Gramps asked.

"The pit reporter," I confirmed. "He was a kid in the paddock, but he's got no other connection. Trust me, not anyone to waste time on."

He'd slay with words, not whatever killed Ron Arvin.

"I saw him," Holly said. "He was in line for the bathroom with me around the time you found Ron and Alexa out back."

Her statement sparked an idea, and I only paid partial attention as Holly kept reading names.

"Chuck and Josh Gaffey. I saw them early. The team says they left with everyone else after giving the cops their basic statement and contact information." She glanced at the rest of us, saw no comment, and kept going. "Paul Lauth, PJ's former boyfriend. Arrived late and left early, missing all the drama. I didn't see him, did you, Kate? Kate?"

I snapped out of it. "Sorry. Paul? I don't remember, but I don't think so."

"Don Strange? I don't even know him," Holly read. "Lyla Thomas, the reporter."

Gramps grinned. "Old Lead-Foot Lyla. She could wheel a car."

"Who's Don?" Ryan asked.

"A crew member who provided protection for PJ. He's working for our tire supplier now." I related the conversation I'd had with Donny, and we agreed he didn't seem like much of a suspect.

"And Lyla's been in the business forever—driving and writing back then, still writing today," Gramps explained. "She's supportive of women in racing, and she'd have gained nothing from killing either of them. No dice on her."

I smiled at his vehement defense, but since I agreed with him, I didn't comment.

"Lastly, Vallorie Westleton and Diane Wittmeier," Holly said.

I shook my head. "Vallorie was a good friend of PJ's who now works in Timing and Scoring, and had no problem with Ron that I've heard of. And Diane, Ron's ex-wife, seemed to get along with him. There was no interaction or drama at all."

"I don't see either one of them being involved. That leaves us with Kevin Hagan, Tom Barclay, and Dean Herrera." Holly put the list down and addressed me. "What's brewing in your head?"

"I wondered if we could figure out who was at the back of the building at the right time—we know Cindy and Banjo vouch for each other in the front lobby, so they couldn't have killed Ron. Let's figure out everyone who used the bathroom in that last half-hour or so."

Holly took only a moment to catch on. "I ask who I remember seeing, then ask the people they remember, and slowly expand our list."

"Maybe someone even saw someone else go outside," I added.

Ryan was skeptical. "These questions won't make people suspicious?"

Red curls bounced as Holly shook her head. "Not if I say the police asked me who I saw in the area—which they did—and I'm trying to remember every name possible. Then I throw out a couple names for them to verify and see who they remember. Piece of cake. I can do subtle. I'll make that my assignment for tomorrow."

"And I'll keep sitting on the stool and reminiscing," Gramps said.

It was eleven o'clock by the time we went our separate ways. Holly gave the signed items purchased from Herrera to Ryan, who agreed to call his FBI contact about our suspicions. I was horrified to see the time, since I still had e-mails to answer.

While everyone else headed to bed, I sat on the couch with my laptop and responded to the urgent messages that had piled up over the day. Half an hour later, Ryan wandered out from my bedroom. Shirtless.

My mouth went dry. "I thought you'd be asleep by now."

"I was waiting for you." He smiled. "How much do you have left to do?"

I clicked "send" on the last e-mail. "Unless I want to know how many people on social media support me, hate me, or want to have sex with me, I'm done."

His smile broadened. "That information important to you?"

"Not so much." I set my computer aside and stood up, moving close to him and running my fingers down his well-muscled chest and stomach.

Then I stilled my hands. "I lied."

His eyebrow quirked up.

"I do need to know one opinion." I smiled and started exploring with my fingers again. "I'm hoping to get a response, you might say, from one particular fan."

The heat in his eyes threatened to set me on fire. He grinned and pulled me against him.

His response is clear, all right.

He started walking backwards, toward my bedroom, never breaking that smoldering eye contact. I lifted my chin, wanting his kiss, but he bent down and put his mouth close to my ear.

"Let me assure you, I'm *very* eager to give you as much feedback as possible."

A thrill ran down my spine, and we covered the last few feet to my room quickly.

Chapter Thirty-five

The next morning was Friday, the day the schedule got really nuts. It was known as "Carb Day," for Carburetion Day, even though the racecars haven't used carburetors since 1963. Next to race day—always the Sunday of Memorial Day weekend—the Friday prior to the race saw the largest attendance. What with our practice session, an Indy Lights race, a pit stop competition, and a concert by a top country star later in the evening, it was a day of activity that brought tens of thousands of fans to the track.

We arrived by eight, and I left everyone at the garage to head to the media center for an interview with a sports magazine writer. After that, I had a meeting with a different reporter, this one from a women's magazine, who was writing about "Fast Women: The Women of the Indy 500." It sounded like a great article, which would cover a bit of history and also current day. The unfortunate result was a joint, sit-down interview with my least favorite driver, Sofia Montalvo. It would be a trial.

For my part, I wished Sofia hadn't hated me from the moment she met me. I wished I had an ally, not an enemy, in the only other female driver in the field. I didn't, but I wouldn't be seen publicly as antagonistic to another female driver. She could play that role if she wanted. I wouldn't.

But Sofia—who was tall with olive skin and sultry looks that contrasted with my short stature and milkmaid vibe—arrived pretending everything was sunshine and unicorns. And when the reporter, another woman, asked us how we supported each other, being the only two women in the field, Sofia outright lied.

"We know we are there for each other," she said, in her light, Spanish accent. "We support each other, should I need Kate or she need me."

I kept a smile on my face. *Which is never.*

The only time Sofia's mask slipped was when the reporter asked us what we thought about the comparisons between me and PJ after my leading the first practice session this year.

Sofia wasn't smooth enough to hide the twist of her lip at the question, though she recovered quickly. "I was, of course, happy for Kate that she did it."

I remembered her sneering comments. *Could have fooled me.*

The reporter turned to me. "Your thoughts on the comparisons, Kate?"

"I've never been the one making them. I'd rather people let PJ be PJ and let me be Kate."

The interview ended soon after that, and Sofia left quickly for another commitment. The reporter eyed me after she left. "Anything else you want to say? I have the feeling I missed some of the story."

I smiled at her. "I think we covered it. Thanks for your time."

She nodded and tapped her pen on the table. "What do you really think about being compared to PJ Rodriguez?"

"PJ deserves her own identity, as do I. I'd like to be considered on my own merits as a driver—not a female driver, either, but a driver." I shrugged. "But until women aren't the rarity in the field, it'll be an issue. I'm simply glad to be here, and I hope the best for every other driver in the field."

She stopped her tape recorder and thanked me for my time, adding, "Scuttlebutt around the media room says you're something of an amateur sleuth. Are you planning to investigate the death that took place two nights ago? Or PJ's death? I mean, in a soap opera, she'd have been murdered, so why not real life?"

I managed to laugh off her questions and get out of there fast. *How about let's* not *go public on my dubious investigation skills?*

After I finished talking with journalists in the media center, it was time for the drivers' meeting—the real one. We'd all attend a ceremonial public drivers' meeting the next day, but this one was for participants only. This was where drivers argued, complained, and generally behaved like fractious children. I stayed out of the discussions and name-calling, keeping my mouth shut. It was safer that way.

By the time that meeting was done, the crowds had arrived for the day. I made my way back to the garage through most of them, stopping every ten feet for a photo or signature. Not that I minded. I appreciated everyone who cared enough to say my name. The ones who called me PJ, not so much. But I kept smiling, glad for the real fans, and ready to educate the others.

"Busy out there," Holly said, when I finally reached the Beermeier Racing garage. "How was the Kate-to-PJ ratio today?"

"Three to one." I continued past her through the engineers' office area and into our driver area.

Holly followed me after a quick peek to make sure the other drivers weren't in the middle of changing clothes. "Twenty-five percent PJs seems like less than last weekend," she said. "Maybe that's progress."

"How's social media?" I asked. I stripped down to my sports bra and underwear, tucked my street clothes in my locker, and pulled out my firesuit.

"Nothing we should discuss. But I had an idea. Maybe a sympathetic reporter could do an article about the disservice it is to compare you and PJ."

"It's a disservice to all women in racing. There aren't many of us, and to lump two of us together as if we're interchangeable promotes the idea we're here as tokens." I stopped and took a breath.

Focus on the car, that's what you can control.

Holly nodded. "I bet I could talk Lyla Thomas into it. Maybe it'll help people recognize that's what they're doing."

"It's a great idea." I finished lacing up my shoes. "Anything else going on?"

"Uncle Stan confirmed Jimmy worked on suspension for PJ's car, like we'd heard. And Gramps is doing his thing—you probably saw him out there with Chuck, chattering away to the crew."

I zipped my firesuit closed. "Where's Ryan?"

"Checking in with the law enforcement agencies here at the track. He'll come into the pits when practice starts. Did you get PJ's time of death?"

I slipped my lip balm into my pocket and put my sunglasses on my head. Then I reached for my phone, which I hadn't looked at since I started my media appointments a couple hours earlier. "Her brother texted, saying official time of death was about eleven that morning, and he confirms word hit the track a couple minutes after noon." I closed my locker door. "We should ask Lyla who she saw. She was in the team garage when everyone found out—or got here right after."

"Copy that. I'll tell the others about the time for PJ. Let me know when you're ready to go out to pit lane."

"After I check in with Alexa and Nolan."

With a wag of her phone, she went back out to the main part of the garage, leaving me alone—or as alone as I could get in the semi-private corner of a team garage. I leaned my forehead against my locker and closed my eyes, feeling the cool metal and focusing on my breathing. I visualized climbing over the low pit wall to get to the car, nodding to Bald John as he helped strap me in and secure the extra padding around my head. Snapping the steering wheel into place on the column and flexing my fingers around it. The rumble of the car as they start it up, and the spring-loaded feel of the throttle. The firm feel of the brakes.

I pictured a confident, controlled departure from the pits—no fish-tailing back end as the tires struggled for grip. Pulling onto the track and getting up to speed. Flying down the pavement, hands busy on the anti-roll bars or the weight jacker in every turn. Seeing what's coming well down the track. A good time, a smooth run. I opened my eyes.

I can hope, and I can do my best.

A few minutes later, after a short talk with Nolan about the plan for practice, Holly and I walked to pit lane. I carried my helmet and stayed focused, only stopping twice for fans and only because they screamed my name. Ryan and Gramps arrived in our pit space as I pulled on my balaclava, helmet, and gloves, and I nodded at them, but didn't speak. At that moment, I wasn't thinking about anything but the car. Didn't care about anything else.

Despite the day being named for our opportunity to tune our cars, we only got an hour of on-track time. It wasn't much, but we'd take every minute to keep working on our race setup. And this was our last chance before the race.

I sat, buckled and settled, for a few minutes as the clock ticked closer to our official start time of eleven a.m. Bald John stood over me with an umbrella to give me some shade, but even with that, I was drenched in sweat before we'd fired the car. Temperatures were in the mid-eighties and humid, given the thunderstorms predicted to roll through that night and into Saturday. Race day would be dry and sunny—according to five different weather reports the team was following. We all hoped they were right.

Finally, the crew fired my engine, and when practice was green-flagged, I was waved out of my pit box.

I gave the car plenty of throttle and released the clutch into first gear, steering around the car in front of me that was still in its box. I fell in line behind a bunch of other cars, and as a group we accelerated around the first two turns in the warm-up lane. More throttle on the back straight, letting the car buzzing around behind me leap ahead.

Sofia, that figures.

My job in this session was to see how the car felt and run a full load of fuel to the end. I ran some in clean air, but mostly in traffic, getting used to different degrees of feeling uncomfortable, and I focused on being smooth, making lots of small adjustments to the wheel or the weight-balancing tools. The team and I kept adjusting through the session, and we inched toward better handling. Toward getting and keeping those wheels under me.

I spent every lap I could working on how to save fuel, primarily by letting off the throttle when I was right behind someone else to let the draft tow me along. Where I could, I also worked on easing off the pedal ahead of a turn to coast through it and rolling back onto it in the turn, to save small amounts of fuel. I might never need to do it, but throughout history, races had been won or lost for want of one or two laps of fuel. A typical stint, or fuel run, was about thirty laps, and at the miraculous extreme, drivers had stretched a stint to thirty-five or six. In the end, I went twenty-nine laps on the fuel load, and the team thought I could easily have done another lap and a half.

We worked on the car continuously until the very last seconds of practice, and I still wanted more. There was never enough time to make it perfect. But as I turned the car off in pit lane, a thrill went through me.

The next time I'm here, I'll be starting the Indy 500.

Chapter Thirty-six

I had a full schedule before I sat in the car again. After changing out of my wet firesuit in the garage, I backtracked to the Frame Savings suite above the grandstands for lunch. There, I spent an hour enjoying food, air conditioning, and conversation with Frame Savings and Beauté executives, as well as assorted guests.

My half brother, Eddie, showed up as I was asked how I felt about my chances in the race for what felt like the nineteenth time.

Still, I smiled. "Pretty good. We've got a decent setup on the car. We'll need some luck, but I think we've done everything we can to prepare, and I'm really grateful and thankful to the team for all of their hard work."

The local Beauté VP wished me luck and headed to the buffet table, and Eddie leaned close. "I've got a different question. How's your grandfather after the other night? It must have been traumatic."

"Seeing a dead body's never fun. But Gramps wasn't out there with us—Ryan and I found Alexa and her father. Gramps only came along later."

Eddie's eyes went wide. "You found the dead guy the other night?"

"Alexa did. We found her."

"Only you." Eddie shook his head. "I meant how your grandfather coped with meeting the big, bad Reilly family?"

Right, the trauma I hadn't even had time to consider.

"We haven't talked about it. There's been a lot else going on."

"Looking for a murderer?"

I blinked at him. "Why would you say that?"

"It's what you do. Why wouldn't you look for whoever whacked the guy the other night? Or who killed PJ?" He saw my surprise and grinned. "It's too delicious for PJ's death to be plain old suicide. Come on, thirty-year-old cold case? That the person who duplicates her accomplishment solves? Tell me you don't think she killed herself. Tell me you think someone did her in."

I drank some water and stared at him. "You have quite an imagination."

He took two steps to his left and nabbed two mini brownies from the dessert table. He popped one in his mouth. "In the banking world, I'm known as an 'innovative thinker,' and they give me raises because of it."

"Stick to banking." I declined his offer of the other brownie.

He gave me an admonishing look as he loaded a small plate with more sweets. "You can tell me, you know. I'm good with secrets."

I sighed. "Everyone says I'm just like PJ, but if that's the case, she couldn't have killed herself, because I know I wouldn't. I'm asking questions, but it's hard to get answers thirty years later."

"I met a guy who hooked up with the series then." He glanced around the room. "Over there. Standish, with the hotel chain."

When he pointed, I finally saw Nathan Standish sitting at a table with Charlene Menfis, the Frame Savings executive and superfan. "I met Nathan in Phoenix this week. He was going to try to find some information for me."

"Get to it, Inspector Reilly." Eddie made a sweeping gesture with his arm.

As I reached their table, Nathan Standish stood up and greeted me. "I understand you know Charlene already—here I thought I held some kind of record for attending the race, but Charlene has me beat."

"You've had better access and insight in your thirty years," Charlene assured him. "This year will be my first year in a suite—it'll be especially great since Sunday's my actual birthday."

I had a thought. "Have you ever gotten a look inside the garages?"

Her eyes got big and she shook her head.

I pulled out my phone and checked my schedule. "If you can be at my garage at eight-fifteen Sunday morning, I'll have a couple minutes to show you around."

She jumped up and down as if she'd won the lottery. "I'll be there, thank you!"

I love this part of my job.

Nathan smiled and apologized for needing to leave. He handed me a small book in a doubled-over manila envelope, secured by a rubber band. "Here's the information I mentioned, Kate. I hope it helps."

I tucked it under my arm, wishing I could dig into it there and then. "Thank you again. I'll let you know."

A few minutes later, I left also, and the minute I stepped foot outside the suite, the butterflies hit. My next activity was something new, and it made me more nervous than anything else we'd do at Indy, aside from qualifying.

The pit stop competition.

It was one of the staples of Carb Day, and though I'd watched it the two previous years, I'd never competed. This year, I was a full-time competitor in the Series and my crew had lobbied Alexa to compete, so I'd be there.

I knew it was silly to be nervous—the pressure was on my crew to change four tires and simulate fueling the car as quickly as possible. My job was to get off the line quickly, drive the short distance to the temporary pit box—marked by tape in the middle of pit lane—stop on my marks, and drive away quickly when directed to by my crew. Simple. The same thing I did multiple times in every race. But minor flubs in a race, whether by me or a crew member, could be made up. Not so here.

Of course, this contest didn't have a larger impact for the race or the season. The prize was bragging rights and a small check. But I didn't want to let my guys down.

In the garage, before we went out to pit lane, Alexa gathered us together. "I won't be in your ears for this one. It's on you. You know what to do—watch the officials and watch each other. And focus. That's what I want you to remind each other right before you go. *Focus.* Now go get 'em."

Sitting out on pit lane, the fans cheering up and down the front straight, we kept repeating the word to each other. "Focus."

Bald John strapped me into the car and Tyler, the kid on the crew, held the umbrella over me for the shade. "Focus," they reminded me, patting my helmet.

"Focus," I shouted through my helmet when they were close enough to hear.

Slowly we moved forward, hearing the roar of the crowd as pairs of cars and crews before us went head-to-head. Hearing groans and cheers as teams lost and won.

Then it was our turn. *Focus,* I told myself. My crew waited down pit lane in front of me, and my engine rumbled. Bald John stayed with me as each crew member lifted a hand to acknowledge their introduction over the track PA.

Bald John stepped back. The horizontal row of round lights lit up red, one by one, left to right. *One, two…five red—now green. Go!*

I spun my tires a tiny bit off the line—and later learned the other driver stopped just before I did—but hit my marks perfectly. *Go, guys, go!*

I was ready, my foot poised, trembling, on the throttle, fingers on the clutch. *Now!*

As the car bounced down on its tires, I launched. My crew had worked their magic—or the other team fumbled or both—and I crossed the finish line before the other car. I braked hard, my heart pounding, and I saw my crew cheering in my mirrors.

Twenty minutes later, we were lined up and ready for the quarterfinal matchup—this one against the previous year's pit stop competition winner. My heart thundered in my ears.

I won't mess up this time. We're beating this guy.

Red lights illuminated, then flashed green. Less than thirteen seconds later, I crossed the line ahead of the other car, not sure if I'd taken a breath.

Twenty minutes and another blistering twelve-and-a-half second-run later, and we made it to the finals.

I had a few more minutes to regroup, and then we were set up again at the starting line, side-by-side with the other finalist, a Dutch driver with one of the three big teams. I heard the PA announcer proclaiming us "the little team that could" and praising our coordination for being new together this year. He also mentioned this being the highest a female driver had ever gotten in the competition. As the announcer whipped the crowd into a frenzy of anticipation over the final run, Alexa broke her own promise, and came over to huddle with all of us.

"You all are awesome, and as far as I'm concerned, you've won already by making it here. You'll get a bonus next week, from me, win or lose—plus a pizza night." She looked around at everyone, her eyes bright. "That said, go kick some ass. Show the big boys what we're made of."

We all reminded each other to focus, and we lined up. I was finally calm, ready for the lights, looking down the road to my marks. Red, green—go!

Go, go, go!

I hit my marks, waited, and sped away from the box as quickly as I could, sure we'd gone even faster than the last time.

We had, but we'd been beaten by six-tenths of a second. I turned off the car and struggled out of the car, dejected. Within seconds, I was surrounded by my crew, who'd run down the lane to hoist me onto their shoulders.

"We didn't win," I got out, as they bounced me around, cheering.

"Doesn't matter." Banjo grinned up at me. "We got closer than we thought we would, and we proved we're a team."

Tyler ran up, whooping. "You don't mess with the 82 car crew!"

Chapter Thirty-seven

Our near-win meant I spoke with four different reporters, including the PA announcer, who let me thank all the fans on-site for their encouragement and support. Lyla Thomas was the last reporter to ask for a quote, and after I gave her my thoughts on the competition, I asked her a question. "Where were you at the track when the news broke that PJ was dead?"

"Headed to her garage." She saw my surprise. "Her car hadn't come to pit lane—nor had any crew. I was on my way to find out why."

"When do reporters usually get here on a practice day?"

"Usually an hour before, give or take. Though it depends on the individual."

"Do you remember more about that day? Anyone who wasn't here but should have been?"

"Thirty years ago?" She laughed.

"Maybe if you think back to where you were, what you heard, and who you saw, it might bring back other memories. What you did after you left PJ's garage, who you talked with then—what report you filed—that sort of thing."

"Let me think about it. I'll let you know. Who are you trying to alibi? Off the record," she added.

"Hagan. And maybe the memorabilia guy, Herrera. For now."

She nodded. "I'll see what I can remember."

We parted with a wave, and I made it back to the garage with barely enough time to change and drink a quick glass of champagne with the crew before literally running from one thing to another for the next five hours—culminating in a dinner hosted by Beauté for executives and guests. I arrived late and left early, but between my heartfelt thanks and the party atmosphere, no one minded. The open bar didn't hurt.

By the time we got back to our apartment complex, it was all I could do to drag myself inside where my two favorite men waited with the latest clues to a double-murderer.

Holly did most of the talking as Gramps assembled ice cream sundaes for the others. She'd started making a list of who'd been in and around the bathrooms near the time of Ron's murder, but she wasn't done yet, and none of the names on her list so far had been alive or in the racing world in PJ's era.

She was also the only one to have come up with a solid, useful fact. Vallorie Westleton, on a rare break from timing and scoring duties, had verified Tom Barclay was at the track when PJ was killed. Vallorie and Tom had both worked for her uncle's team, and everyone was required to be at the track every morning by eight. Since being late had been a firing offense, she knew Tom had been there.

"Between that and Ryan and Gramps seeing him leave the party the other night before Ron was killed, I suppose we scratch him off the list." I was disappointed.

"Vallorie also said she knew the recent rumor about you was fake, and it's not the first time he's leaked that kind of thing to try to drum up business." Holly grimaced. "He goes off the murderer list, but stays at the top of the asshole list."

"Herrera, our forger, should be on that list too," Gramps noted.

I finished my miniscule scoop of ice cream. "I didn't learn anything useful today, but I got information from Nathan Standish—notes, a case study, business thoughts, I'm not sure. But it's from thirty years ago." I yawned so hard my jaw cracked. "If I can stay awake to read it."

The three of them shooed me out of the kitchen and dining area. I went straight to bed, though I took my laptop and the envelope from Nathan with me. When Ryan joined me most of an hour later, I was finishing the last e-mail I had to send.

"I thought you'd be asleep." He shook his head. "What did you still have to do?"

"Confirm when I'll arrive and how long I can stay for every event tomorrow. Verify everyone has the giveaways or that I'm bringing hero cards to sign. Respond to requests for comment or quotes from different media—Holly deals with most of those, but passes the important or specific ones to me. Confirm a time with the fan coming to the garage on Sunday morning. That sort of thing."

"Here I thought the racing driver's life was one of glamour and adulation. You work hard."

"I have it easier than some people." I got up and plugged in my laptop on the desk. "I don't have to do my own merchandising, and I've got Holly to help me with the general requests and social media. But we all have to hustle."

I settled back under the covers, propped up against my pillows, and opened the envelope from Nathan Standish. What I pulled out was a slim notebook, covered in rich, dark leather with the initials "NPS" embossed on the front. I flipped through the pages, finding each one full, top to bottom, of neat printing. Every few pages there was a new date at the top, all in May and June of 1987.

Ryan turned out the overhead light and joined me in bed. He didn't speak, but entwined his legs with mine and opened his own book. I smiled and settled back to read. As I turned to the first page, a note from Nathan fell out.

"Kate," it read. "Please excuse the disjointed nature of my writings. Though I never collected or shared my thoughts more formally, writing down my impressions helped me recognize some of the intangible values of the racing market for our promotional purposes, and these pages served as a valuable complement to structured metrics and ROI. I hope the information is of use to you. Keep the journal for as long as you like; I'll happily arrange for return shipping when you're done with it."

I understood his "disjointed" comment when I started reading. His writings were one part stream-of-consciousness about what he experienced in the racing industry and another part formal language I could imagine him using for more public consumption.

"After my first experience at an Indy Car race last year," he wrote on the first page, "I firmly believe the racing industry holds great potential for marketing purposes. Specifically, fans of racing show a marked propensity for supporting sponsors of favored teams and drivers, even when it costs them time or money to do so. By allying with the right racing entity—note to self: determine which team carries the most positive image—Standish-Conroy properties could leverage the benefits of association with proven winners and perennial fan favorite personalities."

Nathan Standish wasn't slow on the uptake.

Racing was like few other sports, because corporations could sponsor their choice of series, races, teams, or drivers and see their branding all over the track and airwaves, dozens of weekends a year. Plus, racing fans had a long tradition of being dutiful brand soldiers for sponsors of their favorites, as a reward for the sponsorship.

He went on to write about the most prominent sponsors of the era and how they benefitted from the association with racing, specifically national restaurant chains, motor oil, tobacco, and beer companies.

The last thing I remember was Nathan ruminating on the possible value of exposure for an upscale product like Standish-Conroy offered. When I woke to my alarm the next morning, the journal sat on the desk next to my computer.

Ryan smiled when I asked him about it. "Your eyes were closed, and it almost fell on your nose. You didn't notice when I took it from you."

He followed me out to the kitchen where I thanked the technology gods once again for a pre-programmable coffee maker. I poured us both cups, and took a third to Gramps, who sat at the table eating a ham and cheese croissant.

"Where'd you get that, Gramps?"

He pointed to Ryan. "The fridge. Agent Smartypants picked them up for us."

"Good work, Ryan. Want one?" At his nod, I put two of them in the microwave.

"I can get more for tomorrow, if you want," he offered. "I'm not sure what your race-morning routine is."

"I'll be too nervous to eat much, but this will be as good as anything."

"I'll take care of it later."

Though we'd all four drive to the Speedway together, only Holly would go downtown to the parade with me. Gramps and Ryan would stick around IMS or go back to the apartment. Either way, they'd meet us at the track when the bus returned the drivers there around three in the afternoon.

Ryan joined Gramps at the table. "I had a thought about that journal."

"Shoot." I drank more coffee and hoped for it to work quickly.

"You're the busiest one around here, but I've got time. Why don't I review it and flag anything that might be relevant?" When I hesitated, he added, "I can read, you know. Even marketing analysis."

Gramps laughed, and I rolled my eyes. "Funny. I'm wondering if you'd know what's relevant, since you don't know the players like I do."

He shrugged. "Seems like it's worth a shot. I'll have time today while you're waving to crowds."

"I appreciate it. I do need the help. Today'll be wall-to-wall activities again, and tomorrow…" I was struck dumb at the thought.

The race.

"Exactly," Ryan concluded.

Holly finally exited her bedroom and struck a pose, a cheap, plastic tiara glittering in her bright red hair. "Dahlings, it's parade day!"

Chapter Thirty-eight

After starting another busy day with an interview, I sat down with the other thirty-two Indy 500 drivers in the plaza below the pagoda at IMS and signed autographs for thousands of fans. The lines for each table snaked around and around the plaza, making us think we'd never find the end—though of course, the IndyCar staff made sure the line stopped when the session was over.

And it had to stop, because we were on a tight schedule. We had an hour for the autograph session, then a short break before the public drivers' meeting began. During that break, I found Gramps and Ryan and walked them up pit lane past the pagoda.

For the drivers' meeting, a small set of temporary stands, which seated exactly thirty-three drivers, stood in pit lane facing the main grandstands—and facing directly into the sun. In front of our stands was a podium with a microphone, rows of folding chairs for the speakers and VIPs, and the Borg-Warner trophy, the perpetual award for the winner of the race. To the side, facing the podium, were twenty more rows of folding chairs. I walked Gramps and Ryan past security and got them two seats in the back row.

We were early for the ceremony, so I stood with them for a moment, studying the crowd in the main grandstands. That's when Scott Brooklyn appeared, wearing a shirt logoed with the television station broadcasting the race and flipping open a notebook.

He smiled at the three of us. "Good morning, Kate. Ready for the parade?"

"I think so." I sighed internally, but made the introductions.

"Good to meet you, Scott," Ryan said. "Kate's mentioned you."

Scott's smile faltered, and he glanced at me. "Nice to meet you."

"It's not what you think," I murmured.

He frowned, but he nodded and addressed Ryan. "You're here with Kate. Will you be in her pit box for the race?"

It was Ryan's turn to look concerned, and I stepped in. "He and my grandfather will both be there. What do you want to know, Scott?"

He held his hands up, notepad in one and pen in the other. "I like to know who's important to each of the drivers I'm covering—Kate is one of the pits I'll be responsible for reporting on during the race," he added, to Gramps and Ryan. "That way, if you win the race, say, I know who to go to for reaction." When he got no response he sighed. "If you don't want to be mentioned, I won't mention you."

Ryan raised his eyebrows at me, and I gave him an "It's up to you" shrug. Though Ryan had attended a couple races with me over the last two years, the question of our relationship had never come up publicly until now.

"You can talk to me if that happens," Gramps said.

Ryan nodded. "I'll be there, as well."

As Scott wrote down Gramps and Ryan's particulars, he glanced between us. "Boyfriend?"

"Yes." Ryan slid an arm around my waist, and I leaned into him.

"What do you do when you're not at the racetrack, Ryan?" Scott asked.

"I'm with the FBI, but I'd rather you didn't mention that."

I reached out a hand to still Scott's pen. "Don't even write it down. Off the record. If it gets out, I'll know where it came from." I glared at him, telling him with my eyes, *If the Ringer prints this, I'll kill you.*

He held both hands up again. "Fine, fine. Can I say you're a businessman?"

"Call me a security consultant."

"Fair enough." Scott wrote the words down—at least, I hoped he did. He glanced down pit lane at more arrivals. "Nice to meet you both. I'll see you tomorrow." With a wave, he was off.

Gramps was hailed by someone he knew, and he moved a couple steps away to shake hands and slap backs.

Ryan raised an eyebrow. "How well do you know that guy? You seem awfully comfortable with him."

I heard a rare note of jealousy in his voice, and I turned to him with a grin. "It's not what you think. We've gone from adversaries to friends, that's it."

"Okay." Ryan shifted so we both faced the event area. "Tell me about that trophy. Does the winner get to take it home? And why's it so lumpy?"

I chuckled. "You don't know anything about this race, do you?"

"Five hundred miles. More than two hundred miles-per-hour. You kicking ass. That's what's most relevant."

"You're not wrong." I smiled. "The winner of the Borg-Warner doesn't get to keep the trophy, but the trophy keeps the winner. A small sculpture of each winner's face is made out of silver and attached to the trophy—those are the bumps. Then the driver and owner each get a mini trophy, called a Baby Borg, and the driver's has a replica of their face on it."

"That's pretty cool."

"You'll have to get close to it later or tomorrow morning so you can see the faces. The history on it is pretty amazing."

"Being the first woman will be incredible."

"Another of my dreams."

He gestured at the drivers starting to fill the stands. "Better go do your thing."

I squeezed his hand, then waved at Gramps who'd returned to his seat. "I'll see you here or somewhere after the parade." I made my way through the rows of chairs and up into the stands.

We sat in qualifying order, in four rows of eight, with an aisle up the middle and an extra seat in the top row to make thirty-three. I sat in the eighteenth space—third row up on the left, second seat from the left—and I was glad not to be in the very last row, as I'd been the year before.

While we waited for the ceremonies to begin, I pulled out my phone and took a photo of my view. I estimated close to ten thousand people were on hand, in the grandstands, on pit lane, or milling about within earshot—not to mention the scores of media and cameras directly in front of us. I shouldn't have been surprised at the crowd, given the number of fans at the autograph session, but it was still an astonishing sight—another reminder this race was more than just another stop on the Series schedule.

My phone buzzed with a text message from Holly, instructing me to ask Kenny who he'd seen near the bathroom. Kenny O'Toole, another Beermeier Racing driver, hadn't had the qualifying day he wanted, and he would start in twenty-sixth place, which meant he was seated directly behind me. As the ceremony still hadn't started, I leaned back and got his attention.

"Kenny, were you around the bathroom at the back of the shop a bit before Ron was found the other night?"

He laughed and leaned forward. "Are you stalking me bathroom habits then?" he asked, his Irish showing.

I shook my head, rolling my eyes, even though he couldn't see them. "I wanted to know who else you saw back there at the time."

"Well, now, why would I remember that? I've no clue."

"Think about it, Ken. You're standing in line, talking, probably flirting with a woman. The bathroom door opens, the next person goes in. Who's around you? Who are you talking to?"

He closed his eyes for a minute. "Perhaps I can remember… particularly one lovely girl with a skirt as short as her—"

"Save it," I told him. The announcer started to welcome the crowd to start the meeting. "Text me? Names or descriptions. Thanks."

"Shhhhhhh. Some people have no class," I heard from two seats down, twentieth position, on the aisle. Sofia Montalvo.

Stuff it, bitch.

I smiled at her and turned my attention to the meeting, which started with a number of awards, including Baby Borgs and rings to last year's winning driver and owner. The best part happened next: the presentation of starter's rings to all of us who'd take the green the next day. We were individually announced, in reverse order of qualifying, and we each went down the stairs to pose for a photo and accept the special wooden box containing the ring.

The rings were silver, "class ring" style, with a blue stone in the center and "Indianapolis 500" around the bezel. One side had the wheel-and-wings logo of the Indianapolis Motor Speedway and "500," but it was the other side that was the most special. It was personalized with my last name, the speed I'd gone to qualify, and the year. As I admired it, back in my seat, one thought played on repeat in my head.

The Indy 500. Tomorrow.

Chapter Thirty-nine

The rest of the public drivers' meeting passed in a haze of applause as I did my best not to fall asleep in the hot sun. As the race director warned us again to play nice, my phone started buzzing with names from Kenny. I scrolled through the blizzard of them as the meeting ended and drivers filed toward the bus parked at the end of pit lane.

We were headed for the 500 Festival Parade, which drew approximately 300,000 spectators every year as it wound through downtown Indianapolis. Due to our schedule and the crowds around both the Speedway and parade route, drivers were shuttled to the parade staging area via a bus and police escort, to ensure we arrived on time.

Boarding the bus provided dual relief—getting out of the sun and into air conditioning. I found Holly waiting, saving us a row of seats, and handed her my phone. "Names from Kenny."

"Interesting—I'm finally getting some overlap."

I peeked over her shoulder as she added to the bottom of a long list on her own phone. I only recognized half of the twenty or thirty people who'd been in the rear of the shop around the time of Ron's murder.

"That many?" I muttered.

"There were people everywhere. Happening party."

I read the names I recognized aloud. "Kenny O'Toole, Sabrina Ross, Kevin Hagan, Eileen Nguyen, Cecilia Moore, Paul Lauth, Lyla Thomas, Neal Sinclair, Ron Arvin, Alexa Wittmeier, Chuck

Gaffey, Josh Gaffey, Caleb Wise, Stan Wright—wait, Tom Barclay? Gramps and Ryan saw him leave. How could he have been there?"

Holly shrugged. "I don't know the exact time for these sightings. He could have gone to the bathroom before leaving. Or returned."

"Nothing is clear." I took my phone back from Holly, and it buzzed with another text message as a Series rep came through to make sure all drivers were on the bus.

We lurched into motion as I pulled up the text and showed it to Holly. Lyla Thomas had written,

> Remembered we had a press opportunity that morning in '87. Think it started around eleven and ran thirty minutes. Do remember Hagan came blasting in at the end and repeated questions the rest of us already asked. PITA then and now.

"PITA?" I asked Holly.

"Pain in the ass."

"Nice." I laughed as a second text came in from Lyla. I read it aloud.

> Herrera seen buying PJ goods from vendors within minutes of hearing news. But some vendors held impromptu memorabilia flea market in a Speedway parking lot that morning, and I'm told Herrera was there when it opened at nine.

Holly shrugged. "We already thought Herrera was slime, but not a killer. Guess that confirms it."

"I guess so." I perked up. "Maybe the Feds will get him for forgery."

It was only a few minutes before we arrived downtown. We exited the bus and were shepherded into an old, converted church building where we met the cancer warrior prize winner, Maria Febbo, and waited. And waited more.

When the parade eventually started, we went outside to the identical blue convertible Chevy Camaros, each with a different driver's name on it. They were lined up in eleven rows of three, so we'd ride down Indy's avenues in the exact formation in which we'd start the race. Holly, Maria, and I made our way to the eighteenth car in the order—then it was finally our turn to start down the parade route.

Holly rode in the car's passenger seat, but Maria and I perched on the back deck of the convertible, our feet on the rear seats. For a couple miles, back and forth on the downtown avenues, we rolled between checkered flag borders on the pavement and waved at stand after stand of people. They called the Indy 500 "The Greatest Spectacle in Racing," and I was convinced it wasn't for the on-track action alone, but for all the traditions of the event, including the parade.

Sooner than we'd have liked, the parade was over. I said goodbye to Maria—promising to see her the next day in the Frame Savings suite—and boarded the bus with Holly for the ride back to the track. One final appearance, and then Holly and I were off to the final event before race day: a thank-you dinner for sponsors.

I schmoozed my way through the cocktail hour, thanking everyone for attending and getting flashed in the eyes repeatedly by the official photographer, and then I took a break before we sat down to eat. I joined Holly and my half brother, Eddie, near the bar, talking with a good-looking guy in his mid-thirties who I'd seen before at the track.

"Here's the star of the hour," Eddie said, as I approached.

I saluted them with my glass of water. "I'm Kate Reilly," I said to the stranger.

"Kate, this is Josh Gaffey, of Gaffey Insurance," Holly said.

"I'm messy from the hors d'oeuvres." He reached out, smiling, and we bumped fists instead of shaking.

"Glad to put a face to a name," I said. "I've met your father."

He laughed. "I keep expecting to hear he's put down roots on that stool in your garage." Then he sobered. "Though I guess he won't now, with Ron gone."

"They were friends for a long time?" I asked.

"Decades," Josh responded, as he handed an empty plate to a waiter and wiped his fingers with a napkin. "Dad always backed Ron's team, and Ron was a big supporter when Dad was starting the company—always willing to be the sounding board or the guinea pig for new product ideas. Even when Ron was away, Dad visited him every few months, and they wrote back and forth."

"Was he aware of what Ron was involved in?" I asked Josh, adding quietly as an aside to Eddie, "Ron went to jail for drug smuggling in the nineties."

Josh grimaced. "Dad probably knew—I think most people in the paddock did. It was pretty rampant at the time."

"Ron wasn't the only one?" Eddie asked.

I looked around to be sure Alexa wasn't nearby to hear us discussing her father's criminal activities.

"Sugar, the joke was IMSA—the governing body for sportscar racing," Holly explained for Eddie's benefit, "didn't stand for International Motor Sports Association, it stood for International Marijuana Smugglers Association. From what I've heard, it was everywhere, but only a couple unlucky souls got caught."

"Dad always felt bad Ron was one of them. Not that Ron hadn't done it—he never denied it." Josh shook his head. "But he didn't like seeing his friend, who was basically a good guy, in trouble for something lots of others were also doing."

Except few others handled the volume Ron did—or the cocaine with the weed.

I was glad my FBI-agent boyfriend wasn't here for the conversation.

"Sounds like Ron wasn't condemned by his peers for it," Eddie noted.

"From what I remember—I was a kid, but you still feel the vibes," Josh said, "no one thought he shouldn't go to jail, since he'd been tried and convicted. But the reaction was both sympathy and 'I told you so.'"

Eddie shifted his feet. "That's typical anywhere. Something bad happens and someone's always going to shake their heads, say they knew it would all go wrong."

"Hindsight is twenty-twenty." I got the bartender to refill my water. "But I can't understand being willing to take such risks, when it could all go so terribly wrong."

"Says the woman who straps into a racecar." Holly winked at me.

"I'm not going to jail if I do something wrong in the car," I returned.

Josh shrugged. "I think he felt it was his only choice. Dad's always quoting someone who said, 'There's no reward in life without risk.' That's been a guiding principle for us building our business—from mortgaging our own house to save the business to paying out of his own pocket for an injured driver's transportation."

Eddie grinned. "You're literally all about risk, in the insurance game."

"We say it in our mission statement: 'We take the risk for you.' And Dad usually always adds, 'And we'll do what's necessary to serve you.'" Josh paused. "It led to some unorthodox situations—fudging things here or there when we're trying to help a team stuck in some way or trying to get an injured driver transported. But nothing systematically illegal."

"The ends justify the means?" Eddie asked.

Josh sighed. "A debate I've had with my father many times. He'd agree more readily—a consequence of his heyday being those more freewheeling times when 'everyone was doing it,' like Ron."

"You said people didn't condemn Ron, but…" Holly began, then hesitated. "Did you hear of anyone angry with him over the years?"

"Who might have killed him?" Josh shook his head, then stopped and considered. "I hadn't thought about this in years.

But I remember being hurried out of the garage one day, because a guy came in and acted like he was going to attack Ron. I was bummed, because he was yelling great swear words, and I wanted to hear them."

I sensed the quickening of interest in Holly and even Eddie that matched my own. "Any idea who he was? Or why he was angry?"

"I'll ask my dad. He'll know, and he's around here somewhere."

"Not that it's any of our business—that's the cops' job," I admitted. "But it's hard to have seen what happened to Ron without wanting to know more about his life."

Josh nodded. "Something goes wrong and we try to figure out how we might have stopped it from happening—or how we predicted it in the first place. Human nature."

By that point, it was time to sit down to dinner and make nice. As much as it was work, I was genuinely glad for the opportunity to thank everyone involved with my two biggest sponsors for their support of my racing. After the meal, when Alexa got everyone's attention to thank them for being there, I took the mic to reiterate my point.

"I couldn't be here without your help—that's every one of you. By being here, being at the track, telling your friends about our effort, talking about us at the office, sharing on social media—all of that creates the awareness, recognition, and support I need to be on the track. I can't thank you enough. I'll carry all of you with me when I'm in the car tomorrow. Make sure you're watching!"

Everyone applauded and went back to chatting amongst themselves. I worked my way through the crowd that formed around me and eventually ran into Josh.

He toasted me with a half-empty wineglass. "Found out the guy's name who was so mad at Ron—and why. It was earlier the same year Ron got indicted. Ron had been under investigation and he'd stopped receiving drug shipments, so he was running out of money. Rigo Herrera was one of his racing team's suppliers—nothing to do with the drugs—a one-man business supplying machined parts of some kind. He was one of the first people Ron stopped paying when the money ran out. Apparently, though, Ron's team supplied all of Rigo's income—not a good business plan, by the way. Rigo went belly-up, lost his living, his house, his wife—the whole country song. Blamed it on Ron."

"The year Ron got arrested…that was ninety-two?"

"Right."

After PJ. Then something rang a bell. "Rigo Herrera. Did he have a son?"

"One, who grew up hanging out with Rigo at the track. The son's now a big-time memorabilia dealer specializing in racing."

Maybe he wanted revenge on Ron for his father? But how does that tie to PJ?

"What happened to Rigo?"

"Couldn't handle his losses. Probably couldn't handle the shame. He killed himself less than a year later." Josh frowned. "Hard not to lay some of that responsibility on Ron, but people make their own choices."

And did those choices lead Dean to murder?

Chapter Forty

"Ron Arvin ruined Dean Herrera's father's life?" Holly boiled hot water for tea while the rest of us sat around my dining table.

"That's what his father, Rigo, thought. I wonder if Dean agrees?" I replied.

"We don't know when he left the other night." Gramps shook his head. "He could have stayed and walked around the building to the alley."

"But Lyla said he was at the track the morning PJ was killed," I remembered. "Besides, PJ died before Rigo's business went downhill. So he has no motive for her."

"Maybe PJ and Ron's deaths aren't connected?" Gramps offered.

I dropped my head in my hands. "I wish I knew what I was doing."

Holly set mugs of tea in front of me and Ryan and a plate of cookies in front of Gramps. "What does our special agent think of the news?"

Ryan hadn't said much since I'd related what I'd learned from Josh. He frowned now. "I think too many people know you're asking questions about two deaths."

"Josh was a kid when PJ was around," I protested. "Plus he's got no motive for either of them."

"Josh asked someone for Herrera's name," Ryan said. "Who was that? And who was around when he did? Who was nearby when the four of you talked about it?"

I felt my face heat. "You're right. But we were standing away from people, and we weren't speaking loudly—I know because I kept looking around to make sure Alexa didn't hear us talking about her father."

Holly blew on her tea. "Josh was going to ask his dad about Rigo. But that's just Chuck. He was Ron's best friend, and he was heartbroken over PJ."

"So he says." Ryan took a cookie from Gramps' plate.

I frowned. "I don't see motive. But you're the expert. Do you?"

"No," he admitted. "But his name keeps coming up."

I broke a small piece off one of Gramps' cookies, ignoring his protest. "Ron was also around. Uncle Stan. Lyla Thomas, the reporter. None of them have motive either."

"My point was to be careful who you're talking to. The more people who know you're asking questions about a murder, the more likely the murderer will hear about it." Ryan frowned at me. "I've got a bad feeling."

"You think the killer thinks I'm onto him?" I laughed. "I don't know anything."

"He or she doesn't know that," Ryan replied.

That sobered me. "What do we do, stop?"

Gramps and Holly were as wide-eyed as I felt.

Ryan sighed. "I don't expect you can help yourselves, but yes, back off?"

Holly scowled into her mug. "How do *you* investigate, without being obvious? Don't people know you're searching for a criminal of some kind?"

"It's different when you carry a badge and a gun," Ryan said.

Point to the FBI agent.

Ryan looked from Gramps to Holly to me. "How about tomorrow you all cool it? And watch each other's backs?"

The race!

My mouth was suddenly dry, and I drank some of my chamomile tea. "I'll only be alone in the car. But you two," I gestured to Holly and Gramps with my mug, "keep an eye on each other or stay in public."

"I'll be with you most of the time," Holly noted.

Ryan nodded. "I'll stick with Gramps."

We went over the schedule and details for the next day, and then I took my tea to my room, while the others tidied the kitchen for the night. After the non-stop activity of the past couple days, I'd made sure to be home tonight at a reasonable time. Most drivers, and even some teams, did the same to ensure time to relax, rest, and hopefully get a good night's sleep.

If I can calm my nerves.

I sat on the bed with my eyes closed, working on making my mind still, trying to think about getting in the car and starting the race. But my usual meditation and visualization routine wasn't working. One panicked thought after another chased around my brain.

Did we put ourselves in danger asking questions? What did I do? Did I put Gramps and Holly in danger?

I felt my breathing accelerate at the thought of something happening to my beloved Gramps, the only father figure I'd had for most of my life.

And my father…what would happen when I opened the envelope from my grandparents? Would some horrible family secret tear us apart? Tear his family further apart? Would he be better off without me in his life causing problems for his family?

Everything suddenly piled in on me, draining my energy. I was tired of struggling for the truth about the past, tired of battling my father's family—and my own. Tired of weathering the storm of public opinion on social media or in person at the track. Tired of answering the same stupid questions over and over. Exhausted from holding my head up and pretending none of it affected me. Tired of doing it alone.

Ryan found me a few minutes later, curled into a ball, crying it all out.

"Hey, now." He sat beside me and gathered me into his arms. "What's all this about?"

"Everything," I got out, my lower lip and chin quivering. "I'm afraid Gramps and Holly are in danger. I'm afraid I'm being a fool pretending to investigate a serious crime. I'm worried about performing well in the race."

The race! What if I wasn't prepared enough? What if we'd gotten the car setup wrong? What if I screwed something up? What if I don't get any sleep tonight and I'm not in shape for the race tomorrow? I can't let everyone down!

"Easy, now," Ryan soothed. "Take a breath. I've got you."

He does, and isn't that amazing?

I focused on a few deep, regular breaths. "Have I mentioned I'm glad you're here?"

I felt a laugh rumble in his chest. "You have, and I wouldn't be anywhere else." He tipped my chin up to look me in the eye. "I love you, Kate Reilly."

The tears returned to my eyes, this time for joy. "I love you, too." We'd said the words before, but we didn't toss them around like confetti. Seeing the love in his eyes made them more precious.

Ryan shifted to sit with his back against the headboard, legs extended, and I snuggled more comfortably against him. He stroked a hand down my back, continuing to soothe me.

"I don't always fall apart like this before a race," I told him.

"Didn't think so. But this one's big."

"And there's all the other crap—PJ and her family wanting my help, all the media, and the family secrets Gramps brought. I hit overload."

"Totally reasonable. I won't tell anyone superwoman's façade cracked." He kissed the top of my head. "What's your normal routine for the night before a race?"

"Do a little reading, try to stay calm and get some rest."

"If it's reading material you want, I've got Standish's journal marked for you." I felt him chuckle. "Maybe it'll put you to sleep."

I sat up to see his face. "I figured you'd want me to stop investigating."

"I won't tell you what to do, Kate. I'll tell you if I think you're putting yourself in danger or being careless." He frowned. "And I won't promise that won't sound like 'You're being an idiot'—but you've got to make your own decisions. I'm in this for a partner, not a dependent."

I couldn't speak for a moment. There were plenty of men who fed my ego and told me I was beautiful or sexy, but it was a rare man who loved me for my independence and power as a woman. I kissed him. "So glad you're here."

He handed over the journal. "Be careful."

I spent the next hour reading the pages Ryan had marked. Nathan had noted the ups and downs of dozens of sponsors in the months leading up to and following PJ's death, recording information about products, local or national reach, and race-weekend activities. He paid particular attention to other companies hawking services or lifestyle—such as an international shipping company, a limousine service, and watchmakers.

Nathan was as interested in successes as he was in failures and went out of his way to talk with companies that had gotten out of the sponsorship game, including a high-end jewelry company based in the Midwest. "Their target audience was too narrow a subset of the market reached by racing," he concluded. "Racing sponsorship will only work if nearly everyone who sees your message will someday need your services—better still if they need them every month or every week." He went on to note the idea of trying two approaches: business and vacation travelers.

One of the pages Ryan had flagged was a discussion of a failure Gaffey Insurance had experienced. They'd introduced their new business interruption insurance product the prior year and couldn't drum up interest. "Team owners and other sponsors are used to covering their own losses in the event of a problem," Nathan wrote. "Gaffey is frustrated, but still determined to prove the product's value. He tells me he's sure it can be the cornerstone of comprehensive coverage for racing teams and the differentiator for his own success, if he can only prove its worth."

The next page concerned Tom Barclay, who Nathan described as "a clever young man, full of out-of-the-box ideas for his new business." Farther down, Nathan added, "His work for the team this month, as a break after completing his recent graduate degree, has filled him with ideas—particularly that of a business based in counseling athletes, such as racing drivers. We chuckled about the fragile egos drivers have, but he also spoke about helping confidence levels and performance anxiety in pit crew and teams. I told him I thought his ideas were interesting and innovative, and all he needed to launch his practice was one great case study for the value of his services. I wish him well, and I plan to follow his progress."

One great case study? PJ provided that. Could he have left the track that morning after all, and gotten downtown to kill PJ? I still wouldn't put it past him...

Chapter Forty-one

We were all up early the next morning to be ready for our six-thirty escort to the track. I'd slept well, but once I was awake, I was buzzing on adrenaline.

Race day!

The sun was rising, casting everything in blue-gray tones as we followed a motorcycle officer through the empty streets on the north side of Indianapolis. Because IMS was notorious for long lines of cars waiting to enter parking lots on race day—small wonder given its capacity of up to 400,000 seats—the solution for getting drivers, team members, VIPs, and even special tours past the lines was a police escort.

As we approached the track, I estimated a backup of at least a mile already, stretching east on Sixteenth Street, headed for the large, gravel lots directly across from one of the main entrances. As our small group of cars zipped past them, I was grateful all over again for not having to wait.

As much as I didn't like getting up to do it, I loved being at the track early on race day. I'd always found magic in seeing, hearing, and feeling racetracks come alive—and IMS was the most dramatic of any I'd been to, because the contrast was so stark. I knew some staff arrived as early as four or four-thirty, to prep for their day's work or simply to beat the traffic, and they told me of a quiet front straight and pit lane, illuminated only by the digital scoring pylon and the softly glowing pagoda. I didn't think I'd ever make it there that early, but I could imagine the peace of those moments.

By the time I arrived, the sun was up in a clear, blue sky and crews moved slowly around their garages. A chill remained in the air from the small rain shower we'd had overnight. It would be hot and humid later, but at least we wouldn't have rain.

We parked and walked into the paddock from the east entrance of Gasoline Alley, and a thrill coursed through my body like an electric shock.

For more than a hundred years, cars, teams, and drivers have walked this path from garages to pit lane to track. And I get to be part of it again.

Even someone calling me PJ didn't dim my mood. I signed a couple autographs outside our garage, and then we all went inside.

I ducked into the office and collected hot-pit passes for Gramps and Ryan—long, narrow stickers that wrapped around their lanyards and ensured they could be in the pits during the race. "Holly will be with me for the rest of the morning. You're on your own."

"I recommend going out to pit lane and the front straight now," Holly said. "It's amazing to be out there when it's not crowded. Plus you can get close to the Borg-Warner trophy."

Gramps nodded and clapped a hand on Ryan's shoulder. "Do your thing, Katie. We'll take care of ourselves."

I hugged them both, and Ryan kissed me on the cheek. Then I checked the time, dropped my bag in my locker, and headed for my first appointment of the day, two bottles of water-plus-electrolytes in hand. One of my top priorities was hydrating to minimize the effects of dehydration via sweat during the race.

Out on pit lane, I chatted with a TV reporter while we waited for the live broadcast. Holly stood to the side and tapped away on her phone. My heart pounded as I thought of flying down the front straight in just a few hours, which reminded me to start on the next bottle of water.

"I'm glad we have a couple minutes," said the reporter, Michelle, the lone woman on the local station's sports reporting team. "I wanted to work something out with you."

That intrigued me. "What's that?"

"I thought I'd ask you about PJ Rodriguez when we go live." She saw my alarm and hurried to explain. "I've seen the crap you've been taking about her. I want to give you the chance to make a clear distinction between the two of you. Maybe that will help put the comparisons to bed."

Someone in the media wanting to help me, not exploit the comparison for a story?

As soon as I had the thought, I knew it wasn't fair. The real journalists I'd dealt with weren't into the sensation of "Kate as PJ"—that came from the Internet trolls and bloggers masquerading as reporters. "I'd appreciate that."

She winked at me. "Women have to stick together in this business. Besides, what people have been saying to you is downright shitty."

Holly giggled, and I smiled. "No kidding."

A couple minutes later, we went live. Michelle started with the usual: how I was feeling, what I thought my chances were, what attendees should watch for in the race, and what it meant to me to be participating in "The Greatest Spectacle in Racing."

Then she paused. "Kate, I want to cover something you've been dealing with off the track. Some viewers may know about PJ Rodriguez, the first woman to be the fastest in a practice session for the Indy 500. You duplicated her feat this year, which generated numerous comparisons. But PJ never actually qualified for the 500, and in fact, she committed suicide before her second attempt. Now we're here on race day, do you have anything you'd like to say about PJ and yourself?"

"This place and this race are magical—so much bigger and more meaningful than other races, because of the history. For more than a century, men and women have come here chasing a dream, with results ranging from success to heartbreak. PJ was one of the heartbreaks." I paused. "I understand the comparisons, and I have great respect and sympathy for what PJ went through. But what's frustrating is everyone assuming I'm exactly like her and calling me by her name, simply because I'm also a woman."

Am I going to say it? Should I? What the hell...

"Honestly," I dredged up a smile to take the sting out of my words, "it's disrespectful to assume we're the same person. We're both women, and we both showed comparative flashes of speed—but we're different people with different stories. We should all be celebrated for our unique gifts—men and women, drivers or not. So while I've been glad for the opportunity to learn about PJ, I hope people will think about her with compassion and root for me and the number 82 today on our own merits."

"Thank you, Kate," Michelle said, turning to the camera, which swung to center her in the shot. "I know I speak for all of us at the station when I say we're behind you one hundred percent. I'm Michelle Horton, live from pit lane at the Indianapolis Motor Speedway. Back to you in the studio."

As the cameraman lowered the lens and nodded, Michelle turned to me, still smiling. "Well done."

"Thanks for the chance to say it."

"I hope it'll help. Best of luck today. Maybe I'll see you after the race." She shook hands with me and Holly.

On our way back to the garage, we navigated through a growing crowd, and I stopped a few times to sign autographs or take photos with fans. Holly typed up a couple tweets as we walked, quoting my words about PJ.

She saw me eyeing her phone as we turned into Gasoline Alley. "Don't worry about social media today, I've got it handled. You think about the car."

The thought made me smile. "Done."

Chapter Forty-two

Holly and I were walking past the first garage building when my least favorite crew member loomed in front of us—tall, wiry, and in our faces. We shifted to the right, and he moved with us. His scrunched up face scowled.

Jimmy.

My stomach did a slow roll that didn't help the unsettled feeling I already had from pre-race tension.

He sucked on the stub of a cigarette hanging out of his mouth and tossed it to the ground next to us, where it continued to burn. "You on the rag or something, bitch?"

I coughed as he exhaled smoke into my face, then flapped my hand and tried to move away to breathe fresh air. He again moved to block me, but since he focused on me, Holly slipped around his other side and ran for help.

I stopped, furious instead of intimidated. "What the hell is *your* problem?"

"You." His lip curled. "And the old man you sent to ask questions. You think I'm too stupid to figure out he's related to you?"

I studied the lifetime of meanness etched into his face. "I don't think about you."

"'Cept you wanted to know what I thought about PJ, since that's what the old man asked. You sure you want to know?" He pulled a pack of cigarettes and a lighter from his shirt pocket while I stared at him.

"She was worthless." He smiled as he lit up, but it wasn't friendly. "Like you."

Gee, now my feelings are hurt.

"Not everyone agreed," I replied. "Did you do something to make your case?"

"The hell you talking about?"

"Did you mess up her car to make her run badly?"

He was shocked at first, then he doubled over, laughing until he wheezed, his cigarette forgotten in one hand. I realized I could get away from him, but I crossed my arms and waited him out.

"Fuck you." He straightened. "That girl didn't need my help to look awful, it was all on her. The car was fine, and the crew was fine—better than she deserved. We were wasted on her."

He shook his head and took a drag. "She couldn't drive, and you want to blame me? It's true, you're as crazy as she was. Going to take a dive off the pagoda today?"

My breath caught, and I felt hot all over. "Listen, you son of a bitch, nothing you say affects me. Because you're not important. So crawl off with your woman-hating, minority-hating, and probably white-supremacist bullshit, and leave the rest of the world to evolve without you. We don't need bullies."

I smiled at him. "That's what burns you the most, isn't it? That we're not scared of you. We just don't care."

On one hand, I was appalled at the cruelty coming out of my mouth, and on the other, I was proud of myself for responding to decades of discrimination.

"Ugly-ass bitch." Jimmy's face went beet red, and he looked me up and down. "I wouldn't fuck you if you begged for it."

"That'll never happen." I laughed, and my anger and tension seeped away. "Typical bully, go for personal insults. They won't work." I stared at him, letting him see all the disdain I felt. "We're done here."

Moments later I met Holly, Banjo, and Bald John hurrying toward me. I turned them around and told the story, though I had to stop them more than once from going after Jimmy, assuring them it wasn't necessary or worth it.

Back at the garage, I calmed myself down by signing autographs for the inevitable crowd in front of our space. After that,
Holly handed me more fluids, and I sat down with my engineer, Nolan, for an update on the predicted weather and track
temperatures, along with strategies we'd employ depending on
track position and cautions. I ended up late to meet Charlene
Menfis, the Frame Savings executive I'd invited to the garage,
but Holly found her and gave her the tour.

A few minutes later, I met with two reporters in quick succes-
sion, both from big markets—Atlanta and Los Angeles—where
my sponsors had headquarters. Then I headed for the Frame
Savings suite, with Holly promising to meet me there shortly.

I signed more autographs as I worked my way through the
rapidly thickening crowd, feeling my breathing get shallower
the more I was detained along the way.

Can't we get to the race? Skip these preliminaries?

I reminded myself the number of obligations I had was
dwindling, and it would soon be race time. Then I reminded
myself to drink more fluids.

As I finally rounded the corner of the row of suites atop
the main grandstand, I almost ran into Tom Barclay, sports
psychologist and champion rumormonger. We both fumbled
with apologies for the near-miss, until we realized who the other
person was. His handsome, tanned face creased into a big smile.
Mine formed a snarl.

"Kate, good to see you." He gushed. "I hope you're ready
for the day."

Primed by my confrontation with Jimmy and the current of
nerves running through me, I went nuclear. "How dare you?"
I spat.

"Express my concern?" He looked confused, which made
me angrier.

"What gives you the right to talk to me after spreading rumors
about my mental stability?"

"Are you referring to the post on the Racing's Ringer blog?"
His innocent expression didn't fool me. "When the Ringer

asked for comment, we could only do so in a hypothetical sense. Our response had nothing to do with you—we wouldn't even confirm you'd been a customer of ours in the past. I hope you noticed that."

"I don't believe you."

"I have to say, if the rumors are true, I hope you'll come talk with one of my staff." He had the audacity to put a hand on my shoulder.

I swung my arm and knocked his hand away. "Don't ever touch me. You're the last person I'd deal with now. I know where that rumor came from."

He dropped the warm and friendly act and raised a cool eyebrow. "I can only repeat I have no idea what you're talking about. Though I will note, strictly in a theoretical sense, I've always believed all is fair in love, war, and marketing."

It took a moment to find my words through my shock. "Are you *kidding* me? There's nothing fair or right or *ethical* about slandering a customer."

That sent both of his eyebrows soaring. "Slander is a strong word to throw around. I think you'd find it difficult to prove."

"If you'd screw over your customers, it makes me wonder what else you'd stoop to. How about bumping off a fragile competitor to scare others into using your services?"

His eyes narrowed, and he glanced at the mostly empty walkway two flights above the main crowds. "If anyone heard you, I'd make a case for slander right now."

I ignored his threat and hissed at him. "You're saying murder would be too far? Even for marketing purposes—didn't you say all was fair?"

"What are you talking about?"

"PJ Rodriguez, whose death so conveniently drummed up enthusiasm and customers for your services," I taunted. "You must remember her? She was murdered."

"PJ—but that was suicide. Wasn't it? I can't—no…" He turned to brace himself on the railing with both hands and sucked in deep breaths.

Son of a bitch. He doesn't look guilty.

I tried to hold on to my anger, but it drained away in the face of his obvious surprise.

He turned to me, all arrogance and aloofness gone. "You think someone killed her? I never considered it. Why would I?"

I sighed and leaned on the railing next to him. "Her parents are convinced she didn't commit suicide—that she wouldn't have. And I agree with them."

"You thought it was me?" There was more confusion and hurt in his voice than anger, but I figured that would follow soon enough.

"You benefitted from her death—the cornerstone of your career, right?"

"It was that," he said quietly, looking out at the mass of people streaming through Gasoline Alley. Then he turned to me. "I'll be honest, suicide never made sense, but I accepted it—we all did. I'm having a hard time grasping that the bedrock of my career was a mistake on my part. At some point, I'll probably be outraged at your suspicions." He paused and drew a deep breath. "But I had nothing to do with PJ's death. *Nothing.*"

And dammit, I believed him.

Chapter Forty-three

Tom Barclay left, after stilted goodbyes, and I remained at the railing, focusing on my breathing and gathering my thoughts.

So much for that suspect, and so much for tact in handling my suspicions. Besides, Kate, what the hell *are you doing, letting this get to you today? You need to focus on the race. The biggest race of the year!*

I closed my eyes and thought about the car, the track, and dirty air. I was feeling mostly re-centered when I heard Holly's voice.

"Something wrong, sugar?" She handed me another bottle of electrolyte-water.

I took a drink, then described the conversation with Barclay. "Another classic moment proving I should stick to driving, not investigating. Apparently, subtlety is not in the cards for me today."

"A couple hours to the biggest race of the year—if not your career? You should be on edge." She chuckled. "But his reaction was interesting. Hard to see him as a suspect now."

"I think he's off the list." I checked the time, started to panic. "And shit, I'm late."

She patted my shoulder as we turned to walk the final few yards to the door of the suite. "Take a breath. Everyone will deal. Keep focused on the race."

I nodded, trying to follow her instructions as I reached for the door. I spent the next twenty minutes chatting with executives and VIPs from Frame Savings and Beauté, which consisted of agreeing I was excited about the race, I thought our car would be in good shape, and our chances were good for a top fifteen or twenty finish. Plus accepting good wishes and taking selfies with nearly everyone. I told everyone I hoped to see them on the pre-grid or after the race.

My father stopped me as Holly and I made our way to the door. "Thank you for coming by. I know you've got a packed schedule, but it means a lot to our guests."

"You make it possible for me to be here. I'm sorry I can't stay longer, but everyone's welcome in the garage after the race." I smiled at him. "Thank you, for everything."

I saw a glimmer of moisture in his eyes as he kissed my cheek. Then he let us go.

After a quick stop at a tweet-up for fans organized by IndyCar Nation, the Series-sponsored fan community—and another stop at a bathroom—we fought our way back through the now-dense crowds to the garage. I went straight to the hospitality area, grabbed a bottle of doctored water, and plopped down on the cooler's closed lid. I exhaled and tried to send the stress of the morning out with my breath.

"Long day already?" Chuck Gaffey's voice was filled with amusement and sympathy.

I saw him and Gramps sitting on stools and grinning at me. I toasted them with my bottle. "The glamorous life of a racing driver."

Gramps laughed. "I recall warning you as a kid it would be a lot of work."

"I still wouldn't change it." I watched the activity around the car, which sat in one piece in the center of the garage space. "Did you make sure it's put together right?"

"Supervising," Gramps said. "That's our talent."

Chuck laughed. "We made sure they didn't miss a spot in their polishing—not that we need to tell this group anything."

"They're good at their jobs. I'm fortunate to have them all."

Alexa and team co-owner Tim Beerman stepped out of the office area. "It's nine-forty-five. Let's do this," she said as she strode past me to the center of the garage space. She clapped her hands and raised her voice. "Beermeier team, gather round."

We all stopped what we were doing and moved closer. Tim stood behind her, arms crossed over his chest, his typical silent self.

"We're about to take the cars to the grid, but before we scatter to our different responsibilities, I want to say thank you for the effort you've made this month. Thank you to every single one of you for the care you take in doing your jobs. For the support you give each other—and especially the love you've shown me and my father this past week." She paused and looked down at the floor.

When she raised her head, her eyes were wet. "You've demonstrated over and over that we're a team, and that's never more important than today. Go do what you know how to do. Do it to the best of your abilities. And do it because you love your jobs and love being here for this incredible event. Thank you, and have a great race."

Everyone in the room cheered and applauded, then got down to work. My crew went back to the car and immediately started preparing to depart. They'd take it to our space in pit lane first, and then they'd roll it out to our grid position on the track, where it would sit until I got in and took off for warm-up laps.

I resumed my seat on the cooler, content to take a couple more minutes to regroup and watch the action. I was done with my duties for the morning, and aside from stepping outside the garage to sign autographs for fans, I had nothing else to do for the next hour and a half except drink more water, try to eat, and get ready to race the car.

Three standard meals of rubbery chicken, pasta, and steamed vegetables had been delivered for the drivers, and I opened one and picked at it. I was more nervous than hungry, though I knew I needed something. I did what I could and supplemented with a banana, plus two more bottles of water. As I ate, I watched the crew and car leave—with my helmet, gloves, and other gear— and listened to Gramps and Chuck chat about vintage racing, which Chuck was heavily involved in, now that he was retired.

I could see fans outside the garage pausing and looking in at me, so after I finished eating, and before I changed into my race gear, I went outside to greet them. Twenty minutes and a bunch of selfies later, I came back in to suit up. By then, Gramps and Chuck had progressed to talking about Indy 500s of years past. There was only a skeleton crew in the garage, and only Holly sat in the folding chairs of the office area, so we could hear their conversation clearly. As I passed her, I nodded toward the men and raised my eyebrows. She shrugged.

"Ninety-two was a great year, I agree," Chuck said. "And I'm a Rick Mears fan, so I'm partial to ninety-one, when he won his fourth."

"Gotta admit, all of my Indy memories are tainted now," Gramps replied. "I've never enjoyed a race more than last year, purely because Kate was in a car."

As I moved back to my locker and started taking off my street shoes, I heard Chuck laugh. "No one can blame you for that."

Gramps sounded thoughtful. "I don't know what I'd have done if she hadn't managed to qualify. You've been involved with teams and drivers that didn't make it into the field. How do they deal with it?"

There was a pause, and I imagined Chuck shrugging or shaking his head. "It's not easy. To some extent, they're convinced they'll make it. But some come in knowing they're longshots. Others could be legitimate contenders, but something goes wrong that day. It's rough having to pack up and admit your dreams are over—for the drivers, but also for the team. But that's true whether it's qualifying or race weekend."

"Or weeks before, in some cases," Gramps returned. "Like PJ Rodriguez—I'd never heard of her before Kate was fast on day one. But I think about her a lot now, imagining Kate in her shoes, thinking of how awful it must have been for her and everyone around her."

I heard Chuck sigh. "It wasn't easy."

"You were around?" Gramps prodded him.

"Yeah. Poor Ron. He did so much to support her—including using some of his own money to fund her."

Presumably, he had enough coming from running drugs.

I stripped off my shirt and pants and pulled out my Nomex gear.

"Did it seem like she'd give up?" Gramps asked. "I've seen plenty of racers over the years who simply disappear. But giving up in the form of suicide is different."

"Ron didn't think so. That's probably what hurt him the most." Chuck paused. "I know it's easy to say this in hindsight, but I could see it. She wasn't as tough as she acted. There was a brittleness underneath, a lack of confidence. I remember hearing the breaking news of an unidentified driver suicide and thinking, 'I bet that's PJ.' Sadly, I was right. Then it was a matter of doing what any good friend would do, and helping Ron deal with the vultures, attention-seekers, and sensationalist press."

"Were the press as bad back then as they are now? I swear, some of the so-called media outlets that say things about Kate I want to run out of town on a rail." Gramps sounded legitimately angry as I finished tying my shoes and stood to pull on the top half of my firesuit.

"Most of them were okay, but a few were prototypes for the glory hounds of today. Back then, they were still mostly about objective reporting. Until that Kevin Hagan came along and started doing emotional features on everyone."

I reentered the office area, water bottle in hand, as Chuck made that last statement.

"Interesting," Holly muttered, her eyes wide.

I nodded.

Sure. But forget that. Time for racing.

Chapter Forty-four

The traditions, rituals, and ceremonies surrounding the Indianapolis 500 were more prolonged and grand than any other race I'd seen or been part of.

Winners of the 500 have drunk milk since the 1930s, when a three-time winner of the race requested buttermilk as a post-race thirst-quencher, and the local milk board recognized an opportunity. Winning drivers and teams have knelt down to kiss the yard of bricks on the front straight since 1996, when a NASCAR driver did so to pay tribute to the track's history—which led to thousands of fans puckering up for photos every year.

Pre-race activities were equally steeped in tradition. Hundreds of multi-colored balloons have been released on race morning since 1947. And "Back Home Again in Indiana" has been performed since 1946—by Jim Nabors for nearly forty of those years.

Every race weekend had some form of pre-race ceremonies—at the very least, an invocation, national anthem, and instruction to "Start your engines." But at the Indy 500, they went on for hours, slowly building the excitement and adrenaline in the Speedway. Starting at eight that morning, a dozen bands had paraded down the front straight. They were followed by parade cars carrying Indy 500 Festival princesses and sponsors. Then the official delivery of the green flag by helicopter, followed by parade cars carrying past race-winning drivers and the race's grand marshal.

By that point, our racecars were in place on the front straight's starting grid, and teams were allowed ten minutes to warm up the engines—though we wouldn't go racing for another hour and twenty. I knew from attending in the past that the quieting of those engines signaled the start of the televised portion of the pre-race show, which began with a military color guard assembled on pit lane. As the Borg-Warner was rolled out to the yard of bricks for photos, media assembled on all sides of a giant platform bridging the wall between pit lane and the front straight.

Another tradition was driver introductions. We would be called out in reverse order of qualifying, and each row of three starters would climb the steps to the platform, wave to the crowd, and descend steps on the other side for media photos.

With help from the yellow-shirted security patrol blowing whistles to clear a path through the crowd, I made my way for the final time from the garages to the pagoda, my nervous system already ramped up to anxiety mode. Holly was with me, running interference with autograph-seekers. I was happy to respond to fans at almost any time, the two exceptions being right before qualifying and right before the race, when it took all of my energy to stay calm about what lay ahead. To keep breathing.

We arrived at the green room, on the pagoda's ground floor, which was full of drivers, team reps, Series and broadcast crew, and VIPs. I saw the Grammy-winning recording artist there to perform the national anthem in one corner and the Oscar-winning action star who would wave the green flag in another. Mostly I saw my fellow drivers, looking some combination of tense and focused—a few acted relaxed, but that was for show.

"You hanging in there?" Holly asked in a low tone.

"Thinking about the car and the race—everything else is put away for now. Except maybe Gramps or Ryan. Any idea what they're doing?"

"We'll see them on the grid. You want more water?" She pulled a bottle out of the small tote bag she carried.

I already have to pee.

"Sure." I knew I needed as much as I could take in, because the minute I got in the car I'd sweat it out by the cupful.

An IndyCar staffer entered the green room to assemble us into our rows of three. I felt my heart rate kick up another notch, which I wouldn't have thought possible.

Keep breathing, think about putting your helmet on and getting in the car.

In moments, I was exiting the green room to wait under the pagoda behind a tall screen bearing the race logo. Two drivers stood on my left, representing positions seventeen and sixteen. We'd barely formed our row when we were directed to skirt the screen and walk out to be introduced.

I looked around, amazed at the sight of hundreds of thousands of people. The crowds were thick on pit lane and the front straight, packed solid from the rope line edging our narrow walkway for a hundred yards in either direction. The stands in front of us, lining the front straight as far as the eye could see down to Turn 1 and up to Turn 4 were full. I turned to look behind us and saw similarly full stands, as well as people lining every window and deck of every level of the pagoda.

My mouth went dry.

I forgot how big this feels.

As we climbed the six steps, I heard the announcer. "Turning to row six, on the outside, starting in eighteenth and making her second run here at Indy, from Albuquerque, New Mexico, Kate Reilly!"

I waved, smiling, turning to look behind me and up and down the track. I registered a vague increase in volume at my name, but between the cheering of the people in the stands, the ongoing blare of the PA, and the constant roar of my heartbeat in my ears, I wasn't sure if the reaction had been good, bad, or indifferent.

The three of us paused at the top of the platform while the other two drivers were introduced, and then we started down the other side, where we worked our way past special guests— veterans of World War II seated in chairs along the yard of bricks—the Borg-Warner trophy, and prior race winners. We greeted and took photos with most of the VIPs, including the Oscar-winner. When we'd reached the end of the line, we all hurried back along a designated path in the crowd to the green room, where everyone made a beeline for the two bathrooms—all drivers were in the same over-hydrated and nervous-stomach state. Holly was waiting for me after I got through the line, and together, we made our way out to the crowded grid to the strains of Florence Henderson singing "God Bless America."

We stopped where we were—barely onto the crowded front straight—and bowed our heads for the invocation and the bugler's version of Taps.

I heard Holly blow her nose behind me as we started moving again. "Taps always gets me," she said.

I agreed with her, but kept walking, my entire being focused on getting to the car. The Grammy-winner launched into the national anthem, and we reached my crew seconds before the flyover. From that moment, I stopped hearing anything that wasn't right in front of me. I wanted to use the bathroom again, but I knew it was just nerves and the need would disappear the minute I got in the car. I'd already started sweating.

I moved to my engineer, Nolan. "All good?"

He tugged at the sparse hair over his ears. "As we'll get. Have a good race."

My heart rate hit maximum speed, and I wondered if I'd pass out. I glanced at my crew, unable to do more than nod. Gramps patted me on the back and told me he was proud of me. Ryan squeezed my hand and got out of the way. Holly stepped up with my gear, and I handed my phone, sunglasses, and lip balm to her.

I studied the cockpit of the car as I inserted my earplugs. I pulled on my balaclava and opened the neck of my firesuit to tuck the ends inside. Zipped up again, and smoothed the neck flap closed. Took a deep breath.

Almost show time. You got this. Focus, stay in the moment, and kick some butt.

I met Holly's eyes and smiled as she handed me my helmet. "Thanks."

"Anytime, sugar. Anytime."

I looked down the track toward Turn 1 as I pulled my helmet on. I didn't see the crowds, flags, or other cars. Didn't hear the cacophony around me. I saw open pavement and smooth track. Felt speed. I fastened my chinstrap and stepped toward the car.

Bald John helped me get settled, fastening and double-checking my belts and securing the extra padding around my head as Alexa initiated the radio check—between her on the stand and me in the car, between me and my spotters in Turn 1 and Turn 3, and between her and the spotters. I was more nervous and more calm at the same time—nervous for the million things that could go wrong at the start and in the race. Calmer because it was finally time to go.

Enough with the buildup and the waiting. Let's light this candle!

Finally, they said the words. "Ladies and Gentlemen, start your engines."

Nolan swiveled a finger in the air, the crew inserted the starter motor, and my 82 car growled to life under me.

Chapter Forty-five

The thirty-three entrants in the Indianapolis 500 pulled away row by row for three warm-up laps before the green flag. The first was the official parade lap, during which we stayed in formation around the 2.5-mile circuit—I was told fans cheered us the whole way, but I didn't notice.

The circuit took forever, the 110 mph we did for warm-up laps feeling slow. As we moved from Turn 4 onto the front straight, we straggled into one long line, giving each other space to do the small amount of accelerating, braking, and weaving back and forth we were capable of to warm things up while in full fuel-save mode.

Alexa radioed to me as I entered Turn 1 on the second lap. "I know it's not easy, but get your tires as warm as you can, and save fuel."

My heart rate was already near race-pace, but I was starting to settle, to feel in the zone. "Copy."

"Your jacker is currently zero. Bars P4 and P1. Make sure they're where you want them for the start so you're not too loose. Fuel setting 8. Stay out of trouble at the green." Alexa's voice was unusually tight with tension.

Time to go. "Copy."

I weaved back and forth between Turns 1 and 2, putting my hands on the anti-roll bar levers and the weight jacker button for reassurance. On the back straight, I gave the car some throttle, then pounced on the brakes fifty yards later and weaved back and forth more before Turn 3.

One more time down the front straight, focusing on my car. Glancing at the cars around me. Making sure I'm breathing to be ready for the green. Into Turn 1 again.

The next time, we'll be racing.

I touched the throttle to line up next to the middle car from my row, and we went through Turn 2 side-by-side. On the back straight, I switched to fuel setting or "map" 4 for aggressive fuel use at the start. The inside car from our row fell back into line with us. Ahead, the fifth row had similarly formed. The two cars next to me edged forward, and I went with them, closing the gap slightly between rows and feeling the track get narrower as three speeding cars lined up side-by-side.

We don't fit three-wide! Breathe, Kate. We do if we're very, very careful...

We went through Turn 3 together, then the short chute between turns.

One more turn.

My pulse skyrocketed. Still in a tidy row through Turn 4. Heading for the green, starting to pick up the pace. Following the cars in the row ahead as they accelerate. My heart pounding. The sound of the roaring crowd mingling with the crescendo of blood roaring through my veins.

"Be ready," my Turn 1 spotter called as my row came out of Turn 4. "Be ready. Ready. Ready—leaders are accelerating. Green, green, green!"

My instincts tell me to mash the throttle down. My head backs off just enough to not run over the car in front of me.

"Inside. Two inside. Inside," the Turn 1 spotter calls from his stand high atop the outer grandstand. "Now one. One inside."

I fly down the front straight, seeing space to my left and moving toward the center of the track, now that there are only two of us side-by-side. Shift to fifth gear. Look ahead to Turn 1 but see it full of cars jockeying for position and slowing everyone down. Foot off the throttle, braking. Turbulent air from cars all around me. Check my mirrors—yellow car behind me to the outside, coming fast.

"Inside. Now outside," the spotter calls.

I'm the meat in a car sandwich at nearly 200 mph. I follow my line into the corner, hoping the yellow car on the outside will slow down because there's not enough room to get by. It doesn't, and we go through Turn 1 three-wide.

There's no room! The outer car is crowding me.

We round Turn 1 and go into the short chute between 1 and 2. Spotter reminding me of cars inside and outside. Me trying to hold the car steady to keep from hitting anyone and trying to figure out how the car feels for racing.

My car pushes up. I turn the wheel more. The outside car gets closer.

Is the inside car pushing me? The outside car crowding me?

I feel a bump and multiple vehicles dart around me as I fight my wiggling car. Ease off the throttle, get the wheels straight through the turn.

Losing ground to the other cars!

Through Turn 2, I can tell the handling has changed. The front wants to grab and the back end wants to snap around. I'd lost aero downforce on the rear of the car with whatever had been damaged. I wind the weight jacker to the right to add more weight, more mechanical grip, and less tendency to turn or snap to the side that lost aero. Make the front anti-roll bar stiffer—*slowly!*—to decrease mechanical grip and make it grab less up front.

I barely got through Turn 2, trying to keep my speed up. Then the yellow car passed me on the back straight.

Sofia Montalvo.

I pressed the radio button. "She hit me!"

In the moment, my adrenaline high and blood hot, I was sure she'd done it on purpose. Watching replays later, I could concede it had been a racing incident.

"We saw it. Three-wide, hard to be sure," Alexa's voice came back, calm and measured. "How's the car?"

I inched the wheel to the left, turning into 3, and didn't respond, busy making more adjustments and thinking the car would slide out from under me into the wall at any second. Feeling like I was on rollerskates in a butter factory.

Alexa came back on the radio as I fought through the short chute and Turn 4. "We don't see damage—nothing's broken off."

Down the front straight to end only my first lap. "She crowded me, then hit me," I insisted. "Something broke. Handling went to shit."

Bitch.

"Do what you can. Don't want to pit under green. Try to hang on. Fuel map 3." Alexa kept the words to a minimum to be heard with the noise of airflow.

I focused on turning into 1, then dialed my fuel mixture down. *She will not get away with ruining my race. No way in hell will she beat me.*

I channeled my rage into dealing with my suddenly ill-handling beast.

Alexa spoke three laps later. "Lap times steady. Good work. Keep it up."

I didn't bother responding. Kept listening to the sound of the car in the turns and tuning my senses to the feel of the tires through my seat. Nudging the levers to compensate for the shifting weight of the car as I burned fuel and wore down the tires. Dealing with the loosest car I'd ever driven and feeling at every second if I even looked at the car wrong, I'd upset the balance, break loose, and hit the wall.

The only other radio activity came from my spotter as five different cars passed me. I swore as the poor handling got worse with a car next to me taking away my air. But I refused to give up without a fight, and I worked my tools until they did no more good. Then I started lifting to slow my corner-entry speed, cursing Sofia all the way.

I was in Turn 2, lap 20, when my Turn 3 spotter yelled, "Yellow! Yellow! Yellow! Turn 4!" The lights around the track and on my dash flashed. "Car is against inside wall. Watch for debris."

Relief washed through me. I lifted my foot off the throttle incrementally, braked gently, slowing with the other cars on track into Turn 3, waiting for more instructions.

"Looks like debris all across the track. Do your best not to hit any," Alexa called.

I slowed as much as possible through Turn 4 and picked my way through the debris in the tracks of the car ahead of me. Then I changed the fuel settings on the wheel to setting 8, to minimize consumption.

"Pace car missed the leader," my Turn 1 spotter called. "Pick him up next time."

I heard Alexa sigh as she transmitted again. "The wrecked car's blocking pit entry, so extra time to clear it and open the pits. We'll try to see what's wrong as you go by."

"Copy," I said.

"But we'll change your rear assembly." Alexa paused. "That'll be full fuel, tires, and rear assembly change. You'll lose more positions—probably a lap—but it'll give you something to work with again."

"I'll take it," I told her. Then I waited, impatiently, as the field circled the track for a full eight laps.

Let us in! Got to get this car fixed!

Chapter Forty-six

It seemed like forever, but the safety crew finally cleared the driver, car, and debris. When the pits opened, we all came in, which made for a crowded pit lane. Fortunately, the car pitted behind me was still behind me on the track, so I could pull into my box straighter than if I had to pull in around another car—and I was lucky the crew next to us liked me, because they pulled aside the front tire laid out for their own pit stop to ease my entry.

Unfortunately, fixing my car took a long, long time. The crew worked fast, undoing fasteners and removing the rear assembly—including wing, winglets, and pods—then sliding the new one into place and twisting screws to hold it tight. But even with their speed, I sat there forever. Every second was an eternity, especially as cars in front of me pulled out of their pit spaces. Then cars behind me pulled out and passed us. The field passed us on track, and I lost a lap. Still I waited.

"Hang on, Kate," Alexa soothed. "It'll be worth it."

I concentrated on breathing and being ready to go when I got the wave.

There! Go!

I was clicking the car into gear and pressing on the throttle as I heard Alexa in my ear. "Go, go, go!" A moment later, she continued, "You're P32, one lap down, but it's early in the race. Work on the car, we'll get it back."

I tamped down my panic and listened to Alexa and my spotters. When we took the green two laps later, I was at the very back of the field and in more dirty air than I'd ever thought possible. In the pits, I'd reset my anti-roll bars and weight jacker closer to normal, but not all the way neutral—which left the car now pushing like a pig.

Too much understeer!

I started moving my tools immediately, a position at a time, and slowly the handling came back to me.

"How does it feel?" Alexa asked, a few laps into the stint.

"Pretty good," I returned. "Still working on it."

I kept working for the next ten laps, focusing on tuning the handling and even passing the last car on the track ahead of me. Four laps later, we got another yellow. When the leaders pitted, I stayed out to get my lost lap back, then pitted for full service—telling Alexa I didn't want any changes. As we circled for the green, I was last again, but back on the lead lap.

More importantly, I had a car I was starting to feel good about. I finally had some stability—a relative term for a racecar at the edge of grip—and I could work on tuning the performance.

We took the green, and two laps later, someone brought out another yellow flag.

Fortunately, this one was short, for a one-car spin and stalled engine. It took a couple laps to get the field collected behind the pace car and get the car restarted. But he drove right off and around to the pits, ensuring a short caution period.

Because I was at the back of the line of cars anyway, Alexa called me in to top me off with fuel—because we never knew if it would help, and it didn't hurt us. Then we restarted again and settled into a long, green-flag run.

Three laps in, I passed a car with a mechanical problem that was low in Turn 3, slowing and heading for the apron to get to pit lane. I went through Turn 4 and took a breath down the front straight, telling myself to relax. I had a fleeting impression of a wall of color pressing down on me from the stands to my right, but I ignored it, and focused on the car.

Make the next lap better. Faster. Flatter. Catch the red car in front of me.

I stared at Turn 1, not seeing what actually lay ahead—the track and outer wall looking like a barrier at the end of the straight—but seeing the bend of the track in my mind's eye. Seeing through the turn, past the pesky red car in the middle of it. Foot flat on the throttle.

"You're four lengths back from the next car, Kate," Alexa calls. "Go get him."

I inched closer to him, fighting against turbulence and dirty air, making myself lift less and less through Turns 1 and 2.

Steady. Smooth.

Wind pushing me in the middle of Turn 2. Back end a little loose. Weight jacker to the right to keep more weight on the right rear. Push another click, finally feels stable.

On the back straight, soften the rollbar again, because I'd been good through Turn 3 the last time. Creeping up on the red car four lengths ahead of me. Moving the weight jacker back as I get closer, feeling the dirty air. Good through 3.

Hands barely turning the wheel into Turn 4. Car not turning. Shift the wheel left more. The car finally responds, sluggish. Soften the front bar.

Shooting down the front straight. Wind the weight jacker down again before Turn 1. Still good through that turn. Flat out. Weight jacker again in the short chute, preparing for 2. Better through there, the back end still a little unstable.

Soften the rollbar on the back straight, inching up on the red car. Two lengths now. Good through 3. Watching the red car's lines. Unwind the jacker for 4.

Down the front straight again, I feel the tow from the red car sucking me closer to him. Feel the dirty air making the car push in some moments and scary loose in others. A length and a half apart now. I adjust for Turn 1, keeping close to the red car. Fight the turbulence. Adjust for 2, still close. Close enough behind him on the back straight to consider passing there—I pull out to the left, foot flat. But I'd started my run on him too late in Turn 2 and can't get it done.

Do it on the front straight.

"Keep at it, Kate. You'll get him." Alexa tells me.

Lift at Turn 3, then roll on the throttle to be flat through Turn 4—this time too close to the red car through the turn. I lift slightly and lose the attempt.

Staying close to the other car around the track, dealing with the air, planning for the next lap. Lift again at 3, build speed and throttle through the short chute and into 4.

Just the right distance away.

I stayed flat through 4 and carried speed onto the front straight. Caught the tow just right. Inching closer. Closer. Closer—*now!* I pull out.

"Outside," my spotter tells me. "Still outside."

I slingshot past the red car.

"Outside—clear!"

I move my tools for Turn 1 before I turn in and keep digging, keep adjusting the car's balance to compensate for wind, clean and dirty air, and my tires starting to wear. I caught the next car three laps later and passed him on the back straight. Passed another car nine laps later, and another three laps after that. The car was working well, but mostly I was getting past cars that had been slower than us in practice sessions. As I climbed up the order, they'd be harder and harder to pass. But I'd keep trying.

Alexa came on the radio after I'd gone twenty-four laps. "P20. L6 to pit. How's the car?"

She was telling me I was in twentieth place and we'd pit in six laps. "Loose. Front wing."

"Copy," Alexa replied, understanding I wanted a front wing adjustment.

The next time around, Alexa gave me the vitals and told me what they'd change. "P15. L5 to pit. Quarter front wing out."

"Copy." I saw cars starting to make green flag pit stops.

The car slid in Turn 2 and I held on, hoping. It was too late in the stint for many adjustments, because my tires were shot. Anything I did at one end of the car by now would unbalance the other. I made it through the turn, flying down the back straight, aiming for the next car, some ten lengths ahead.

Lifted gently for Turn 3. Car slipping more. Into Turn 4, seeing more cars peeling off into the pits.

"P7. L4 to pit," Alexa told me.

I took a breath down the front straight and felt my heart rate increase.

I have a couple laps' more fuel—don't think about it.

I focused on keeping my car pointed down the track for the next lap, dealing with the slide, making any adjustments possible, lifting where they weren't. Turn 4, the car ahead of me turns into pit lane.

Across the start/finish, remembering to breathe and adjust my tools. Telling myself to focus on the feel of the car in the moment and nothing else.

"P3. L3," Alexa said.

Focus on the car!

The next lap was a blur, the only thought in my head to not screw up. Turn 4. More cars pitting. I flashed past the start/finish holding my breath. I heard the crowd roar as I focused on Turn 1.

Alexa finally radioed. "P1. L2."

My whole body shook. While part of my mind dealt with adjusting the car and turning the wheel—and not crashing— another part went somewhere else. Somewhere shocked. Somewhere euphoric.

For a second, I sat there in complete silence, almost unable to see from the vibrations of the car, the wind, and myself. When I got to the back straight, the wave of sound hit me. I heard the car noise, and I heard the crowd.

Holy shit, they're cheering for me.

I knew it was temporary. I knew it was a game of mileage— solely due to when we'd stopped for fuel and how long we could stay on the track. I didn't care.

I'm leading the Indianapolis 500, The Greatest Spectacle in Racing, for two laps. This is the best moment of my life.

Chapter Forty-seven

I resumed my mid-pack position after pitting a couple laps later and making the adjustment we'd discussed. The tweak helped, and I wasn't fighting the car so much for stability, especially in dirty air. It wasn't entirely stable—I still adjusted to get back to the sweet spot of handling, while in traffic, and as the tires wore—but that was normal for Indy, and I had the tools to work with it.

Our next couple stints were uneventful. I picked off one car each stint, and cycled up to second or third—never again to the lead—right before stopping. The car felt better than it had all month, and even with the increasing heat of the track surface and the changing tire conditions as they went from fresh to worn, it stayed manageable and, at moments, good.

Then, on lap 158, after more than a hundred laps of green flag racing, the big one happened. Right in front of me.

Two cars had gone down the front straight, nose to tail, and going into Turn 1, the following car misjudged his spacing and bumped the leading car in the right rear. Bumped him in the worst place on the track—aside from the exit of 4, where we all tended to be loose anyway. Because of the impact, both cars were unbalanced. The second car—the bumper—spun around first, his rear toward the outside and his momentum propelling him up the track fast, right into the wall. The bumpee wiggled and almost saved his car, but ultimately suffered the same fate.

Because of their trajectories, the bumper hit the wall and slid along it, leaving a long black mark on the white barrier where tires and carbon fiber bodywork scrubbed away. The bumpee was less lucky: he hit the wall hard, destroying most of his back wing assembly, and bounced off, spinning and traveling back down the track, into the path of the rest of us. At that point, he was powerless to control the car—since the suspension was bent, the tires were in the air, rather than on the pavement, and the brakes were useless.

The two cars immediately behind the crashing duo were veterans who'd been trading positions for the last five laps, putting on an incredible display of skill as they went through turns side-by-side and kept their noses clean. But as they went into Turn 1—one car staggered slightly ahead and to the side of the other—they had nowhere to go. They ran right into the first two cars.

The lead veteran was lower on the track. He slammed into the front corner of the spinning car such that tire met tire and launched the veteran's car airborne for a couple yards. He slammed back onto the track minus one front wheel and most of his front wing, helpless. The other veteran was tucked in behind, half a front wing higher and a split second behind—which gave him more time to lock up the brakes and generate tire smoke, but not enough time to avoid impact. He hit the car that had scrubbed along the wall, sending both of them jolting down the track.

In the end, all of the drivers were uninjured, except for bruises, a sprained wrist, and crushed hopes. But the cars were destroyed.

At the moment it happened, I didn't know the details, though I was positive none of the four would finish the race. That was clear, based on the debris field, which, as the next car in line after the two veterans, I ran through. Luckily, I was ten lengths back, so I was near the start/finish when my spotter started screaming in my ear.

"Yellow! Yellow! Turn 1! Brake, brake, brake! Go low!" My spotter yelled at me.

I felt a jolt of adrenaline. I got on the brake and shifted my hands to the left to move down the track, trying hard not to unsettle the car. Careful not to tip myself into a spin with sudden actions.

Shit, shit, shit.

Then I was in the turn, trying to pick my way through almost stationary cars and an enormous swath of carbon fiber, metal pieces, and tires strewn across the track. At more than 150 mph I went left onto the apron to avoid a rear wing that slid to rest right in front of me and stayed there through Turn 2, still slowing as quickly as I dared.

If I haven't cut a tire, it'll be a miracle.

I moved onto the track again on the back straight, and immediately felt the wobble.

"Did you hit anything?" Alexa asked.

"Maybe? Car feels terrible."

"Good job to get through there," my spotter said. "Well done."

"Agreed," Alexa said. "Let us know if you feel a tire starting to go, and we'll watch for it on the monitors. But we want to try to keep you out there even if you do. We don't want to stop under closed pits. Fuel map 8." Closed pits meant we couldn't enter, but in emergency situations, such as a flat tire or not enough gas to continue, cars could enter the pits for only that service—changing a single tire or taking a couple gallons of fuel. For the remainder of service, we'd have to stop with the field once the pits were officially open. Obviously, doing so would put us at the back of the pack, and I knew everyone on the team was hoping and praying I wouldn't have a tire issue.

I changed the fuel mixture to the caution setting, as instructed, and then hung on for a fraught two laps while my car tried to buck and vibrate all over the track.

After I'd complained on the radio for the third time, Alexa responded. "We're sure you just flat-spotted the tires getting slowed down. Stay out until the pits open."

I made it, and when I pulled away, I was in twelfth position—a jump due to the attrition of the four wrecked cars that had been ahead of me, but also to the speed of my crew, who got me out ahead of one of my competitors.

"Great stop, thanks, everyone," I called, once I'd gotten back on track and in line.

"Forty laps to go, Kate," Alexa said. "No one can make it on fuel, so we'll all be stopping. We're going to do a normal stint, and if we don't get a yellow, we'll do a quick splash near the end. Everyone will probably do the same." She paused. "You're currently P12. Let's try to pick up a couple more places. Keep it clean."

Translation: first priority is finish the race, second is finish higher than I am now.

"Copy," I returned. I checked my mirrors. "Who's behind me?"

"The Wildman. Sofia Montalvo behind him," my Turn 3 spotter replied.

Shit. I'll be dive-bombed into Turn 1 by an overeager rookie.

The driver in question had earned the nickname for his flamboyant moves on the track that worked about half the time—there wasn't much in between brilliant speed and catastrophe in his repertoire yet. With Sofia behind him, I had a double target on my back. I didn't trust the rookie much, and Sofia, not at all.

"Spotters, tell me who's coming up behind me," I radioed.

"Ten-four."

"Ignore who's behind you," Alexa barked. "Focus ahead. Catch the car in front of you, and let what's behind you sort itself out."

Look where you want to go—it's true of steering out of a spin or driving in a race.

I knew she was right. If I drove by my mirrors, I'd go slower and end up being passed. "Copy."

A few seconds later, we passed the start/finish again, and Alexa radioed, "One to go for green. Restart in fuel map 4."

It seemed like an eternity before we were accelerating through Turns 3 and 4 toward the green flag.

"Green, green, green!" called my spotter.

I kept my promise and focused forward, on the car in eleventh place, spending the next ten laps staying as close to him as possible and trying to work out where I might pass. We were evenly matched, but I was determined to get it done. I tucked close to him on the straights, letting the tow pull me along, and started poking my nose to the inside, once getting all the way alongside him on a straight. But he was protecting the line, and I couldn't get ahead of him into a turn. I was still working out how to get to the inside before him when The Wildman did me a favor.

I later learned Sofia had gotten around him behind me, though he'd stuck to her like a burr after that. I'd put a gap between myself and the two of them early in the run, so I wasn't paying attention, but fifteen laps into the stint, The Wildman showed his rookie stripes. Apparently impatient with his inability to get past her—she received a warning for blocking him—he went all in at the entry to Turn 1. He dove for the inside of Turn 1 with the smallest of overlaps with Sofia's car—but she was already turning in, holding her line to the apex. His front wing caught her rear wheel pod, sending them both into the wall and giving everyone the yellow we needed for fuel.

I wouldn't have to worry about either one of them again in the race. I felt a glimmer of satisfaction at Sofia's result, followed by a flicker of guilt. I shoved it all away to think about later and focused on the quick pit stop we'd make for the fuel to get to the end. Everyone would be coming in, so pit lane would be busy.

I was almost as nervous for that one stop as I'd been for the start, but we all held it together. My team did their jobs flawlessly, and I pulled away without stalling the car. Halfway down the pit lane, I passed a scrum of cars and crew members waving their arms. When I got onto the track, I called to Alexa, "What happened?"

I heard shock in her voice. "Two cars from the same team screwed up entry into their boxes, turning one around."

The first rule of racing was don't wreck your team cars.

She radioed again. "That puts you P10. Let's stay there for the last twenty laps."

A top ten at the Indy 500?

My mouth went dry. "Copy that."

It was the biggest partial-stint of my life. I didn't win. I didn't make the podium. But in the closing laps of that race, I fended of multiple challenges from a former Indy 500 champion right behind me, and I kept my car clean.

Three hours and twenty minutes after the green flag flew to start the race, I took the checkers in tenth place. And I'm not ashamed to say I cried.

Chapter Forty-eight

My crew was still high-fiving and hugging each other as I pulled into the pits after the cooldown lap. Four of them climbed over the wall to secure the car and help me out, but after I stopped and shut down the engine, I held up a hand. I sat there for a minute, hands still on the wheel, catching my breath. Reliving the laps of work, the passes, the nerves, and the feeling of driving across the yard of bricks, under the checkered flag. I pounded the wheel with my fists and shouted "Yes!" under my helmet.

Finally, with a nod, I waved the crew in. Banjo removed the pads around my head, while Bald John took the steering wheel off so I could climb out. I stood, but before I could get out of the car, the men surrounded me, shouting congratulations, slapping my back, and hugging me. I yelled thank yous, and I returned every hug, a grin they couldn't see on my face. My fingers shook as I removed my gloves, helmet, and other gear.

Finishing the Indy 500 at all was an achievement, but a top ten? Amazing.

When I turned around, Holly stood at the low pit wall, ready to collect my equipment and hand over a cool, wet towel and a bottle of water. I could see Alexa on the pit box, talking with a small group of reporters. Beyond that, I caught a glimpse of Gramps and Ryan standing at the back fence of pit lane, as people streamed past.

"Nice work," Holly said, grinning from ear to ear.

I beamed back at her. "Unbelievable." A crew member climbed over the wall next to me, and I thanked and hugged him on the way.

"Not unbelievable," she corrected me. "Lucky, but deserved. You and the team worked hard. Keep that in mind for the media."

"True." I held the wet towel over my face, stood still, and breathed for a moment. "Wow," I said through the fabric.

Holly laughed. "Wow is right."

I opened the bottle of water and drank it down in one go. I was hot and dehydrated—and soaking wet. But happy.

"There are reporters waiting," Holly said.

I nodded, looking for Gramps and Ryan again, but not seeing them. Then suddenly, they appeared to my left, climbing over the wall next to our depleted stacks of tires. I went to them, and the second he was back on two feet, Gramps swept me up in a bear hug.

"My Katie," he murmured against my ear. "Congratulations, my girl."

I felt tears threaten again. "It wasn't a win," I tried to joke.

"It was as good as one, and you know it." He stepped back and patted my cheek. I could see love and pride in his eyes, and they filled my heart. "Now give Ryan a hug. He nearly wore his hands out, wringing them, worrying over you the whole time."

"He did?" I glanced from Gramps to Ryan, my eyebrows raised. "That's s—" I almost said "silly," then I came back to reality. *More than two hundred and twenty miles per hour, Kate.* "Sweet," I amended.

Gramps kissed my cheek. "You go do the rest of your job. We'll find you later."

Ryan stepped forward when Gramps moved away. He held my shoulders and stared into my eyes. "You're amazing."

"You've seen me race before."

"This one's different. Watching you out there, so totally in control of that much speed, I felt…"

I waited, wondering how he'd finish the sentence. Other men in my life would have been turned on, jealous, or diminished. It came to me that this was a vital moment in our relationship, right here, in the pit lane at Indianapolis, with me sweaty and stinky in my firesuit.

Ryan smiled. "I was proud. Humbled. In awe. Grateful to be with such a tough, special person."

I should never have wondered.

I hugged him. "You always say the right thing."

He squeezed me, then stepped back. "More later, speed demon. You've got more work to do." With a smile, he nodded toward the pit box.

I went back to where Holly stood, chatting with four men and Lyla Thomas, and climbed over the wall to stand next to the group. By unspoken rule, they let the IndyCar radio guy go first—television and radio always had tighter deadlines, especially if they were broadcasting live.

"We'll go live on-air, Kate," the reporter began, and paused for the go-ahead. He smiled, drew breath, and then spoke. "Congratulations, Kate. How are you feeling after your best finish here at Indy?"

All of the reporters held out their recording devices to catch my response, though I aimed for the radio microphone. "I'm feeling fantastic. What a great day and a spectacular result for the Frame Savings/Beauté car. I can't thank the Beermeier Racing team enough for giving me an outstanding machine, and especially my pit crew for being so focused and solid with every stop." I paused and took a breath. "If you'd asked me before the race how high I thought we could aim, I'd have said a top fifteen. You know, I dreamed of higher, but hardly dared think it'd be possible—not because we didn't have a good car, but because of the relative youth of our program. But here we are, with a top ten that feels like a win." I smiled at everyone.

The reporter nodded. "Do you realize that only two women have finished higher than you here, in the history of the race? Can you comment on that?"

For a moment, I couldn't speak at all.

Pull it together! You're live!

I stole Ryan's words. "I'm proud to hear that. It humbles me to be part of the incredible tradition of the Indy 500 at all, but to be the eleventh woman ever to race here, and now this? It's hard to put into words the honor it is. But again, it was so much more than just me. I share that honor with the entire team." I grinned. "It's especially cool to share it with my team owner, the woman calling the shots on the radio for me today, Alexa Wittmeier, one of the other eleven women."

The radio reporter thanked me and signed off on the air, then lowered the mic and thanked me again, shaking my hand before he left. The other reporters pressed closer. I spent the next twenty minutes answering serious racing questions ranging from "What kind of adjustments were you and the team making to your car throughout the race?" to "Does this give you confidence for the remainder of the IndyCar season?"

I also fielded the inevitable ridiculous queries, such as "How did it feel to be a woman leading the race?" and "What's your response to the idea that you're one of the best female racers around today?"

Before answering the last one, I exchanged a look with Lyla Thomas, who rolled her eyes at the questioner. I smiled. "Someday I'd rather be thought of as one of the best racers around today, not just one of the best women."

The reporters all left shortly thereafter, except Lyla, who lingered for another question. "Do you think this will finally put the PJ comparisons to rest, Kate?" When I didn't answer right away, she added, "On or off the record, your choice. I'm curious."

"I hope so. I feel sympathy and respect for her, and I'm sad she never got the chance to fulfill her potential. But I'm a different person in a different car in a different era. I hope people see Kate when they look at me, and if today's finish helps, great." I nodded. "You can quote me if you want to."

She thanked me, saluted with her micro-recorder, and took off down pit lane toward the media center.

I sat down on the wall, feeling like a balloon losing its air. *What a day.*

Alexa and Nolan stepped down from the pit box, Nolan carrying two laptop computers under his arm. His hair stuck straight out on end, no doubt the result of hours of tugging on it during the race.

He stuck out a hand. "Hell of a job, Kate. Thanks for the effort."

I pulled him in for a hug, which he always seemed to like but was too shy to initiate. "Thank *you*, Nolan. You gave me a great car."

He nodded and shuffled off. Alexa smiled after him then turned back to me. "How does it feel to make history?"

"You'd know, wouldn't you?" I stopped and thought about it. "Amazing. Empowering." I thought more. "Exhausting."

She laughed and slung an arm around my neck. "I remember it well. Come on, let's get you back for some clean clothes, and then we'll celebrate."

Chapter Forty-nine

My crew already had the champagne and beer out by the time Alexa and I returned to Gasoline Alley. Up and down the Beermeier garages, everyone was celebrating. We'd all finished well—me in tenth, Mick in twelfth after not one but two cut tires during the race, and Kenny in fifteenth.

Banjo pressed champagne into my hand before I could even change, insisting, "You gotta toast with us."

I took a sip with the boys, then hurried off to get into dry clothes. Kenny was still in our locker area, tying his shoes. We congratulated each other on our finishes.

"Aye, I'll take fifteenth. Mind you, it's not tenth in only my second year of trying." He eyed me sideways, a smile curving his mouth. This had been his fourth running and his best finish so far.

I shook my head as I opened my locker. "Plenty of luck. How was your day?"

"Car was good, but the bastard yellows caught me out twice."

I peeled my wet firesuit off the top half of my body. "I must have gotten all your luck. For once, the yellows fell exactly right."

"Then you owe me a pint for taking my share of luck." He stood and smiled. "I'm off to share a toast with my crew. See you tomorrow night at the banquet, if not before."

Once he'd gone, I finished removing my wet clothing, rubbed myself down with a towel, and got dressed in jeans and a team polo. I didn't rush back out to the party, but instead took a moment to tidy my locker and reflect on the day.

I thought of the bubbly waiting for me in a humble plastic juice cup and compared it to the race-winner's bottle of milk, drunk in front of thousands of spectators and dozens of media. I'd caught a glimpse of him, one arm and shoulder through the traditional wreath of mixed green leaves and thirty-three orchids. He'd been grinning, staring at the Borg-Warner trophy, and wiping milk from his face.

Being sticky from dumping milk over yourself was a small price to pay for being in victory lane—and I'd give anything to be there. But all in all, I was content with champagne in plastic cups with my team.

Maybe next year it'll be milk....

I smiled at the thought and went back out to join the fun.

While I'd been changing, my father, his family—my family—and a handful of the VIPs who'd been in the Frame Savings/Beauté suite had arrived.

My half brother, Eddie, spotted me and whooped. "That was amazing! I didn't breathe for the last twenty laps."

"You and me both."

He stepped out of the way for the others to congratulate and hug me. My father, his wife, my half sister, Lara, Beauté executives, and even Charlene Menfis, the Frame Savings VP I'd toured at the start of the day—everyone glowed with excitement and success. As I spoke with them, Ryan appeared at my side with a new glass of champagne for me.

He spoke into my ear. "Enjoy yourself. I'll drive everyone home." Then he moved off to talk with Eddie and Lara. I had a moment's concern about my father and Gramps running into each other again, but since I didn't see Gramps around, I decided he'd gone somewhere to avoid having to interact.

Everyone wanted to hear how the race had felt from inside the cockpit, and especially how I'd managed to avoid the accident that had happened right in front of me. I told and retold the story, answering the same question over and over, but I didn't mind. If I could put my sponsors in the cockpit with me and help them experience the thrill I felt behind the wheel, any effort was worth it. And from the looks on their faces, they felt some of the same wonder I did to have been part of this historic race.

Half an hour later, I walked the Beauté executives and my father's family to the door of the garage, wished them a safe drive to their hotels, and thanked them again for their support. I took a moment to lean against the block wall of the garage and breathe. There was still activity in Gasoline Alley as teams returned equipment to their garages and lingering fans snapped photos or cornered drivers for signatures. Tom Barclay rounded the far corner of the garage building, coming from the track, and as I watched, he walked directly to me.

"Kate, congratulations." His expression showed him to be unsure of his reception, but he extended a hand anyway.

What the hell.

I shook. "Thanks. A pretty good day."

"Do you have a minute? I won't keep you long, but I wanted to explain something." He was subdued.

I nodded, leaning against the garage wall again.

He stuck his hands in his pockets, hunching up his shoulders. "What you said earlier made me think."

"I'm sorry again. I shouldn't have—"

He stopped me with a gesture. "It's fine. You made me face that the catalyst for my business might be a lie, which was a little rough."

"That doesn't mean your business isn't worthwhile."

He smiled, a hint of his typical arrogance showing through. "Thank you, but I'm not questioning my career—I know I've helped hundreds of people."

At least I didn't damage his ego.

He went on. "The key was I realized I hadn't questioned a foundational assumption, which I'd then built a series of actions—and a business—on. Even worse, something else you said made me recognize another baseline assumption I'd taken at face value." He sighed. "This is the one I need to explain and apologize for."

I had no idea where he was going with this. "Sure."

He closed his eyes for a moment. "Last week, I was talking with an individual I've worked with in the past, and in conversation, this person mentioned being a friend of yours and being concerned about you. Wanting to help you. Saying you felt the stress of the race, especially given all the comparisons to PJ Rodriguez. You were apparently feeling vulnerable and not as focused as usual, but you weren't yet admitting to any of it. This individual thought perhaps you could use some help from me to get through the month. Then, of course, when your assistant came to ask me about our services, it only validated what I'd been told."

I studied him. "Do former clients often walk up to you and say 'I know someone who needs your help,' and you believe them? And you spread rumors about that person being unstable?" I was pleased to hear the calm tone of my voice.

"You misunderstand. First, it wasn't brought up right away. It was well into our interactions—" he stumbled over the word and flushed beet red.

I took a wild guess. "It was a woman."

He opened his eyes wide.

I took it another step. "And you slept with her."

"How could you know that?" He gaped at me and turned a deeper red.

I resisted the urge to roll my eyes, though I probably didn't manage to hide my disgust. "Was the story of poor little Kate pillow talk? And did you approach her?" *Who the hell was this bitch?*

"She approached me, but she didn't bring you up until later. After." He shuffled his feet. "It's embarrassing to feel taken in. It's been a long time since a woman her age was interested in me. I should have known better."

"You believed her and spread rumors?"

He snapped his eyes to mine. "I didn't do that. I'd never do that, I swear."

"If you didn't, then—"

"She must have," he finished.

"Who the hell would want to damage my image? Who hates me…?" Then I knew. "Sofia Montalvo." It wasn't a question.

He'd gone pale, and he wrung his hands. "I believed her—her interest in me and her concern for you as a friend. I assumed she had the best intentions, since she spoke so warmly of you and your talent. She was concerned your skills not be lost like PJ's were."

I couldn't stop a shudder.

That woman is creepy.

"But once I started questioning things today," he went on, "I realized I had only her statement to go on. And after she wouldn't even look at me today on pit lane, I had to question everything she'd said to me."

"Finally," I muttered.

"Once I questioned my baseline assumptions about her, I saw every one of her actions in a new light, and it changed my perspective. Turned everything I thought I knew upside down." He grimaced. "It's embarrassing, professionally and personally. I'm truly sorry for the issues it's caused you."

I had to be fair. "If you didn't tip off the Ringer, you didn't do anything. You were taken in also."

Question the baseline assumption and it turns everything upside down….

I struggled to connect that idea to something, but I wasn't sure what.

He shook his head. "I didn't. In fact, I'll contact him and demand a retraction."

"Only if it comes up again. I think it's blown over now."

"Then I'll owe you one for the future. Again, I'm sorry."

I patted him on the shoulder. "It's fine, Tom. I understand."

Now go away, so I can think!

After five more apologies, he left, and I remained outside, leaning against the garage wall. I knew I should get back to the party, but I was trying to chase down whatever was stuck in the back of my mind. Like a word I couldn't remember, it hovered just out of reach. I looked around the garage area. There was

Donny—Don—PJ's former crew member and now a tire guy, exiting another team's garage. There was Josh Gaffey, entering Kenny's garage space at the far end of Beermeier's row. There was Paul Lauth, PJ's boyfriend—*wait.*

Josh Gaffey? Gaffey Insurance? No. Chuck Gaffey.

Chapter Fifty

Look at things from a new perspective, like thinking about my father's family. Question the baseline assumption.

When I did, an awful lot of pieces fell into place. I'd taken Chuck at his word that he was so distraught over PJ's death he almost quit racing.

Ryan told us to question what everyone said. What if Chuck's story wasn't true?

Sure, his company had lost money making a payout to Ron Arvin for PJ's death, but that had proved his new product had value. His business had steadily grown through the years. Except for the reported stumbles and money problems—having to mortgage his own house, Josh had said—at the start.

The Ringer mentioned a rumor of mishandled funds. Was that Chuck struggling to keep the business afloat?

Plus Chuck had heard about PJ via a "breaking news" report, meaning he might not have been at the track when PJ died.

What about Ron's death? How could he be responsible if they were best friends?

Maybe Ron had figured out what Chuck had done, and Chuck had to shut Ron up—but would that have happened now, after all these years? Sure, Chuck was at the team party, but I didn't see any motive for him to have killed Ron.

"Kate?" Tyler, the young transmission expert, stuck his head outside the garage. "There's a photographer here who'd like a photo with some of your sponsors."

I thanked him and hurried back inside the garage. My mind still spun with ideas and connections, and I worked hard not to stare at Chuck Gaffey, who sat on his customary stool and chatted with Gramps and some of the crew. I wanted to tell Ryan what I'd figured out, but he stood by the office area talking with Alexa. Plus, the photographer was waiting. I posed for photos alone next to my dirty and battered car, hoping my mental distress didn't show on my face, and then our fuel sponsor's representatives joined me.

When we finished, Holly dragged me to an empty corner of the hospitality area. "What's going on in your head?" she whispered.

"Can't I hide anything?"

"Not from me or your grandfather," she said, gesturing across the garage to Gramps, who looked at me with a question in his eyes.

My heart skipped a beat. Next to Gramps, Chuck also watched me, and as much as I tried to be smooth and smile, I was afraid the horror I felt for him showed on my face. I made a lame attempt at a smile, then pointed at Gramps and waved him over, hoping to get him away from Chuck.

Alexa tapped my shoulder, wanting me to take a photo with her and representatives from the company that supplied our brake parts. When we finished, Alexa walked the reps out of the garage and I turned, looking for Gramps. But he wasn't next to me. He wasn't on his stool, and he wasn't in sight. Neither was Chuck.

"Where's Gramps? Where'd he go?" I could barely breathe.

Ryan looked up from his phone at the sound of my voice. "What's wrong?"

"Gramps—Chuck." I gulped air as Ryan and Holly moved closer. "I think Chuck did it. And now I don't know where Gramps is."

"Chuck?" Holly repeated. "But he—oh."

Ryan didn't ask questions. He grabbed the nearest crew member, Tyler. "Where did Horace go—Kate's grandfather? Did you see him? Was he with Gaffey?"

Tyler was blank. "They're not over there?" He turned to the stools they typically occupied and scratched his head. "Geez, I have no idea."

I wanted to shake Tyler until his teeth rattled.

Ryan darted across the garage to Uncle Stan, and I followed. "Did you see Kate's grandfather leave? Was he with Gaffey?"

Uncle Stan saw Ryan's worried face and my frantic one. "Stepped outside together, couple minutes ago. Chuck wanted to show Horace something, but I don't know what or where. What's wrong?"

"Call the police—call security and have them send the FBI and others on site. Tell them we have information about Ron Arvin's killer," Ryan said, moving toward the door.

"Tell them he's got a hostage," I added.

Ryan stopped and turned back to me and Uncle Stan, as Holly and Alexa joined us. "No, don't." He kept his tone low. "We don't know Chuck's the guy. We don't know Gramps is a hostage. We're going to find the two men and see what's going on, because it's almost time to go home."

"Chuck is what guy? And who's a hostage?" Alexa asked.

I clutched at Ryan's arm. "Gramps is in danger. I'm sure of it."

"Tell them to hurry," he told Uncle Stan, then turned to the rest of us. "You all stay here."

"Like hell," I returned.

"I've got the gun and the training."

"He's the most important person in my world." I spit the words out, focusing on anger instead of fear. "You're wasting time. I'm going with you or I'm following you."

"We'll deal with the cops," Holly assured him.

"What's going on?" Alexa demanded.

"You go." Holly shooed us away. "I'll explain."

Ryan looked at me. "Shit. Come on."

But we didn't have far to go. We turned right out of the garage, away from the main corridor leading to the track, and toward the row of hospitality tents, now being dismantled and packed up. Around the corner of the garage building opposite mine was a gate that led to one of the roads in the speedway, as well as to a dozen different parking areas. Gramps and Chuck stood arguing outside the gate, while a bored and tired yellow-shirt fanned himself listlessly fifty feet away.

Ryan grabbed my hand to slow my headlong rush. He murmured, "Remember, we're looking for Gramps so we can leave. Nothing dramatic. No accusations."

I took a deep breath, my first since realizing Gramps was in the company of a two-time killer. I matched Ryan's stride and forced a smile. "All right."

I walked ahead of Ryan. "We're ready to leave, Gramps, but we didn't know where you went." I slung an arm around Gramps' shoulders and turned to Chuck with a fake smile on my face.

Gramps was stiff, but he smiled at me. Chuck didn't.

Apparently Chuck wasn't fooled by my acting job, because he moved faster than I thought possible. In seconds, he'd wrapped his left arm around my throat in a choke hold, pulled a knife from a sheath on his hip, and held it against the side of my neck.

Chapter Fifty-one

"Stay back!" Chuck hissed, as he dragged me around the corner, into a walkway between the back wall of the last garage and the side of a now-deserted concession tent. The parking lots around us were filled with big rigs and motorhomes—lots of slab sides unbroken by windows. No one in sight to help.

I stumbled along in Chuck's grasp, panting for breath between my panic and the arm clamped around my throat. I felt a sting from the knife tip pressed into the flesh of my neck, and I cringed, trying to move away from it but unable to.

Ryan had his gun out and pointed our direction by the time he and Gramps followed us around the corner. Gramps was agitated, wringing his hands, but Ryan stayed calm, focused on Chuck and me.

Ryan ignored Chuck's instruction and moved to within ten feet of us. "What's going on, Chuck? We were looking for Horace to leave for the day, and now this? What's this is all about? Let Kate go."

Chuck laughed, but without any humor. "How stupid do you think I am, FBI boy? Put down the gun or I'll slit her throat."

I stopped breathing and heard Gramps gasp.

"What is it you think we know, Chuck?" Ryan didn't move a muscle.

I felt Chuck shake his head and shift so he stood directly behind me, out of the line of fire. "I'm not playing this game," he said.

"Then what are we doing here?" Ryan replied.

"You're in the way. Our media darling Kate is my insurance policy." Chuck laughed. "I do like my insurance policies."

I thought he sounded deranged, and I choked down the panic and nausea threatening to rise in my throat. I met Gramps' eyes, and the fear in them as he watched me made me ache.

Ryan still hadn't lowered his gun, and I stared down its barrel. His voice was still calm, but I caught a flicker of fear in his eyes. "Whatever you've done, don't make it worse by hurting Kate."

I moved slightly to ease a cramp in my back, and Chuck tightened his grip. I had trouble drawing breath, and my hands flew to Chuck's arm, tugging at it.

"Let her breathe!" Gramps pleaded.

"I said, stay back." Chuck wiggled the knife at my neck, and I felt a sharper sting of pain. But he did loosen his grip, and I sucked in air.

Ryan didn't move his body, but his eyes flicked from Chuck's to mine. "It's okay, Chuck. We'll stay back here."

"Let's get on with what I need to do," Chuck snarled. "Starting with you putting down the gun. Don't try to be a hero. No one wants to see their precious Kate hurt."

Ryan still didn't budge. "If we do as you say, you won't hurt her?"

"That's right. She's just my insurance policy. Put your gun and phone on the ground over there—Horace's, too." Chuck nodded toward the white tent wall. "Nice and slow. No tricks. Don't make me twitchy." He moved the knife to emphasize the point, and I winced, wondering how much I was bleeding.

Ryan hesitated a long moment, and I imagined him mentally working through possible scenarios, but then he nodded and complied, keeping his movements slow and deliberate. Gramps looked frantic, but he stayed still, chafing his hands. Ryan returned to his original position, poised on the balls of his feet for action, hands loose at his side.

Chuck nodded. "Now, I need to get in my car, drive to the airport, and get on my plane. Then I'll let Kate go. If you stay out of it, she won't be hurt. Her safety is your choice."

I didn't understand. "How are you going to take me to the airport? You can't get through security like this."

"I'm sure he means a small airstrip, with a private plane," Ryan said. "One big enough to get you to somewhere with no extradition…the Cayman Islands, say?"

Chuck smiled. "Something like that."

"How is this going to work?" Ryan asked.

"Horace is going to take my car keys from my right jacket pocket," Chuck said. "Then he'll retrieve my car. Kate and I will get in—she'll be driving—and you'll let us leave. When I get to the airport, I'll take her on the plane with me until right before we take off. Then I'll let her go."

I didn't like the sound of his plan, and neither did Ryan. "It'll never work," he warned.

Chuck rolled his eyes. "You sound like a bad movie. You think all of a sudden, I'll believe you and decide to give myself up?"

Gramps swallowed. "Where's your car?"

"In the lot behind us, far end," Chuck jerked his head in the approximate direction. "White Porsche 911. You can approach slowly now. Keys in my right pocket."

Gramps glanced at Ryan, who nodded. I hoped someone had a plan or that the police would arrive soon. Gramps took one step at a time toward Chuck, his eyes darting between Chuck's face and the knife at my throat.

Can I do anything when Gramps gets close? No, he might get hurt also. Chuck will be the most distracted when Gramps gets back with the car. Do something then. And why didn't I ever take martial arts classes?!

Gramps approached slowly, extracted the key from Chuck's bomber jacket pocket, and walked backwards away from us, looking anguished as he met my eyes. I projected back confidence, and I saw the same determination reflected in Ryan's face.

We're going to get out of this.

Chuck nodded. "Now go get the car. Don't talk to anyone or signal anyone. Don't take too long. Remember, I've got your granddaughter's life in my hands."

Gramps clutched the key. "Don't hurt her."

"Then be back here in five minutes," Chuck responded. "Go."

With a last glance for me, Gramps set off at a fast shuffle down the lane, quickly disappearing from view behind the concession tent.

Ryan kept his eyes on me and Chuck. "You can still back down from this, Chuck. Get in the car alone and leave Kate here. We won't stop you."

Chuck snorted. "You'll have cops waiting for me." He shook his head. "If you do as I say, I won't hurt her. Just let me take care of business—that's all it's ever been about. I did what needed to be done."

"What needed to be done for whom?" Ryan asked.

"For me and the greater good of the racing world."

I couldn't hold in my outrage. "How was killing PJ for the greater good?"

Ryan sucked in a breath, and Chuck tightened his grip on my neck, his arm scratchy with hair and slick with sweat.

"Do you realize how many small teams I've saved with my business interruption policies?" Chuck snarled near my ear. "And in turn, how many other local businesses those teams have kept afloat—suppliers, manufacturers, and the like? How many families those businesses continue to feed to this day? I knew my policies would work—knew they would save businesses and lives. I was bold, and I had vision—I deserved to get a fair chance to fulfill my destiny of helping people. What was one worthless life stacked up against hundreds of others?"

"You threw her off a building and made it look like suicide to further your business?" I spat out.

Chuck was silent for a long moment, then he sounded dreamy, almost reverent. "She wasn't concerned until we got onto the roof—she trusted me, believed I had something to show her." I felt him shake his head. "She didn't even struggle, not after a tap on the head stunned her. And then she flew."

My stomach rolled, and I wondered if throwing up on Chuck

was a way to break free. "You're not God. How can you make that choice?"

"Easy," Ryan murmured.

"Did you make the choice for Ron, too?" I had to know.

"My best friend, Ron. My partner in crime." Chuck sighed. "Ron agreed to buy the new policy after PJ's spectacular run that first day and agreed to ensuring she wouldn't race."

"But he seemed upset by her death," I said.

"He was soft," Chuck sneered. "He planned for an accident that would break her leg or something—but when she and I were staying at the same hotel, I saw the opportunity for a solution she'd never be able to talk about." I felt him shrug. "Ron lost his nerve while he was in prison. He said PJ was weighing on him. He swore he'd never told anyone, but I didn't trust him."

"You killed him, too?" Ryan asked.

"Sometimes needs must, as my mother used to say," Chuck replied.

We heard the sound of an engine, and I tensed, readying for action. Chuck also tensed, tightening his hold around my neck again. I gasped for breath as Gramps executed a shaky three-point turn in front of us, then pulled to a jerky stop.

I looked at Ryan, opening my eyes wide, trying to signal, *Let's act now.*

He gave me the tiniest of head shakes. I was confused, but I didn't make a move.

I hope he's got a plan.

Gramps got out, leaving the door open and the car running. "Kate, are you still all right?"

"She's fine," snapped Chuck.

"I want to hear it from her. Katie, are you all right?" he asked. "Does your neck hurt too much?"

Was I bleeding? Did Gramps have a plan?

I moved my head slightly. "I'm all right. My neck's a little sore."

"Is it as bad as that time you had a rollerskating incident?" He held my gaze.

Rollerskating? You were the one, Gramps—Oh! But what's the trigger?

Gramps could see when I understood, but Ryan looked confused.

"Not that bad, yet," I said, lowering my hands and flattening them.

I saw a flicker of understanding in Ryan's eyes, and Gramps looked relieved.

"Stop right there," Chuck snarled. "No more talking. The two of you, stand out of the way." He started moving me forward.

We were a single step past Gramps and Ryan when Gramps shouted, "Tell me one thing!"

Go, Kate, go!

I threw myself away from the knife and fell to the ground, flinging my arms and legs wide. The suddenness of the movement tore me out of Chuck's grasp, but pulled him forward with me. He tripped over my legs, and might have fallen on top of me, but for Ryan, who'd also leapt into action at Gramps' shout. He tackled Chuck from behind and wrested the knife away. By the time I sat up, Ryan had Chuck down on the ground, arms twisted behind him, subdued—ready to hand over to the six officers who'd swarmed around the sides of the concession tent, guns drawn.

It was over.

Chapter Fifty-two

An hour after Chuck was hauled away in handcuffs by the Indianapolis police, Gramps, Ryan, and I sat in the Beermeier Racing garage with Alexa and Holly, while Uncle Stan and a couple other mechanics puttered around, continuing to pack up their equipment. We'd given the cops our statements and assured them we'd go to the police station the next day for follow-up. I'd also texted my father and told him not to worry about anything he'd see on the news, that I'd explain later. Then we dealt with the aftershocks of the stress and drama.

"What I want to know is how the cops got there. You guys called them? Gramps, you worked out a signal with them?" I looked from one person to another.

Uncle Stan nodded. "I called track security and told them to get the local cops and anyone they had on-site—since they had officers from various organizations here for the race. But Holly and Alexa were the most help."

I turned to them, my eyebrows raised, and Holly dimpled up.

"We followed you." She nodded. "Snuck up to the corner of the garage, peeked around once, listened to what was happening."

"Like super spies." Alexa smiled for the first time since the showdown. She'd been blank with shock at first after discovering her father was murdered by his supposed best friend. "I ran back to tell Uncle Stan what was going on, and we kept a call open on our cell phones to relay information."

Gramps took a deep breath. "They were waiting behind that tent when I went off to get the car. They had an officer hidden inside the car with me, but they told me it'd be better to take him down before he got in. They wanted me to shout something and to try to get you to get away or fall down."

I turned to Ryan, sitting next to me on a cooler. "And you figured out the plan? Or you were just ready to jump?"

"I figured someone got to Gramps while he was gone. And I was ready to move when Chuck was closest to me and distracted. I hoped you'd drop at the same time—which you did. The other officers were a bonus."

I relived the blinding fear of that moment of action and shuddered. "You all saved the day. Thank you."

"And maybe your life," Ryan added, putting an arm around my waist and shifting me closer.

"Except I owe you all an apology." Alexa shook her head when we protested. "One of the mechanics found an envelope with my name on it buried in a storage bin this morning, right as we were going out to the grid. I shoved it in a pocket and never thought about it until Chuck took your grandfather. It explained everything."

She pulled a scruffy white envelope out of her pocket and slipped two familiar folded, yellow notes out of it. She handed one to me. "I could have prevented everything if I'd read these earlier."

With shaking fingers, I unfolded the paper she handed me. It was written in the same hand and language as the anonymous notes I'd received, but everything else was different. It contained more than one sentence, and the tone was apologetic. Most important, it was signed.

I read it aloud to everyone: "Kate, I swore I'd never tell anyone, but I know who killed PJ—except she wasn't supposed to die. That was his doing. She was only supposed to be unable to race, for the publicity. I left you anonymous letters to make you figure out what happened to her, so I didn't have to break my word but PJ would still get justice. All I know is I can't bear this knowledge alone anymore—God knows how he sleeps at night. If you're reading this, something happened to me. It'll be Chuck Gaffey's doing."

I looked up at Alexa, who had tears in her eyes. "It's signed Ron Arvin."

She held up a twin note. "This was addressed to me. It said the same, plus some personal stuff." She turned to me. "I'm sorry I didn't read them sooner."

Gramps, who sat next to her, leaned over to hug her, then held her as she broke down. "It's not your fault, sweetheart," he murmured, patting her back.

"Shoot, sugar," Holly said. "You haven't even had time to grieve yet, have you?"

Alexa pulled away from Gramps and wiped her eyes with a tissue. "His death was such a shock…I'd just gotten him back, then he's gone again, permanently." She blinked, fighting back tears, but her voice was steady. Angry. "Then to deal with the fact that someone killed him—deliberately took him from us. And now? That it was Chuck? I keep thinking I need to see Chuck—to face him and ask him why. *Why?*" She turned to me. "You know, don't you?"

"I think so."

"All started with PJ." Uncle Stan leaned on a push broom near us.

Alexa frowned. "How did you figure that out, thirty years later?"

I'm still not sure.

I shook my head. "Talking to different people and comparing their memories. Asking specific questions. Guesswork. It was a group effort." I gestured to Gramps, Holly, and Ryan.

Ryan was caught between amusement and amazement. "You all did the sleuthing. I came in at the end."

"What made you think it was Chuck?" Alexa asked.

"We never really did." I grimaced.

Holly nodded. "We believed his story about being devastated when PJ died, so heartbroken over the idea of losing people to this sport that he almost quit entirely."

"I've heard him say the same thing," Alexa said.

Uncle Stan snorted and leaned his broom against the wall. "Always thought it was a pile of crap."

I turned to him, surprised. "Really?"

"I watched him over the years. Saw the calculating look on his face after the person he was talking to turned away. Figured he was in it for himself alone." He shook his head. "Mind you, I didn't think he was so far gone as to be behind PJ's death. But I suppose it's all of a piece."

"I wish I'd seen him as clearly." I was embarrassed to have missed it.

Uncle Stan put a hand on my shoulder. "Shows you're not a cynical bastard, like me. You still see the good in people. I've gotten over it." He winked at me.

"Who did you think had killed PJ, if not Chuck?" Alexa wondered.

"We'd only gotten to people who benefitted from her death." I hesitated, not sure how to explain the rest.

"Tell her," Gramps said. "She'll understand."

Alexa nodded. "You thought my father might have done it."

I hope this doesn't get me fired.

"We had to consider it as a possibility," I admitted. "He got more successful afterwards, with more sponsors, bigger drivers. And, of course, he'd gotten the insurance payout from Gaffey for loss of business with PJ's inability to race that year. But there were also others we knew had benefitted."

Holly held her fingers up one at a time. "Kevin Hagan, the reporter. Dean Herrera, the memorabilia guy. Tom Barclay, the sports psychologist. Even Nathan Standish, for a minute. Plus your father. Of course, that all changed when he was killed."

I sighed. "It showed how wrong we were."

"It also gave you more to work with," Ryan noted, "once you decided there was a connection between the deaths."

"Not that we knew what the connection was," Holly said.

I realized how arrogant we sounded, thinking we could solve Alexa's father's murder. "I know the cops were working on finding your father's killer, but we had information they didn't—the connection to PJ. We figured it had to be someone who was around back then and now. Also someone who wasn't at the track when PJ was killed and who was at our party last week."

"Pretty clever." Uncle Stan leaned against the garage wall next to us.

I shook my head. "It didn't feel clever. We kept turning up evidence of people doing borderline illegal or unethical stuff, but nothing seemed to point to murder."

"Like what?" Uncle Stan asked.

"Dean Herrera was the worst. It seems like he's selling forged goods—all those items he sells signed by famous drivers might not be. Certainly some stuff signed by PJ doesn't seem to be. Any news on that?" I asked Ryan.

"I'll know more next week, but I expect the FBI will question him," he replied.

Holly jumped in. "Kevin Hagan was a reporter with AP in PJ's time, and he won prizes for the long features he did on her life and death. It doesn't seem like he's ever done anything wrong, but no one likes him. Or respects him. And we couldn't ever figure out why he'd kill your father, Alexa, though he was around that night."

"And Tom Barclay?" Alexa asked. "I've always liked him."

Holly grinned. "Kate wanted it to be him, especially after that rumor came out about her feeling unstable and seeking help."

"Turns out, he didn't plant that story, but he didn't deny it." I nodded at the surprise on everyone's face. "I confronted him earlier today, and he was stunned when I told him PJ might not have committed suicide. He found me after the race to apologize and tell me I'd made him question fundamental assumptions."

"What did that have to do with anything?" Ryan asked.

"In his case, it meant he realized he'd been used by Sofia Montalvo to make me look bad—meaning she sent the Ringer the rumor about me." I waved off everyone's anger about Sofia. "When he said he'd questioned core beliefs and doing so made everything turn upside down, I did the same."

I glanced at Ryan, chagrined. "Like you told us, only days too late—question everything. I realized the only reason we weren't looking at Chuck Gaffey, whose name kept coming up over and over, was because of his own story."

Holly nodded. "If you didn't believe he was heartbroken, all the rest of the pieces fit. He benefitted, he wasn't at the track the morning PJ died, he was at the party where Ron was killed—he was even on my list of people in the back of the shop."

"I was convinced, but had no proof," I said. "Here in the garage, I tried to get Gramps to move away from Chuck, but Chuck probably saw on my face that I suspected him. Then the brake people were here for a photo, and Gramps was gone." I fell silent, reliving my panic.

After a long moment, Ryan shook his head. "There's one thing I don't understand." He paused. "Rollerskating?"

Chapter Fifty-three

I laughed at Ryan's question. "One year when I was a kid, I had a rollerskating party for my birthday. Even Grandmother and Gramps got out there with us, but poor Gramps." I giggled. "He couldn't make it five feet without falling down."

"I was the hit of the rink that night." He flushed. "Never could get the hang of those suckers."

"It became a family joke." I smiled at him. "Anytime anyone fell down, it was 'a rollerskating incident.'"

Gramps nodded. "When the cops asked if there was any way for you to get away from Chuck or at least to drop to the ground, it's all I could think of."

"It worked. I knew exactly what you wanted me to do," I said. "Didn't understand why, but it was strange enough I figured someone was helping you."

"Clever," Ryan said. "I was hoping we could stop him before he got Kate in the car and took off for the airport—since I didn't know what airport and how quickly we'd be able to get someone there to try to stop him."

Alexa knew the answer. "Eagle Creek Airpark is about five miles away."

"We'd never have gotten anyone there in time." Ryan shook his head. "It's a good thing we didn't have to."

Alexa drew a deep breath and turned to me. "I'm glad that for whatever else he did in his life, my father had a role in bringing

PJ's killer to justice." She paused. "It'll always be hard to know he was part of the scheme in the first place. But at least he helped in the end. I think he'd be glad of that."

"He was more than just part of it, Alexa. He actively encouraged it with his anonymous notes," I explained. "Early on—as early as the second day of practice—I got notes in my locker. At first, I thought they were threats, but by the third one, I knew he wanted me to ask questions about PJ."

Holly nodded. "They succeeded."

"Another thing." I leaned forward. "He was trying to make right what he'd done. He wanted redemption."

We were all quiet, then Uncle Stan spoke. "Ron found it in the end. He knows."

There wasn't much else to say after that, and we slowly collected our belongings and went our separate ways. The four of us returned to our apartment, and while I showered, Holly and Ryan went out to pick up dinner.

"Anything but chicken and steamed vegetables," I'd told them when they asked what I wanted, and I was delighted with their choice: big juicy burgers, piles of crisp French fries, and mounds of coleslaw. We sat at the table, feasted, and talked about the race—without saying a word about Chuck Gaffey.

But I hugged Gramps extra close and long before we all went to bed that night. Ryan did the same for me when I woke at two o'clock from a nightmare of the knife against my neck and that white Porsche.

Monday, Memorial Day, dawned bright, sunny, and breezy in Indianapolis, and for the first time in weeks, I felt like all was right with the world again. My two big activities for the day were cleaning out my locker at the track and attending the Indy 500 Victory Banquet that evening. I also had a few other odds and ends to take care of, including meeting PJ's family at a coffee shop right after the lunch hour. Gramps and Holly wanted a lazy day at home before the evening's party, but I took Ryan with me.

Elena and Tony had heard the news, and we'd all read Lyla Thomas' reports online, but what I didn't anticipate was how clearing PJ's name would have transformed her family. Elena looked ten years younger and joyful. Tony's humor was much the same, but without the grim edge underneath.

They thanked me, effusively. Embarrassingly. "It wasn't me alone—lots of other people helped, including Ryan."

They turned to thank him, and he shook his head. "None of us thought we could actually unravel a crime that old. We were lucky."

I nodded. "We're all glad PJ can be remembered as she deserves to be."

Elena blinked back tears. "You returned our daughter to us. We can't ever thank you enough." She reached into her purse and came out with a small box, which she set on the table in front of me.

I kept my hands in my lap. "You don't owe me anything."

"It was PJ's," Tony said. "I think she'd like for you to have it."

I was surprised and intrigued, so I opened the box and found a small medallion on a metal bead chain. I looked at Tony and Elena for an explanation.

"It's a medal of St. Christopher," Elena told us. "She always wore one. I know she'd like you to have something that was important to her."

It reminded me of the triumphant photo that accompanied Lyla Thomas' interview, and it was the perfect way to remember her. "I'll treasure it, thank you."

As we stood in the parking lot outside the coffee shop, saying goodbye, Tony's phone rang, and he frowned before shoving it back in his pocket, unanswered.

Elena frowned. "Another one?"

"The same," he replied.

"Reporters?" I asked

"That *cabrón,* Kevin Hagan," Tony said. "He leaves messages telling me he's the only person to tell PJ's story now, because he was the one to tell it then."

"Are you going to talk with him?" Ryan wanted to know.

Elena turned fierce. "I hated the story he told then, and we will say nothing to him now. He's about glory for himself and doesn't care about his subjects."

Tony smiled. "We'll give Lyla Thomas the exclusive. She's always treated PJ and you right."

There's another kind of justice.

The other stop we made was the Frame Savings condo in downtown, where my father and his family were staying for the week—and where my stepmother, Amelia, had a plate of cookies and a pitcher of lemonade waiting. We sat around the large living room, its floor-to-ceiling windows open for the breeze and the view of the Soldiers and Sailors Monument, and I told them the story. I also thanked my father and Eddie for their help. My father, predictably, got stuck on the danger we were in the evening before.

"My grandfather was at the most risk," I reminded him.

"But you could all have been—"

Amelia put a hand on my father's arm. "They weren't. They were smart and resourceful."

"Don't forget lucky," Eddie put in, making Ryan laugh.

I nodded. "It's over now. PJ is laid to rest—hopefully in the media as well—and tonight we'll focus on racing and nothing else. All right?"

They all agreed, and my father walked us to the door. He cleared his throat before he opened it. "I assume your grandfather will be at the banquet this evening?"

I nodded. "At the same table. Will that be a problem?"

"Not for me. I hope it's not one for him."

I glanced at Ryan. "Ryan's spent more time with him the last couple days. Has he said anything?"

"Nothing specific, but I think he's mellowing." He looked at James. "He'll be fine tonight—but don't expect any heart-to-hearts. Though I think you'd like each other, given the chance."

James' smile was rueful. "Perhaps that can be a future goal. In the meantime, Kate, let me know how I can help you."

When I read the information from my grandmother.

I felt the weight of those secrets on my shoulders, and I straightened. Took a deep breath. "I'll let you know. That's what family's for—support when we need it."

My father's eyes got shiny, and he cleared his throat before opening the door. "However, tonight, we forget all of that, and we celebrate a great effort, a great driver, and a bright future together."

I kissed his cheek and took Ryan's hand. "I like the sound of that."

To see more Poisoned Pen Press titles:

Visit our website: poisonedpenpress.com/
Request a digital catalog: info@poisonedpenpress.com